THE HOUSE BENEATH THE

What dark secrets lie in

THE HOUSE BENEATH THE BLACK HILL

Chris Green

To Bev
I hope you enjoy it

YOUCAXTON
PUBLICATIONS

ISBN 978-1-914424-98-4
Published by YouCaxton Publications 2023

YouCaxton Publications
www.youcaxton.co.uk

To the people of Herefordshire where I have found so much pleasure in the company of others.

Foreword

WITH THE EXCEPTION of the national political figures, Lloyd George and Ramsay MacDonald and of Frank Owen and Frederic Romilly (the two principal candidates who contested the Hereford seat in 1929), all the characters who appear in this novel are entirely fictitious.

Clodock is a pretty little village nestling under the Black Hill beyond which are the magnificent Brecon Beacons and all that is Wales. St Clynog's church is one of the many gems of church architecture to be found in the County. The local inn, the delightful Cornewall Arms, remains in private hands and has miraculously managed to avoid the brewery inflicted make-over that has spoiled the character of so many of our public houses. High house is entirely a figment of my imagination although I have dwelt in it for so long now that I expect to see it when I pass through the village.

This is not primarily a political novel but, for those interested in politics, the Liberal candidate Frank Owen won a remarkable and unexpected victory in Hereford in the 1929 General Election. These were unsettled times in British politics which, with the emergence of the Labour Party leading to a steady decline in support for the Liberals. The 1920's saw a series of General Elections, power switching from the Conservatives in 1922 and 1923 to a short-lived Labour minority government in the latter part of 1923, followed by a return to the Conservatives in 1924.

Frank Owen was only to serve as MP for two and a half years. On losing his seat to the Conservatives in 1931, He is famously quoted as saying 'I was elected by the highly intelligent, far-sighted people of the constituency of Hereford in 1929 – and thrown out by the same besotted mob two years later.' Owen went on to pursue a highly successful career as a journalist and author and wrote one of the best biographies of his good friend Lloyd George.

I am indebted to all those who have generously given me support and advice while writing this novel. In particular I would like to mention my good friend David Stoll who provided me with positive and helpful feedback after an early reading of the novel. I continue to be indebted to my wife Sheila for her long-suffering and warm support over the many hours I spend locked away writing in my log cabin at the bottom of the garden. I am also immensely grateful to Flo and Pete Hawkins for providing me with the opportunity to write undisturbed in their delightful cottage nestling in the Shropshire hills, and to Alicia Carey and her warm and friendly staff colleagues at Hawkwood College where I have so often found inspiration and the chance to explore new ideas. Finally, a few heartfelt words of appreciation for the support of Bob Fowke, Managing Editor at YouCaxton, and all his colleagues, for the professionalism and efficiency with which they have turned my novel into a reality.

Prologue

THE ORCHESTRA IS tuning up. Nick is almost the last person to enter the cathedral for the second part of the evening's concert. His face is a little flushed from the three glasses of champagne nervously consumed during the interval reception in the hospitality marquee. He is grateful to have been seated on the end of the row. He can take his seat without disturbing anyone and stretch his long legs out into the aisle. His sister Kate is sitting beside him. She knows how apprehensive he must feel. She knows he will not want to talk to anyone before his new work has been performed. She sees it as her job to protect him from having to engage in conversation with fellow composers and friends who have turned up to support him. There will be plenty of time for that later. He needs to be free to cherish this moment without distraction. It is the moment he has been waiting for ever since completing his Master's in composition at The Royal Academy. It is the moment every young composer dreams of and hopes will come, before it is too late, before the opportunities have passed by and all that remains is a part-time teaching position and the occasional invitation to write something for an amateur choir or orchestra.

But now, he is numbered amongst the few who are more fortunate. Following a number of modest Festival commissions and a more substantial crowd-funding community-opera project, he managed to land the big one, a BBC Commission to write a large-scale orchestral work for The Hereford Three Choirs Festival to be performed by the London Symphony Orchestra. This is the evening of the world première, broadcast live on BBC Radio 3, and unlike so many a 'first performance' which turns out to be the only performance, his new work is included in the LSO's forthcoming European Autumn Tour programme and is to be performed in Paris, Berlin, Vienna, Prague and Warsaw.

He remembers the sense of exhilaration the first time one of his compositions was given a public performance. That was in the Wigmore Hall, a song cycle of four extracts from Wordsworth's

Prelude for which he had won the Royal Academy's prestigious Elgar Prize. His sister turns to look at him, smiles, and reaches down to squeeze his hand. Although she is five years older they have always been close. She knows this is by far the most important moment of his professional life. She sees his eyes are closed. This is how her brother shuts out the world on such occasions. She can sense his apprehension from the short breaths he is taking but she is equally sure he is savouring the moment. She takes a quick look back down the nave. She is relieved to see how full it is. She knows how her brother had feared that most of the audience would leave during the interval, once they had enjoyed the Beethoven and Vaughan Williams he suspects they really came to hear. Thank goodness for the considerable media attention the story behind his new work has received. From the animated conversations taking place around them she senses that the audience is in a high state of anticipation, hoping they may be about to witness something exceptional.

The ripple of conversation dies away when the leader of the orchestra enters from the side, to the left of the stage, and is greeted by a generous round of applause. This he acknowledges with a half bow before taking his seat and exchanging a few pleasantries with his immediate neighbour. The lead oboe plays an A, the members of the orchestra go through their final tuning and the cathedral falls silent. Everyone is waiting for the conductor and soloist to make their entrance. Kate wonders why it always seems to take so long. Is it because they are not quite ready or is it deliberately staged to add to the sense of drama? At last, they appear. The soloist is ushered in by the conductor. With an encouraging smile, he gestures for her to precede him. They make their way forward to the centre of the platform where they turn to acknowledge the enthusiastic applause. The soloist is wearing a long, crimson, evening dress, tied round the neck, leaving her slender shoulders exposed. Her hair is tied back in a high bun with two long golden strands hanging down on either side of her face. She takes her seat and sits in a very upright position with her hands clasped tightly together. Kate thinks how beautiful she looks. More accustomed to performing in the opera houses of Europe and America than on the concert platform, Kate imagines she will be feeling particularly anxious.

Nick has opened his eyes now and is quietly taking everything in. He has a contented smile on his face. He is pleased he suggested the young Polish soloist. Although he has never seen her perform, he has enjoyed listening to many of her recordings. There is a certain melancholic timbre to her voice that he felt was ideally suited to the part she has to sing. It was also important to him that whoever was chosen should bear some resemblance to the source of his inspiration.

The conductor raises his baton and, as his hand falls, the strings deliver the opening notes of Nicholas Mortimer's Symphonic Poem *'Remember me when I am gone away.'*

Chapter 1

NICK DOESN'T HAVE any strong religious convictions, nor does he consider himself to have a particularly wild imagination. He can see good in most religions and accepts there is a spiritual dimension to our lives which it is not easy to define. What he would have said before experiencing the strange events that inspired his new musical composition is that, on the whole, he was sceptical about the existence of the supernatural.

It all began when he received a telephone call from a Yorkshire solicitor informing him that his Great-aunt Emmeline had died. The solicitor told him that her funeral was to take place at the Clayton Baptist Church in Bradford the following week. He said that both he and his sister Kate were mentioned in Miss Mortimer's will and, if either or both of them were able to attend the funeral, they might like to call at his office while they were up in Yorkshire so that he could provide them with the details. Otherwise, he said, he would be happy to write to them but would prefer not to discuss the details over the telephone as they were rather complicated. Nick said he would talk to his sister and get back to him the following day.

As it happened, Nick was expecting Kate for supper that same evening. Her husband Bill Willoughby is a Labour MP and a member of the House of Commons Foreign Affairs Select Committee. He is abroad on one of his regular overseas visits. Kate herself produces insightful documentaries for a small independent film company and is nearly always working on an interesting story, which makes for entertaining conversation. She arrived at Nick's flat just before 8pm that evening a little the worse for wear, having taken her team out to the local pub to celebrate putting their latest film to bed. It had been about a local government scandal and had been commissioned by Channel 4. She was in high spirits and soon had Nick in fits of laughter when she told him about the County Council chief executive they had filmed climbing into a broom cupboard in a vain attempt to avoid being interviewed.

Nick was enjoying their conversation so much he nearly forgot to tell his sister about the call from the Bradford solicitor. She was as surprised as he had been to hear the news. Great-aunt Emmeline was their paternal grandfather's younger sister. Nick could only remember meeting her once and that had been the best part of thirty years ago. Kate thought it must have been at some kind of family reunion, possibly their grandfather's sixtieth birthday. The occasion had all but faded from Nick's memory. However, Kate, being that much older, said she had a clear picture in her head of their great-aunt, dressed from head to foot in black, sitting in a high-backed chair, as stiff and austere as could be. She remembered how much they had been in awe of her, the more so since their mother had told them to be on their best behaviour. They had been warned that the old lady subscribed to the Victorian view that 'children should be seen and not heard'. Kate also remembered their mother telling them that their great-aunt was a leading member of the local Baptist community and that they should mind their P's and Q's. Doubtless, to their young ears, this had made her sound even more worthy of their respect, even although they didn't have a clue what it meant to be a Baptist.

They had had no further contact with their great-aunt over the years that followed. Their paternal grandfather Edward Mortimer had lived in Bradford throughout his life. A successful businessman, he had served for many years as an Alderman on the local council. His wife had a weak heart and had died before either Nick or Kate were born. Their father, Andrew Mortimer, was Edward's only son and was born towards the end of the Second World War. He was educated at Bradford Grammar School where he was inspired by the knowledge that the composer Frederick Delius was one of the school's celebrated alumni. His enthusiasm for Delius, together with his natural musical ability, nurtured within him a strong affection for the Pastoral School of English music and especially the works of Delius's contemporaries, Vaughan Williams and John Ireland. After leaving school Andrew had studied English at Leeds University where he wrote occasional articles for *The Yorkshire Post*. The Editor had been so pleased with the quality of his writing that, after completing his degree, he had been offered a permanent position on the newspaper, mainly helping to cover the cultural life of the county. It wasn't long before his talents were spotted by a member of the editorial team on *The Times* and, in the Autumn of 1968, he moved to take up a new position in Fleet Street as a theatre critic.

He had met Nick and Kate's Mother Sarah at the Royal Court Theatre while covering the opening night of David Storey's new play *The Contractor*. At the time she had been working there as a volunteer steward, and it was she who had shown him to his seat before the performance. He had been instantly charmed by the warmth of her smile and the alluring tones of her unusually deep voice. He had spotted her again in the bar after the performance where they had soon become involved in a fervent discussion about the merits of the Storey play. They had continued their conversation in one of the less expensive restaurants down the King's Road, after which he had walked her back to her flat in Flood Street and, as they say, 'the rest is history'. A photograph of the young couple, taken around that time, reveals Andrew to have been well above average height with thick, black, almost shoulder-length hair and a rather embarrassed grin on his face. Sarah, on the other hand, appears to have been not in the least self-conscious. She was tall, like Andrew, slender-waisted and, as was very much the fashion at the time, wore her long fair hair tied back in a ponytail.

It turned out to be a partnership made in heaven and Andrew and Sarah enjoyed thirty exceptionally happy years together. He successfully pursued his journalistic career until retiring soon after his sixtieth birthday. She had an equally fulfilling career in the world of theatre ending up as General Manager of an Arts Council funded small touring company. After retiring in 1997 he and Sarah moved to the West Country to run a small B&B. Sadly their time together there was cut short when Andrew was drowned after his dinghy was caught in a cross current and capsized while he was sailing off the North Devon coast. After her husband's traumatic death, Sarah wanted to be nearer to her children, so she moved back to London, where she now lives in a rather smart first floor flat just north of the Fulham Road. She has no other close family of her own being an only child and losing both her parents when she was in her twenties, her father to a heart attack brought on by excessive drinking, and her mother to ovarian cancer.

Andrew Mortimer never got on well with his father Edward back in Bradford who, from all accounts, had treated him badly when he was a child. As a result, the family hardly ever returned to Yorkshire during Nick and Kate's childhood. Indeed, when their grandfather died in 1994, it took Sarah all her time to persuade Andrew to attend his father's funeral. As a result, Nick and Kate grew up in a world largely bereft of the influence of elderly relatives; so much so, that they had pretty much forgotten about their great-aunt Emmeline's existence until that unexpected 'phone call from the Bradford solicitor.

Once Nick had broken the news of their great-aunt's death to Kate, it was inevitable that they should spend much of the evening reminiscing about their childhood. Kate had rather more memories of their rare visits up north and still carried pictures in her head of cloudy grey skies, endless streets of stone terraced cottages fingering their way along the hillsides and of grander commercial and municipal buildings, churches and assembly halls, soot-blackened by years of industrial smoke and grime. She also remembered their being taken for long walks over the wilds of the Pennines where they saw sheep sheltering against grey stone walls and heard the forlorn cry of the curlew. Although Nick had been too young to remember any of these things, he did retain a dim recollection of being hoisted up onto his father's shoulders one wet and dreary afternoon when his little legs would take him no further.

It was a long time since they had talked together of such things. When Nick asked Kate how she felt about going up for the funeral, he wasn't in the least surprised by her enthusiastic response.

'Yes, of course we must go. I'm feeling quite nostalgic about the North,' she said. 'The funeral's on the Thursday morning, so we'll have to travel up the day before or we'll never make it in time. I suggest we arrange to call in at the solicitor's sometime on the Friday and, if you're up for it, we could stay on over the weekend. I feel Spring in the air so, with any luck, we'll get some decent weather. I can't wait to see how much things have changed since we were last up there, all those years ago.'

'I think your suggestion of an extended visit is a great idea,' said Nick. 'There isn't much happening on my front at the moment. My school's broken up for the Easter holiday and I could do with a change of scene.'

'It just so happens that Bill's off on some kind of international gathering in Canada at the beginning of next week so I'll have the car and we can drive up there together. It will make it so much easier to revisit some of our childhood haunts. I'll book us into somewhere to stay while we're up there, my treat.'

'Thanks Kate, if you're sure. By the way, I've just thought, do you think anyone's told Mother? I don't suppose she'll want to come to the funeral but we should at least ask.'

'I doubt she'll want to come,' Kate replied. 'You know how little time she had for Father's side of the family and she was appalled at the way Grandfather treated him. I don't suppose she's been included in the will. In any case, Emmeline can't have had much to leave, she never got married and I don't think she ever went out to work. She probably just got by on whatever her father left her. To be perfectly honest, I'm surprised that we get a mention in her will. Anyway, I'll give Mother a call in the morning and find out what she wants to do.'

'So, from what you're saying, it looks like my dream of owning my own home and of being mortgage-free will have to wait a little longer,' Nick said, grinning. 'Thank goodness you don't go on at me about getting a proper job all the time like Mother does. I find her attitude profoundly ironic considering the decades of grossly underpaid years she spent working in the theatre! She doesn't even rate my teaching job at the local Comp' and she's always going on about "those awful children" from the council estate. Actually, the kids are just great. I love working with them. They're surprisingly responsive when you think of the deprived background so many of them come from. I have friends who teach privileged middle-class children and yes, of course, they get better results in terms of their musical attainment, but so they should and where's the challenge in that?'

'All right Nick, there's no need to go off on one!' Kate said.

'I'm sorry Kate, but I do sometimes feel I'm being hounded by Mother. She obviously thinks I'm a failure. Anyway, moving onto other matters, how are you and Bill getting on these days? It must be strange being married to someone who's away so much. What with his other parliamentary duties, you don't even seem to see much of him when he isn't abroad on one of those Government sponsored goodwill missions.'

'Nick, you really must stop challenging me about my relationship with Bill. It's as though you're expecting it to go wrong,' Kate said, looking at Nick askance. 'Being married to a career politician may not be everyone's cup of tea but it suits me fine. Don't forget, I have a career too and Bill totally accepts that, which is more than many men would do in his position. He's also kind and thoughtful and we rarely have a cross word.'

'I'm sorry, I shouldn't have asked.' Nick said. 'It was insensitive. But I care about you Kate and I hate to think that anyone would take you for granted.'

'Well perhaps it's time you took a look at your own life instead of worrying about mine,' she said. 'Isn't it time you found someone to share it with? After all, you're not far off your fortieth.'

Kate looked at Nick triumphantly. She had always found a way of turning the conversation around when he touched on one of her sensitive areas and her relationship with her husband was one of them. Nick raised his hands in surrender:

'All right, all right,' he said. 'I guess I deserved that. The truth is I simply haven't found anyone I particularly want to spend much time with, not since Olivia and I broke up.'

'But that was nearly two years ago!' Kate exclaimed. 'I know Olivia dumped you but surely you must have got over her by now. The truth is, you don't get out enough. Let's face it, when you're not teaching up at the school you spend most of your time locked up in your flat here, beavering away on your next great musical masterpiece. That may be good for posterity but it isn't doing you any good. I know you too well, there's no way you're a natural recluse. You need to get out more, go searching for that perfect muse who will provide inspiration for your creativity and something nice and warm to cuddle up to at night!'

Nick knew she was right but didn't want to discuss the matter any further. He was still smarting from the way in which Olivia had walked out on him.

'I hear what you say and I promise to try to do something about it when we get back from Yorkshire,' he said, 'and, by the way, when and where do you want to meet up next Thursday? I can get the tube over to your place, if you like.'

'We'll be heading for the M1,' she said, 'so it's probably best if I pick you up here in Crawford Street, then we can head straight up north via the Edgeware Road.'

'I don't know, door-to-door service; I'm a lucky fella to have a sister like you. By the way, the solicitor said bring your passport as they will need proof of identification.'

Kate said she would set off as soon as the worst of the rush hour was over and would aim to get to him by mid-morning. She begged him to look out for her as parking was such a nightmare in his street.

After Kate had left Nick poured himself a last glass of wine. Stimulated by their plans for the following week he didn't feel quite ready for bed. He turned the lights out in the sitting room, went over to the window and drew back the curtains to look out over the street below. His flat was on the second floor, providing him with an excellent view of the cafés and bars that lined each side of Crawford Street towards Seymour Place and beyond. It was well past 11pm but there were still plenty of people about, gathered in small groups, not wanting their evenings to end, lingering over final farewells before heading off home. Although he could hardly afford the small flat he rented from the prosperous business syndicate that had bought up several of the houses along the street, Nick enjoyed living in the heart of the West End. He was often asked how he managed to write music surrounded by so much noise from the passing traffic and the constant bustle of human activity but, for him, this had never been a problem. He found it so easy to shut out external distractions that Kate had once remarked that he must have inherited his father's genes, for there are few noisier places than a busy newspaper office. Apart from a few months based in Manchester on a composer residency programme, Nick had never lived anywhere other than London. He had often wondered if, like so many of his colleagues, he would find greater inspiration in the peace of the countryside, but the opportunity to find out had never presented itself. He went to bed buoyed up by his sister's visit and the thought of their trip to Bradford the following week. It would be good to get out of London for a day or two. He was looking forward to the opportunity of finding out more about his roots and the mysterious great-aunt who, despite family feuds and the passing of so many years, hadn't altogether forgotten them.

Chapter 2

WHEN KATE ARRIVED outside Nick's flat she was pleased to find him standing outside the front door waiting for her. They made good time leaving London and, despite a brief delay due to road works between St John's Wood and Swiss Cottage, they were soon passing through the outer suburbs.

Kate was busy keeping an eye on the traffic and hardly spoke as she negotiated the challenging complexities of the North London traffic system. Meanwhile, Nick was happy listening to the radio and day-dreaming. However, once they reached the motorway, which was unusually quiet, Kate relaxed and they found themselves sharing childhood memories, especially about their father whom they had both missed very much since his untimely death.

'Do you think Dad would have agreed to come to Emmeline's funeral if he'd still been with us?' Nick asked his sister.

'From everything we've heard about his relationship with Grandfather Mortimer I very much doubt it,' Kate replied. 'I don't suppose we'll ever know exactly what caused the rift between them but it must have been something pretty serious. Dad was so warm-hearted and everyone adored him. I can't believe it was his fault. We know Grandfather was very disappointed when Dad refused to go into the family business, but would that have been enough to cause them to eventually abandon all communication? I suspect it might have been different if Grandma had still been around. From what Mum's said, I don't think Grandfather ever got over her early death. It seems it left him bitter and self-pitying as though he had been cheated in some way.'

'Well, I suppose that's understandable but you'd have thought it would have made him want to be even closer to Dad. After all he was his only child.'

'I guess there's no accounting for human behaviour. Until she died, I imagine he was so busy building up his business he would have left everything to do with running the house and bringing up their child to Grandma. He probably resented having to take on those responsibilities even if he was able to afford to pay for help.'

'I suppose so but I still find it all very odd. I can't get my head round how any normal father could reject their only child. It almost feels like some weird form of self-harm as he was just as much the loser as Dad.'

'I know, but then people often behave in the way you least expect. Trying to look at it from Grandfather's point of view: as well as losing his wife, his son has turned his back on the business empire he has spent the best part of his life building. No doubt, like many successful businessmen in those days, his natural ambition would have been to see his son inherit the business. And what does Dad do? He runs off and takes a low-paid job on the local newspaper.'

'I still don't get it,' Nick said. 'At least you'd think Grandfather would have come round when he saw how good Dad was at what he did. After all he'd reached Fleet Street before he hit thirty, and that's no mean achievement.'

'It may well have been too late by then. They'd probably passed the point of no return.'

'Yes, but why didn't Dad make a bit more effort to put things right between them? It seems so much against his character. He was always wanting to make peace and couldn't understand why people held long-standing grudges against each other.'

'I know, I don't understand that either. There must have been more to the rift between them than we've been told. I suspect Mum knows more than she's willing to say, but whenever I've tried to raise the subject she doesn't want to talk about it. By the way, I gave her a call as I promised but, as we thought, she didn't want to come up to Yorkshire with us. She seemed surprised to hear we're mentioned in Emmeline's will. She was even more surprised that she's only just died. I think she must have assumed she'd died years ago and nobody had bothered to let us know.'

Nick looked at his watch, 'I don't know about you, Kate, but I'm getting a little peckish. Do you think we might pull of somewhere for a bite of lunch?'

'Good idea, but I don't fancy the expensive rubbish they throw at you in Motorway cafés. Let's take the next exit and see if we can find a decent country pub.'

Nick readily agreed and they were soon heading across country towards Chesterfield.

'Isn't that the place where the church has a crooked spire?' Kate asked.

'Yes, I believe it is. However, as the wife of a left-wing Labour MP I'm surprised you haven't come up with a more personal connection with the town. After all, wasn't it where Tony Benn got himself re-elected to Westminster sometime back in the 1980's?'

'So it was. I should have remembered that. Benn is one of Bill's political heroes. He often talks about his courage in standing up for the miners during their long and bitter strike under the Thatcher Government. Sadly, they don't come like him anymore!'

'Well, I'm no socialist, but I have to admit that, the older he got, the more I found myself agreeing with him,' Nick said.

'Yes, he always seemed to come out on top when he was on *Any Questions*. I think he mellowed quite a bit as he grew older.'

'I always thought it rather odd that he and Enoch Powell were, reputedly, such good friends. You'd think there'd be a million miles between them.'

'From everything Bill tells me there's a massive difference between the public stances most MP's take and the way they behave off-stage, so to speak. I believe Benn and Powell had a great deal of respect for each other's intellects,' Kate said. 'Look, we don't seem to be doing very well on the lunch front. There's a turning coming up on the left. How about I take it and, with a bit of luck, we'll hit a village with a nice old pub before too long?'

They found just what they were looking for in a peaceful hamlet beside a slow-running brook, a proper country pub with exposed beams, a log fire burning in a large inglenook fireplace and a modestly priced menu of home-cooked food. Well refreshed, they were soon back on the road and heading up the M1. It wasn't long before they had passed the signs to Sheffield, Barnsley and Wakefield and, just a few miles before reaching Leeds, they veered off to the left on the final few miles of their journey to Bradford.

Kate had booked them in to the Ibis Hotel which, she explained to Nick, was close to the city centre, well positioned for their visit to the solicitors' offices on the Friday morning. Also, according to the reviews she had read, it was within easy walking distance of

Sultan's Restaurant, one of the best Asian restaurants in town. It was a fine spring evening so, after booking into the hotel, they chose to take a walk around the city centre before heading off to find the restaurant. They were surprised and impressed by the abundance of fine Victorian stone buildings in and around Centenary Square.

'They don't build them like that these days, more's the pity!' Nick said pointing at the magnificent City Hall with its tall, slender, clock tower. 'And don't you just love the old Alhambra Theatre there with its splendid circular domed tower? Just look at how sensitively they've extended it with that enormous glass structure. It looks like some kind of arboretum.'

'Yes, it's an imposing building all right but it must cost a fortune to run these days.'

'You bet it will!' Nick said. 'But future generations certainly won't thank us if we fail to maintain these wonderful symbols of our cultural heritage! Incidentally, talking of our cultural heritage, I wonder where St George's Hall is?'

'That's Bradford's concert hall, isn't it?'

'Yes, it's where they've put on classical concerts since it was first built but I think it was always intended to be more than just a concert hall. These days you're as likely to see the Rolling Stones as the Hallé on stage there. It's one of the largest concert halls in the North of England. Surely it must be somewhere close to the centre?'

'Look, there's a street map over there, let's see if we can find it.'

It didn't take them long to discover that St George's Hall was indeed in the Centre, just round the back of the City Hall from where they were standing.

'Perhaps we can take a closer look at it sometime over the weekend. I'm too knackered to traipse around much more this evening. Why don't we go eat and take an early night? We've quite a day ahead of us tomorrow,' Kate said.

Nick readily agreed and they headed off to find Sultan's restaurant which more than lived up to their expectations.

Chapter 3

NICK WOKE EARLY the following morning. Looking out of his bedroom window he was relieved to see the weather had remained fine and that the sun's bright reflection was captured in the shop windows across the street.

When he and Kate had talked about their great-aunt's funeral the previous evening they had assumed that few people would turn up for it. Kate had said she couldn't imagine anything more depressing than attending a funeral in some dark and unadorned Baptist chapel on a wet and overcast morning. Nick's own religious leanings, such as they were, had led him towards High Anglicanism with its rich liturgical and musical traditions. Thus, he too had his misgivings about the likely nature of his great-aunt's funeral.

However, over breakfast, he found his sister to be in a particularly buoyant mood. She said she hadn't slept so well for a long time and was very much looking forward to the time they were to spend together revisiting some of their old haunts.

'Your old haunts rather than mine,' Nick said. 'As I've already told you, I have very few memories of our childhood visits up here. I suppose I was just too young to take anything much in.'

'Well, I shall enjoy driving you around and sharing my memories with you. You never know, it may awaken a memory or two for you too. But, we've got the funeral to deal with first and then we need to fix a visit to the solicitor's office to find out about the will. What was his name?'

'Prendergast,' Nick said. 'There's a good old Yorkshire name for you. As we're not expecting there to be many showing up for the funeral, and we won't know any of them anyway, we should be able to get away pretty smartly after it's all over. We may even be able to arrange to visit Mr Prendergast this afternoon.'

'Yes, I agree. I can't see there'll be any reason for us to hang around after the funeral. If we can get the solicitor sorted today it'll give us three whole days for our trip down memory lane.'

As it turned out, they couldn't have been more wrong about how the day was to pan out. Far from being the dark and dingy, red brick, Victorian building of their imagination, Great-aunt Emmeline's Baptist church was a comparatively new building, set in an attractive park-like area, with well-laid-out flower beds ablaze with colour. Although they arrived half an hour before the scheduled time of the service, a large crowd had already gathered outside the main entrance to the church. at first Nick and Kate held back from joining the throng that is until the truth finally dawned on them. All these people were not, as they had imagined, leaving after a previous service or event. They were there for the old lady's funeral. Far from being a friendless old maid, it appeared that their great-aunt had been a popular member of a thriving community. Nick grabbed Kate's hand and they made their way tentatively forward. They felt very much strangers in the midst of this large gathering of local people engaged, as they were, in hearty conversation. Kate was about to suggest they made their way discreetly into the church when they were approached by a large, red-faced, middle-aged woman who gave them a warm smile and held out her hand in greeting.

'How d'you do? I'm Eve Duckworth, I don't think we've met before. It's such a sad day isn't it. She was a wonderful woman, had a heart of gold. I can't tell you how much she's done for our community. We're all going to miss her terribly. Have you come from far?'

'We travelled up from London yesterday.' Kate replied

'London, that's a long way. So how come you knew Miss Meredith?'

'Well, to be honest, we didn't really know her at all,' Kate said. 'I realise that must sound rather odd, but you see she was our father's aunt and there was a bit of a family fall out, years and years ago. Father moved south, got married and had us two. We only made very rare visits back up here to see the family and that was when we were little children.'

'Ah, so your father must have been Edward Mortimer's son. Miss Emmeline didn't talk about him very often except to say he had been a disappointment to her brother, although she never explained how or why. She was very close to her brother you know and I believe he was a great support to her. Hey George,' she called out, gesturing to a tall, lean, figure with heavy dark eyebrows and a neat little moustache.

'Come and meet this young couple. They're Miss Emmeline's great-niece and -nephew, would you believe?'

'Hello, pleased to meet you and welcome to our little community. I'm George Barnes by the way. So, you must be Mortimers too. I don't remember Miss Mortimer ever mentioning you, but then I don't remember her ever talking much about her family, apart from her brother that is and he must have passed many years ago. I believe your grandfather was quite a big noise here in Bradford. A successful businessman and a senior alderman on the Council. I never met him, but they say he was a formidable character and highly respected. But then you probably know that already?'

'Actually, we know very little about grandfather,' Kate said. 'As we've been explaining to Mrs Duckworth, I'm afraid he and Father didn't get on so we hardly ever came up North when we were kids.'

'Such a pity when families fall out,' Eve Duckworth said, 'especially as it's so often over something not in the least bit important.' Kate wondered whether this last remark was Eve's way of probing for a little further information.

'Nick and I have never really found out what was behind it all. Whenever we tried to raise the subject, Dad wasn't in the least bit forthcoming. All he ever told us was that he had fallen out with Grandfather because he refused to go into the family business.'

'So, what took him to London?' George Barnes asked.

'The offer of a job in Fleet Street,' Nick replied. 'He started his journalistic career up here on the Yorkshire Post, but no serious journalist ever turns down the offer of a job on a national newspaper.'

'So, he was a journalist was he. What sort of things did he write about?'

'Well, first and foremost, he was a theatre critic, although he did write regular feature articles on the broader cultural front, you know, BBC Charter Reviews, cultural contents of party manifestos, or lack of them, that sort of thing. He was quite often interviewed on the radio and rather less often on TV. But, of course, that was quite a while ago now, before he retired and he and Mother moved down to Devon to run a B&B.'

'Do they still live down there?' Eve Duckworth asked.

'No, Dad was drowned in a boating accident in 2001, just a couple of years after they'd moved down there. As I'm sure you'll understand,

Mother's heart went out of running the B&B after that and she moved back to London to be near us.' Kate replied.

'Oh, how sad! It must have been such a difficult time for you all. But these things happen I'm afraid and, at such times, we must seek our strength from the good Lord!' Eve said earnestly. Looking at his sister, Nick thought he saw a slight smile of amusement pass across her face. 'But do tell us a little more about yourselves,' Eve continued. 'It must be awfully expensive living in London these days. How do you earn your livings?'

'Well, it's not so bad for me,' Kate replied. 'I'm married to an MP and have a good job myself in the film industry. It's a bit more challenging for Nick. He writes music and has to supplement his more modest income by teaching and whatever else comes along.'

'I don't know, the careers you young people have these days, they're so much more exotic than the opportunities that were open to our generation!' George Barnes remarked. 'So, what's it like being married to an MP?'

'The honest answer is that it's tough at times, especially as we don't see enough of each other. But Bill and I share very much the same set of political ideals and values and we enjoy campaigning together. One thing's for sure: life is rarely dull!'

'I'm sure it isn't,' George said with a noticeable degree of respect in his voice.

During the brief exchange between his sister and their new acquaintances, Nick had been preparing for the moment they turned their attention to him. It was a moment he was dreading. He had always found the business of responding to well-meaning, but often ill-informed, questions about his career to be thoroughly tiresome. There were so few people who had any real understanding of how big a struggle it was to earn a living writing music or, indeed, in any of the creative professions. He had never forgotten the occasion when, at a post-concert reception, he had overheard the wife of the chairman of the sponsoring company ask that evening's soloist, the distinguished international pianist Cecile Ousset, what she did for a living! Such ignorance abounded even in the most moneyed environment. On this occasion, however, Nick was saved by the bell, quite literally as it happened, because the church bell began to toll and George Barnes gestured for them to make their way inside. As they passed through the porch they were introduced to the minister who seemed to be as surprised and delighted as the others had been to learn that Emmeline Mortimer had surviving relatives.

Once inside the church, Nick and Kate looked around and were amazed to see how many people had turned out to pay their last respects to their distant relative. There wasn't an empty seat to be seen and there were almost as many people standing at the back as were seated. By the way she summoned them to follow her, it was evident that Eve Duckworth was a woman of authority in this community. She led them down the aisle towards the very front. On reaching the second row of seats she leaned forward to whisper something in the ears of a young couple who were sitting at the end of the row. They immediately stood up, smiled, and invited Nick and Kate to take their seats and made their way to join those who were standing at the back.

The only church funeral Nick had ever attended had been at the Anglo Catholic church of All Saints, Margaret Street, in London's West End. That had been a splendid occasion, a requiem mass, with the choir singing Fauré's *Mass for the Dead* and the clergy dressed in purple vestments. The service that followed could hardly have offered a greater contrast. For all the simplicity of the occasion, indeed perhaps because of it, both Nick and his sister were profoundly moved. The sun was shining brightly through the clear glass windows onto the pure, white, unadorned walls The interior of the church was full of light. There was nothing pretentious about the music, a couple of popular hymns and a rather touching folk song, sung by a young man in jeans who accompanied himself on the guitar. The whole congregation joined in the hymns and prayers with an enthusiasm rarely found in the established church.

At various points during the service individual members of the congregation, both young and old, many with tears in their eyes, stepped forward to share their personal reflections on the life of the deceased, full of praise and gratitude for a life well spent. Nick and Kate were astonished to hear of the high regard in which she had been held. There was no doubting that the community's affection for her was genuine. By the time the minister stood to give his eulogy Nick half-wondered whether there was anything left to be said. However, there was a great deal more to come because it soon became apparent that Emmeline had been the church's principal benefactor and had been largely responsible for funding the very building in which they sat. Nick and Kate were a little embarrassed when the minister mentioned them by name, saying how delighted he was they had made the effort to travel up from London, especially as he believed they were her only surviving relatives.

After the service everyone gathered in the church hall where light refreshments had been laid out. By now, both Nick and Kate could have done with something stronger but had to make do with a cup of tea served from a large silver urn. It was a cheerful occasion, the celebration of a life well-served, of someone the community had admired and loved. Such a fuss was made of the young couple that, as Kate remarked to Nick later, she couldn't help feeling like the Prodigal Daughter!

They had spoken to almost everyone and were on the point of leaving, when they were approached by a tall, gaunt looking, elderly gentleman with a moustache and side whiskers, who introduced himself as Ronald Prendergast, solicitor to their late Great-aunt Emmeline. In appearance and manner he was everything you might expect of a 1930's northern lawyer. He politely expressed his regret at their great-aunt's death and enquired whether it would be convenient for them to call at his office in Manningham Lane later that afternoon, to which they readily agreed.

Chapter 4

IT WAS JUST after 4pm when they arrived outside the offices of Greenhalgh, Martin, Prendergast & Co. They were impressed by the fine Georgian house which the firm occupied. They were shown into Mr Prendergast's office which was at the rear of the building. It was a large room with a fine moulded ceiling and a view from the two panelled casement windows out onto an attractive, small, walled garden. There were a number of comfortable looking leather upholstered chairs set around a long reproduction regency table. Well executed oil paintings in heavy gold frames adorned the walls and there was a large desk in one corner from behind which the solicitor stepped forward to greet them.

'Thank you so much for taking the trouble to call round today. Please do take a seat at the table,' he said. 'It is so good to meet you at last. Ah, I can see you look a little surprised at that but, you see, as Miss Mortimer's solicitor for the past thirty years, I've long known of your existence and, how shall I put it, yes, of the somewhat strained nature of relationships within the family. You see, I was your grandfather's solicitor too, towards the end of his life. I know that he and your father fell out and that your father moved to London where he found himself a wife and had two children. Believe it or not, I tried hard to persuade your grandfather to remember your father in his will. But he would have none of it. He was a very wealthy man and I thought he might welcome an opportunity for some kind of reconciliation. But, I'm afraid, he felt your father had let him down by abandoning the family business.'

'Grandfather must have been incredibly bitter,' Nick said. 'Dad hardly ever spoke about it. I think he found it too painful. There's nothing he would have liked more than to stay in touch with the family up here in Yorkshire but, sadly, it wasn't to be. As a result, of course, Kate and I have grown up knowing very little about our northern roots. Only the other day we were sharing the few childhood memories we have of coming up north, but it's all very sketchy.'

There was a knock on the door and a smartly dressed young women entered carrying a tray laden with a colourful tea service which she set down on Mr Prendergast's desk. She poured the tea, passed the tea cups round, and then withdrew as discreetly as she had first appeared. After they had helped themselves to milk Mr Prendergast cleared his throat as though in preparation for the delivery of a major oration.

'Shall we get down to business? You may not know this but your great-aunt was a comparatively wealthy woman. She was devoted to her father and, as an unmarried daughter, she took on the responsibility of caring for him in his later years. In appreciation of this he bequeathed her a considerable amount of property including a number of terraced houses and a row of shops with flats above. And then, when her only brother Edward, your grandfather, died, he left her the proceeds of the sale of his business and other substantial savings he had in stocks and shares. Your great-aunt was able to live very comfortably on the income from property rentals and her investments. However, she cared little for the things of this world and lived a simple life, choosing to dispose of a large part of her income by supporting local charities and the local Baptist Church. She was especially generous to her many private tenants taking a much lower rental than the local commercial market would suggest. Indeed, on those occasions when one or other of her tenants faced hardship, she would invariably waive their rental payments altogether until they were in a position to commence paying again.'

'It sounds like she was a truly remarkable woman,' Kate said. 'What a pity we didn't get to know her.'

'Yes, she was a very remarkable woman and so selfless in her giving, never asking for, nor expecting, any expression of gratitude. Indeed, I remember her saying to me, on more than one occasion, how uncomfortable she felt when one of her beneficiaries took it upon themselves to thank her for her generosity. She was a true philanthropist, a pillar of our society. It was a great privilege and a pleasure to have her as one of my clients.' Mr Prendergast paused to wistfully wipe a tear from his eye. 'But, let me continue. In her will, as you might expect, she has left the lion's share of her estate to the church and to the charities she has long supported. She also gifted a number of her properties to long-standing tenants, leaving the remainder to the church to be let to the needy at peppercorn rents.'

At this point, the solicitor stood up and walked over to his desk where he picked up an imposing looking document which they soon discovered was a copy of their great-aunt's will. He sat down again at the table and leafed through the document until he came to the place he was looking for.

'Now this is the interesting part as far as you two are concerned. Let me read it to you.' He wiped his spectacles with a white cotton handkerchief and then continued. 'And to my great-nephew Nicholas Edward Mortimer and to my great-niece Katherine Elizabeth Mortimer, I bequeath to each the sum of £150,000, together with an equal share in the freehold of the property known as High House, situated in the village of Clodock, in the County of Herefordshire, together with the adjoining garden, meadows and woodland.'

Nick and Kate looked at each other in amazement and then back at Mr Prendergast.

'That's incredible news, I can hardly believe it!' Nick exclaimed. 'How enormously generous of her, especially as we haven't been in contact with her since we were kids. I wouldn't have been surprised if she'd forgotten about us altogether.'

'I agree. It's extraordinary, how very generous of her,' Kate said, looking genuinely astonished.

'Perhaps it isn't for me to say but your great-aunt always spoke well of your father. I gained the distinct impression that she felt her brother should have made more of an effort to seek a reconciliation with his son. She was never one to bear any kind of grudge herself. I feel sure that by including you in her will she was trying to make up for her brother's past mistake, as she saw it.'

'Well, I don't know what to say,' Kate said. 'I think Nick and I are very fortunate. I'm only sorry that we aren't able to thank her. But then, from what you say, she wouldn't have wanted that.'

'No, indeed,' the solicitor said, giving her a kindly smile.

'Can you tell us anything about the place she's left us in Herefordshire, what was it called? High something wasn't it?'

'That is correct, High House. I'm afraid I'm not able to tell you very much about the house itself. Indeed, until your great-aunt passed away and I was going through her estate, I'd quite forgotten about its existence. However, I've subsequently done a little research and, as I understand it, she originally inherited High House as part of her brother's estate. I believe that sometime, way back in the early 1940's, he purchased a Hereford-based engineering company that had gone into liquidation and the house was included in the sale. From the little Miss Mortimer told me about it, I don't believe your grandfather went down to Hereford more than once and I doubt he ever visited the Clodock property. His main interest was in the engineering business in which he invested heavily, selected a new senior management team and had the company back on its feet within a few years. That was, of course, in the early 1940's when there was a desperate need for skilled engineering work to produce materials for the war effort. Not long after the war, your grandfather sold the business as a going concern. However, it would seem that, somehow or other, at the time the business was sold, High House was not included in the sale and remained, unnoticed, within your grandfather's property portfolio for a number of years. When the existence of the property was finally brought to your grandfather's attention, he instructed a Hereford estate agent to put it up for auction, but it failed to reach its reserve price. As a consequence, the agent was instructed to rent it out and it was initially let to a local market gardener who used the property's large garden and outbuildings in which to grow and store his produce. The market gardener moved out in the late fifties and it appears that High House remained empty for some thirty years, that is until the South Herefordshire District Council contacted this office in 1986 to advise us that they were considering issuing a compulsory purchase order on the property as the house was in a serious state of disrepair and there was a considerable local housing shortage.'

'This all happened a short time after your grandfather's death and at a particularly difficult time for this firm as Mr Burrows, our senior partner, had just taken early retirement, due to illness, and it was he who had looked after your grandfather's affairs. It was at this point that I was invited to become a partner and it was agreed that I should take over responsibility for the Mortimer Estate which had now, of course, passed into the hands of Miss Mortimer. I remember your great-aunt was most distressed to hear of the communication from the District Council. She insisted on travelling down to Herefordshire immediately, with one of our clerks, to inspect the property and to meet with the District Council to discuss an acceptable way forward. Once they'd visited the house and weighed up what needed to be done, they called in at the Council Offices in Hereford. Miss Mortimer explained that she had only recently inherited the property and apologised for the fact that it had been neglected for so long. She undertook to commission a local builder to carry out repairs immediately to put a stop to further decay and the Council officers were quite happy to accept her undertaking. In reality, I suspect they were mainly concerned to deal with the complaints from local residents and not too troubled about the house's future use.

Once a local builder had repaired the roof, replaced much of the guttering and a number of the windows, we placed the property into the hands of a well-established estate agency in Hereford. However, they were unable to find any family interested in either buying or renting it. To be fair, a great deal of work still remained to be done in the way of internal renovation and decoration and then, of course, the village of Clodock sits on the Welsh Border and is very much off the beaten track. In the end the agents came up with an antique dealer who was looking for storage space, and the house was let to him until he retired to the south coast at the turn of the century. Since then, I'm afraid, the property has remained empty. After the antique dealer left, Miss Mortimer instructed us to put the house back on the market but the agents were again unable to find a buyer or tenant for much the same reasons as before. However, you will be pleased to hear that your great-aunt insisted that the Hereford agent should keep an eye on the house, and I have every reason to believe that you will find it in a satisfactory condition. I imagine you will wish to visit the property yourselves in the not too distant future. The keys are held by Ratcliffe, Pullin and Jones whose offices you will find in King Street in Hereford. I think you will find them to be most helpful.'

Mr Prendergast paused for a moment to look at his watch, sighed and said 'Dearie me, just look at the time. I hope you'll forgive me for having gone on at such length, but I felt you would want to know everything I could tell you about the property your great-aunt has bequeathed you. But now I'm due to see another client. If you would be so good as to leave your bank details and proof of identity with my assistant, on your way out, I'll make arrangements for the money you've been left to be transferred into your respective accounts. If there's any other way in which I can be of further assistance please feel free to contact me at any time. It's been a pleasure to meet you both. I hope you enjoy the rest of your stay up here in Bradford and I wish you both well for the future.'

Nick and Kate thanked the elderly solicitor for the considerable trouble he had taken in explaining the contents of their great-aunt's will. Having shown their passports and left their bank details with his assistant, they set off on the short walk back to their hotel. On the way Kate collected her road map from the car and they poured over it in search of Clodock, the tiny Herefordshire village on the Welsh borders, where they were now the proud owners of a house they had never seen. They were staggered at their great-aunt's generosity and over supper that evening they talked excitedly about 'High House' and what they might do with it.

'I've often thought about having somewhere out in the wilds where I can lock myself away and write my music. You know, for me it could be a dream come true,' Nick said

'Yes, I can see that,' replied his more practical sister, 'but we haven't seen the house yet. No-one's lived there for years and it probably needs an awful lot doing to it.'

'You're such a pessimist,' Nick said laughing. 'I'm hoping for a stone cottage with a fine view of the Welsh mountains. It's interesting that it's got a bit of land with it. I wonder if, originally, it was some kind of small-holding?'

'Could well have been. With a name like 'High House' you'd certainly expect a good view. But don't you think the name suggests something a little more imposing than a cottage?'

'Well, there's only one way to find out,' Nick said. 'We'll have to drive down there and take a look. I can't wait to see it! Do you know what? I rather wish we hadn't booked in to stay here over the weekend. If it was left to me, I'd be off down to Herefordshire first thing tomorrow morning.'

'Sorry Nick, but you'll just have to be patient. I'm keen to see it too but, as you know, there are also things we agreed to do here before we go back to London. The forecast for tomorrow is pretty decent so why don't we take a trip out of town and go for a walk across the moors. You never know, we might even find that spot Mum and Dad took us to all those years ago. And then on Saturday we could see if we can find the Grammar School where Dad went and didn't you say you wanted to visit St George's Hall?'

Nick raised his hands in surrender. 'Of course, you're absolutely right, we should make the most of our visit up here. I'm just being stupidly over-enthusiastic. Actually, there are one or two other places I'd like to visit while we're up here. There's the German church where Delius' family used to worship; I think it's some kind of community arts centre these days. And then there's that pub with the extraordinary name 'Delius Lived Next Door', that could be fun.'

'That all sound good to me,' Kate said. 'I'd like to visit the cathedral too before we drive back to London on Sunday. I thought perhaps we could attend their Sunday Eucharist. I know you're always interested to find out what the choir's like and whose music they're using.'

'Good idea,' Nick said. 'I'm happy with all that but, before we get back to London, I'm determined to tie you down to a time when we can make that visit down to Herefordshire.'

'No problem there. I can't wait to see it either. How about next weekend? Bill doesn't get back from his overseas trip until the middle of the following week, so this high-quality taxi service will be at your disposal! Will that be soon enough for my ever-demanding little brother?'

Chapter 5

ONCE BACK IN London, Nick spent much of the following week scouring the internet. He was determined to find out everything he could about the village of Clodock and the immediate surrounding area, before travelling down there with Kate. When he searched for it on Google Earth, he was disappointed not to be able to locate the house itself. He wondered if it was now known by a different name. Neither he nor his sister had ever visited the Welsh Marches. Indeed, the only time Nick had crossed the border had been to attend a performance of his choral anthem 'Christ is Risen', at Llandaff Cathedral some years previously.

His researches revealed Clodock to be a small settlement with most of the houses gathered around a twelfth-century church dedicated to St Clydog, a sixth-century king of the ancient kingdom of Ewyas, who had been martyred somewhere around 500 AD. Nick was particularly pleased to discover there was a pub in the village, 'The Cornewall Arms'. A short distance away was Longtown, a larger village with another pub, 'The Crown', a village shop and the remains of a Norman castle built on the site of a Roman fort. Both Clodock and Longtown were situated at the foot of the Black Mountains that separate England from Wales. The nearest town of any size was Abergavenny, some 9 miles to the South. Hay-on-Wye, the small Welsh town famous for its bookshops and annual literature festival, was fourteen miles to the North and the County Town of Hereford some twenty miles to the East. The whole of the Western part of Herefordshire appeared to be almost entirely agricultural, with most people living in the scattering of small villages that lay close to the Border. The other side of the Border, beyond the Black Mountains, was populated by hill farmers, their sheep and not much else until you reached beyond the Brecon Beacons.

Meanwhile Kate, who was much closer to her mother than Nick, had 'phoned her earlier in the week to tell her of their unexpected inheritance. She had been delighted to hear the news but was sceptical about the practicality of their taking on responsibility for a house so far away from their London homes. As she knew Nick was always hard up, her immediate reaction had been to suggest they put the house up for sale, especially as the second-home market was currently so buoyant. When Kate mentioned this to Nick he had been appalled at the idea, while she herself remained open-minded, at least until they had seen the property.

'For all we know it could be a complete wreck,' she had said, 'and, if so, where's the money coming from? I don't think Bill will be all that impressed at the idea of investing in somewhere so far from London.'

Nick had decided to bite his tongue for the time being. He had half expected his sister would be less enthusiastic about owning and maintaining somewhere so far away. He clung on to the hope that her enthusiasm would grow once she had seen the property.

As they had a good three-hour journey ahead of them, Kate picked Nick up from Crawford Street early on Saturday morning. Always the one to plan ahead, she had surfed the internet in search of somewhere where they could stay overnight while down in Herefordshire. However, she had soon discovered that, with the holiday season now in full swing, everywhere within a reasonable travelling distance of Clodock was already fully booked. Somewhat reluctantly, for she was fond of her home comforts, she had asked Nick how he felt about camping out in their new home for a night or two. This was exactly what he had wanted to do all along but had held back from suggesting, knowing of his sister's preference for more luxurious living. As a natural organiser, Kate had then come into her own, promising to sort out sleeping bags, blankets, towels, enough easy-to-prepare food to last them a couple of days, bottles of still water and a primus stove and kettle. Nick got off lightly with Kate only asking him to provide a bottle or two of wine.

They had arranged to pick up the keys to High House at midday. The roads were surprisingly free of traffic and the journey took less time than they had anticipated, so much so that they had time to stop for coffee in the attractive market town of Ledbury. When they reached Hereford they parked outside the Green Dragon hotel in Broad Street whence they walked the short distance past the cathedral and into King Street where the estate agents' offices were located. They arrived just as the cathedral bells were sounding twelve o'clock midday. They were seen by a Mr Jones, an amiable, elderly man, smartly dressed in a dark grey lounge suit. He explained that he had only recently become responsible for High House but that, judging from the files, it was some years since his company had received any instructions from either Miss Mortimer or her solicitors.

'The last record we have of the letting of the property was to a Mr Ronald West,' he said, pulling out some papers from within a thick manilla file. 'I believe he was an antiques dealer who only used the property for storage purposes. Following Mr West's departure in 2002 we received instructions to put High House on the market or to find another tenant. However, as you will appreciate when you drive down to see it, as properties go, it isn't everyone's cup of tea. I understand we were unable to persuade anyone to show any real interest in buying it. Clodock is well off the beaten track and the house is very much in need of modernisation. For similar reasons, we couldn't find anyone interested in renting the property. Tenants expect so much more these days: central heating, modern bathrooms and kitchens and all that kind of thing. And then, on top of all that, it isn't everybody who wants a property with quite so much land these days.'

'Yes, Mr Prendergast, our great-aunt's solicitor, said something about a meadow and some woodland. How much land is there, do you know?' Kate asked

'Upwards of nine acres I believe, mostly woodland, but there's a large garden which I'm afraid you'll discover is very overgrown.'

'Wow! That does sound quite a lot to look after', Nick said. 'Anyway, returning to your company's efforts to either sell or let High House, has there been absolutely no interest at all since 2009? I mean, is it still up for sale, or what?'

'It's our normal practice to review all the properties on our books every year,' Mr Jones replied. 'However, there's a note here, dated September 10th 2010, which says 'no action required, awaiting further instructions.' As to why we have received no further instructions since then I'm not able to say. Frankly, it's all a bit of a mystery to me. I can only assume that, somehow or other, Miss Mortimer, or her solicitors, either gave up on the property or have simply forgotten about it. Strange as it may seem, this is not altogether unknown in this part of the world. I can think of a number of properties in various parts of the county where it has been difficult, if not impossible, to trace the owner. More often than not it only becomes an issue when a property falls into serious disrepair and there are complaints from the local community, as appears to have been the case in respect of High House, some years ago. At that time, as you may already know, Miss Mortimer gave instructions for major repairs to be carried out to the external fabric of the property before the agreement was signed by Mr West.'

'It does seem a little odd. You see we have been told that our great-aunt was pretty meticulous in the way she handled her affairs.'

'Indeed,' Mr Jones said, looking a little uncomfortable. 'Anyway, if I may move on, although we haven't received any recent instructions concerning High House, Mr Samuel Benjamin, a retired parish clerk who lives in the village, has been retained for some time to keep an eye on the property for a very modest annual fee. He has a key and reports to us regularly in respect of any essential repairs that may need to be carried out. In his latest report, I'm glad to say, the only problem he raised was concerning a minor rodent infestation in one of the outbuildings. This was subsequently dealt with. I've informed him of your visit, but I'm afraid he's away this weekend and won't be able to meet you on this occasion. When you visit the house you'll find the electricity supply has been disconnected and, to be frank, I think you would be wise to have the entire system carefully checked over before you seek a reconnection. Of course, I don't know what you plan to do with the property and, doubtless, you'll want to look over the place thoroughly before you reach any definite decision. But please be assured we're here to help in any way we can.' Mr Jones opened the drawer of his desk and handed Nick an envelope containing a large clutch of keys of different sizes, all of which had tabs attached to them on which were written 'study', 'back door', 'cellar' and the names of the various doors they would open. 'Should you need any help while you are down at the house, apart from this weekend of course, you will find Mr Benjamin and his wife most helpful. They've lived in the village all their lives and are a mine of local information. They live at the white cottage at the edge of the village, just up the lane from High House. I've included details of their address and telephone number in the envelope along with the keys.'

After thanking Mr Jones, they headed back to Kate's car. On the way, Kate was unable to contain her anger at what she saw as the agent's casual manner. 'I can hardly believe it,' she said. 'They've had High House on their books for years and years and yet never really bothered to contact Emmeline or Mr Prendergast for further instructions. Don't you think it's downright irresponsible? Surely they must have some kind of obligation to ensure they get regular instructions in relation to properties on their books.'

'Well, I suppose that works both ways. You could say it was equally irresponsible of Mr Prendergast not to have asked for Emmeline's instructions.'

'Yes, that's true,' Kate responded. 'I couldn't help feeling a little sorry for poor old Mr Jones. It's obvious he's been landed with a load of the late senior partner's files without anyone giving him a proper briefing on their contents. It doesn't look as though he's ever actually visited High House himself, which is pretty unsatisfactory from our point of view, although I suppose he may not yet have had the opportunity to do so. But hold on a minute. Just look at that.' They had reached the top end of King Street and the great Norman Cathedral rose up majestically in front of them. 'I can't wait to have a look in there but I suppose it will have to wait for another day.'

'It certainly will,' Nick said. 'I want to look round the cathedral too, but that will have to wait. We've just become the proud owners of a place in the country and I'm dying to see it'

'Me too!' Kate exclaimed. 'I do wonder what it's like. I can't really picture it in my mind. When we first heard we'd been left a country property I imagined it to be a pretty little stone cottage, nestling in some trees, with a stream running through a garden full of wild flowers.'

'You always were a romantic!' Nick said, laughing, as they approached Kate's car. 'Anyway, we'll soon find out. It sounds like it's quite a big house. We can only hope it's in a reasonable state and that we haven't been left a money pit.'

'I'm afraid there's no satnav on this car, but you were always rather good at map reading. You'll find a local Ordnance Survey map in the glove compartment,' Kate said. 'I hope it won't be too difficult finding our way out to Clodock and, don't forget, the shortest way may well not be the quickest.'

Nick unfolded the map and spread it out between them. 'Well, it looks to me as though our best bet will be to take the A465 out of Hereford. It'll probably be signed 'Abergavenny'. And then, when we reach a place called Pontrilas, it looks like we should take a right turn and go through Ewyas Harold, Dulas and Longtown and then we're almost there.'

'All right,' Kate said as she carefully reversed out of their parking bay and began to head down Broad Street. 'I guess the most difficult part may well be trying to find our way out of Hereford, but here goes. Look out for signs, Nick.'

Once they had crossed the river by the old bridge, locating the A465 turned out to be easier than Kate had feared and they were soon making good progress, heading south towards Abergavenny. In the distance, to their right, Hay Bluff and the Black Mountains stood sentinel over the Welsh Border, providing a natural barrier between the English and the ancient Celts. After they had turned off the A465 at Pontrilas and passed through the sprawling village of Ewyas Harold, the road became little more than a country lane and the going became much slower. At last, they passed through the bottom end of Longtown, spotted the sign to Clodock, close by the 'Crown Inn', and set off on the last part of their journey.

'I think we should take it slowly,' Nick said. 'It's a pity there's no signal or we could have used google maps. High House could be absolutely anywhere from here on.'

'The thing is, we're don't really know what we're looking for,' Kate said. 'We may not even be able to see the house from the lane, if you know what I mean.'

They soon reached the tiny hamlet of Clodock, a scattering of cottages close to a very ancient looking church. 'There's a fork in the lane just ahead,' Nick said. 'I wonder whether we should go left or right.'

'I expect whichever way we choose will turn out to be the wrong one, sod's law!' Kate said. 'But hang on a minute, there's someone in the churchyard over there, Nick. Why don't you get out and ask him if he knows where High House is?'

'I hope he doesn't turn out to be the village idiot!' Nick said grinning. 'Anyway, here goes.'

Kate watched from the car as her brother approached the stooped figure in the graveyard, who she could see had been strimming round the gravestones. After what seemed to be an unnecessarily lengthy exchange between the two of them, the man raised his arm to point to somewhere beyond the village, touched his cap and returned to his labours.

'That took you long enough!' Kate said, when Nick returned to the car.

'Yes, well the old boy seemed rather surprised that anyone should be asking after High House. He mumbled something like 'can't think why you'd want to go there, no-one ever does.' When I told him we were the new owners he gave me an odd look as though he thought I was nuts or something.'

'Maybe that's not all that surprising. The house has been unoccupied for so long, and doubtless the whole place's totally overgrown.'

'I suppose so, but you know what? There was something else about his reaction, something in the expression on his face and in the way he said 'you be careful then young man,' as I was leaving. It was almost as though he was giving me a warning.'

'Now you're being really over-dramatic!' Kate said laughing. 'Come on, let's go to find out what mysterious secrets await us at High House. Which way do we go at the junction, left or right?'

'Left, and then it's just a few hundred yards further along, on the right-hand side. The old boy said you can't actually see the house from the lane, but to look out for the tall stone gateposts at the entrance to the drive.'

There was no mistaking the entrance to High House. The stone gateposts stood tall and majestic and were set in a high stone wall that appeared to run the entire length of the roadside front of the property. Although the right-hand gatepost was covered in ivy, it was still just possible to make out the name of the house, carved out in elegant Roman script. The cast-iron gates had, doubtless, long since been removed, either as a contribution to Britain's war effort or simply pillaged. Once they had driven through the entrance, the drive curved round to the right and steadily downhill along an avenue of what Kate thought were probably lime trees. The drive was heavily overgrown, a tangle of grasses, brambles, thistles and wild flowers. It was clear that no vehicle had passed down it for a very long time. Kate drove cautiously for fear of falling into an unseen pothole. Once they reached the end of the avenue of trees the drive curved sharply round to the left, giving Nick and Kate their first glimpse of High House.

The tall stone house stood back from a large open area which, they imagined, had originally been laid with gravel. In the centre of this was a raised flower bed with a large stone plinth bearing the statue of a Greek or Roman goddess, with an arm raised imperiously to the sky.

The house certainly didn't, in any way, resemble the cosy stone cottage of Nick or Kate's dreams. However, for a structure that rose so imposingly in front of them, there was something surprisingly welcoming about it. It was unquestionably late Victorian, or early Edwardian, but there was none of the usual overbearing firmness of line or element of fussiness in the form of wooden trellis-work on porch or balcony. Herefordshire sandstone lends a certain softness and warmth to the county's architecture and High House was no exception. The dappled pink stone of the façade positively glowed in the early afternoon sun. To the left of the centre of the frontage there was a modest porch framing a sturdy-looking front door. There were large casement windows to either side, two to the left and three to the right. The first floor boasted a similar number of smaller windows and above that there was yet another floor, built into the eaves, with tiny windows looking out over the front. The house was crowned by three tall chimneys with twisted stacks.

Nick and Kate climbed out of the car and stood staring up at the house.

'Blimey!' Nick said, after he had had a moment to take it all in; 'It's big, really big, nothing at all like I had imagined.'

Kate turned to look at him and then back at the house. 'Do you know, I'm at a loss for words. You're right, it's a big house all right, a very big house. At least it doesn't look in all that bad nick, if you'll excuse the pun!'

'Well, that's more than you can say for the garden, or at least for what we've seen of it so far. That really has returned to nature.'

'We'll unpack the car later shall we? I can't wait to explore inside,' Kate said. As they walked towards the front door the house towered above them, seeming to grow more imposing with every step. Nick rummaged through the keys the estate agent had given them and soon found the one marked 'front door'. It was by far the largest key in the bunch and was made of solid brass. He was surprised by how easily it turned when he inserted it in the keyhole. The large door opened with a slight creak and they found themselves looking into a sizeable hallway, with doors leading off to either side, and an impressive broad staircase rising up at the far end. The hallway continued down the side of the staircase, beyond which it looked as though there was a corridor leading deeper into the house.

'Wow!' Nick exclaimed. 'Just look at the fantastic carving on the staircase. What lovely coloured wood – it looks like mahogany.'

'Yes, and what about the floor. I know it's covered in a layer of dust, but aren't those just some of the prettiest floor tiles you've ever seen? They look Victorian all right. Give them a good old scrub and they'll clean up beautifully. Mind you, I'm not sure who's going to do the scrubbing!'

'Come on, let's start here,' Nick said, opening the only door on the left of the hallway. They found themselves in a moderately sized, unfurnished room with a fine stone fireplace. It had moulded ceilings and two large casement windows looking out onto the driveway to the front of the house. The walls were lined with bookshelves which, to their surprise and delight, still housed a substantial collection of books. They concluded that this room had probably been a study.

On the opposite side of the hallway there was a considerably larger room, with an even more splendid stone fireplace, and three large casement windows, again looking out onto the drive. Unlike the first room, this one was full of furniture. There were two sofas, at least half a dozen armchairs, and a stack of other furniture piled up at the far end of the room. There was also a somewhat threadbare chaise longue and, to Nick's delight, a 'baby' grand piano. After bashing out a few chords on it, he was pleased to discover that all the keys were still working, although the piano was in desperate need of a good tuning.

'It looks as though the antique dealer left some of his stuff behind,' Kate said, examining the furniture more closely. 'I'm afraid there isn't much here that'll be of use to us. Most of it's well past its sell-by date.'

'Yes, I can see we'll be having a mighty big bonfire. But isn't this a fantastic room. It's so wonderfully proportioned and those huge windows let in such a lot of light.'

'Yes, it's a lovely room. I should think it was originally the drawing room. Mind you, it looks like there are more downstairs rooms we haven't yet explored, shall we move on?'

The room next door was unfurnished, apart from an enormous oak sideboard which looked as though it had stood there since the house had first been built. Once again the room boasted a handsome stone fireplace. 'Somebody must have been kept pretty busy keeping fires alight in all these rooms!' Nick exclaimed.

'You can be sure there would have been a maid or two in a house this size,' Kate said, chuckling. 'Have you noticed the magnificent wooden floors in all these rooms? They'd have taken a fair deal of polishing.'

'So, shall we go to see what's down that corridor at the far end, beyond the hall? My guess is it leads to the kitchen.'

In fact, the corridor led not only to the kitchen but to a number of other smaller rooms. One of these had a large sink in it and appeared to have been some kind of pantry. Apart from a downstairs cloakroom, the original function of the remaining rooms was unclear, but Kate supposed that one of them might well have provided a sitting room for the cook and other servants, and that the others were probably used for storage. The kitchen itself was quite small for a house of its size. A large range cooker ran along one wall. A good part of the rest of the room was taken up by an enormous kitchen table. Through a rounded archway, there was a scullery with two substantial white ceramic sinks and built-in, floor-to-ceiling cupboards, all of which they found to be empty. The two windows at the far end of the kitchen looked out onto the garden at the rear of the house. Between the windows and the archway through to the scullery, there was a door leading out onto a paved area, on one side of which there were several outbuildings.

Once they had finished exploring the downstairs, they returned to the hall and headed for the staircase. On their way up they stopped on a half-landing to admire the wood panelling that lined the inner side of the staircase. Kate licked her fingers and rubbed clean a small section of the panelling. The rosy hue of the exposed area suggested it had been cut from red oak. On reaching the spacious first-floor landing they found three large bedrooms, all of a similar size and all with small, black, cast-iron fireplaces. They were surprised to find that one of the bedrooms was still furnished, with a handsome oak bed, dressing table and wardrobe to match, bedside tables and two wicker bedroom chairs. At the far end of the landing there was an enormous bathroom with an old-fashioned porcelain pedestal bath, standing on ornate cast-iron legs. There was also a washbasin with a huge crack in it and a toilet with an over-head flush-chamber.

Continuing on from the main staircase, a more modest flight of stairs led up to an attic floor. Here they found two small bedrooms, nestled into the eaves, and a third door into a further room which was locked, and for which Nick was unable to find the key. One of the bedrooms was filled with a clutter of small items of furniture, many of them damaged or broken, and there were two piles of cardboard boxes which they decided to look through more closely on a future occasion.

It was mid-afternoon by now and they hadn't eaten since leaving London that morning. Kate had prepared a picnic and suggested they took it outside in the garden. Nick set off in search of a suitable place, while she unloaded the picnic basket and two garden chairs from the boot of her car.

Nick soon returned with a cheery smile. 'I've found a perfect spot,' he said. 'It's round the back of the house. There's a sort of terrace area. It's less overgrown than the rest of the garden.'

'Sounds good to me,' Kate said. 'Perhaps you'd carry those two chairs, I'll bring the lunch.'

They settled down on the paved terrace where Kate had soon unpacked a couple of small baguettes, butter, a round box of camembert, tomatoes and hard-boiled eggs. She poured them each a mug of coffee from a large silver thermos. They were hungry after their long journey and exploration of the house. Initially overwhelmed by everything they had seen since arriving at High House Housethey ate in silence, trying to take everything in.

Nick was the first to speak. 'I don't know about you Kate, but this really is nothing like I'd imagined. I thought we might find ourselves applying the odd coat of paint to a small stone cottage, somewhere up a hillside and, of course, to giving the place a jolly good clean, but I never thought we'd find ourselves dealing with something on this scale. This is a serious project, wonderfully challenging don't you think?'

'You can say that again, thoroughly daunting if you ask me! My gut feeling is that it's too much for us to take on. I mean we don't even know if we've got running water and the electricity has been cut off. What if we find the whole place needs rewiring? The place is probably swarming with mice and rats who've been nibbling their way through the cables for years. Just imagine what it would cost to rewire a place this size.'

'There's no denying it's a big project. But surely the important thing is the house generally looks to be in a decent state of repair. The builders who took on the renovations and repair work all those years ago, after the Council complaint, seem to have done a decent job. As far as I can see, the roof looks sound enough and, superficially at least, the windows don't seem to be in too bad a state. You're right, of course, the first question is whether or not we've got running water and we can check that as soon as we've finished lunch. As to the electrics, well, we'll just have to look into that. I certainly wouldn't want to trust the existing system without someone passing their professional eye over it. The wall sockets and light switches must have been there for years. I think it's pretty likely the whole place will need to be rewired and, as you say, that won't come cheap. However, perhaps we can get some sort of limited power supply for the time being, you know, enough to provide a bit of lighting and a power point or two, so we can at least plug in power tools and things like that. Anyway, that's something we can think about later. In the meantime, we can manage with oil lamps and candles. I don't know about that big range cooker in the kitchen but I suspect it's solid fuel, and we may even be able to get it working. Who knows, with any luck, it may even heat the water.'

'If we have any that is!' Kate interjected. 'There you go again, the same old Nick! Such a romantic, and always so sure everything's going to be all right.'

'Well, it will be, trust me Kate. I'm really excited. Just imagine what a great place this would be for us all to get together, you know, Mum, you and Bill and your kids, when you get round to having any that is and . . . '

'And most of the population of Herefordshire,' Kate said laughing. 'It's an enormous house and, seriously, how often do you think we're going to even half fill it? As you said yourself, it's a potential money pit if ever there was one. I reckon it'll cost thousands to get the place properly habitable.'

'But surely Kate, that's the whole point.' Nick said, looking a little downhearted. 'We don't have to do it all at once. We can do it in stages. We don't need to touch the top floor at all if we don't want to, and we can manage without central heating and that kind of thing. It's a retreat, not our permanent home. We've got the money that Emmeline left us. I'm quite happy to dip into that.'

'Don't get me wrong Nick, I'm not necessarily against taking this on. But we must be realistic. I don't think it makes sense to go ahead with any major work until we've had everything properly costed. We must have a clearer idea of the size and scale of what we may be taking on.'

'I agree, of course I do. We'll need to make a list of all the essential things that need to be done and get them costed, as you say. We've got the whole of tomorrow to take a closer look at things. In the meantime, we have to decide where we're going to sleep tonight. The whole house is pretty grubby and covered in years of dust. So, I was thinking we might set up camp in that smaller room on the ground floor, you know, the one with the bookcases. There's no furniture in there so it should be relatively easy to give it the once-over.'

'Good idea. All the stuff I thought we might need for a bit of a clean up's in the back of the car. Perhaps you'll give me a hand to carry it into the house. I'm happy to make a start while you look into the water situation. Oh my God, there's a point! We'll be a bit stuck if we don't have any water and can't use the old mop and bucket.'

Always the meticulous planner, Kate had thought of everything and Nick marvelled at the impressive range of cleaning utensils that were soon neatly lined up in the hall. While Kate started work on the room they had chosen as their base camp, Nick made his way through the kitchen to the scullery to see if they had a water supply. The handle on the large brass tap over the sink was so tight he couldn't get it to turn. He looked around for any kind of heavy metal object with which to attack it. Eventually, he found a short, cast iron, metal bar in one of the cupboards. He couldn't imagine what had been its original function, but it served the purpose and he was soon able to turn the tap more freely. To his disappointment, not a drop of water came out, even when the tap was fully turned on. Then it dawned on him, of course, there must be a stopcock somewhere, but where, that was the question? It had to be somewhere before the pipe reached the scullery. He followed the pipe down and then at floor level through into the kitchen. He found the stopcock, low down, inside a cupboard, built into a recess by the door which led out into the back garden. It was an old-fashioned device with a small wheel which, to his relief, turned quite easily. Almost immediately he heard the sound of water gurgling through the pipe. He returned to the sink in the scullery where, after a considerable amount of hissing and coughing as the air was released, a great volume of dirty, brown, water came rushing out. Nick let it run and watched the water gradually become clearer. When he could see no further discolouration, he cupped his hands under the tap and took his first sip. It was ice-cold and tasted delicious, a far cry from the heavily chlorinated waters of the Metropolis. He hurried through to the study to tell Kate.

'Well, that's one of our major challenges happily resolved,' he said, 'Taste this.' He handed her a cup he had found in one of the cupboards.

'That's so good,' she said, 'It tastes like it's come straight from a spring.'

'I'm pretty sure it has. I followed the pipe to a cupboard where I found the stopcock. I don't quite know where it goes after that, but my guess is that it runs under the house and disappears somewhere into the hillside above the drive.'

'I suppose we ought to get it tested. You never know what nasty bacteria may be lurking in it, especially as it's such a long time since the supply was last turned on.'

'Yes, that's a good idea. I expect there's someone working for the Council who specialises in that sort of thing. However, I reckon it's safe enough to drink it for the time being, but if you have any doubts, you can always boil it. At least it'll be perfectly safe to wash in.' He looked round the old study. 'I don't know how you know where to start. Everything looks absolutely filthy.'

'It is. There are many years of accumulated dust, not to mention the mouse droppings, spiders and all sorts of other creepy crawlies who've made this place their home. However, now we've got water there's just a chance we may be able to win the battle and, at least, get this room cleaned up. There's a small calor-gas stove and a kettle in the boot of the car. If you wouldn't mind fetching them we can put some water on to heat up. Then I can make a proper job of wiping down the shelves and window sills and you can mop over the floor. You'll probably have to go over it two or three times.'

After a couple of hours of hard physical labour they had the room looking distinctly more habitable although, even with the windows wide open and despite a heavy dousing with disinfectant, there still lingered a slight smell of mould and decay.

'As long as we leave the windows open, I reckon we'll be all right sleeping in here,' Kate said. 'I think we've both done enough for now. It's been a long day and I'm knackered. Why don't we get a breath of fresh air before it gets dark. I'd like to explore the garden, or what's left of it, and the woodland beyond.'

'Just what I was thinking,' Nick said. 'There's hot water in the kettle so we can clean up a bit first. I don't know about you but I'm seriously grubby.'

'Good thinking,' Kate said, heading for the kitchen. They had soon scrubbed up and were feeling the better for it. As they stepped out through the kitchen door into the garden at the rear of the house, the sun was directly ahead of them, sinking slowly into a gold and orange sky over the Black Hill.

'What a view,' Nick said, 'and it's so quiet.'

'The birds must have gone to bed, but they'll have plenty to sing about when they wake up in the morning.'

'We'll have plenty to sing about too, this is pure heaven!'

'I wonder which way we should go?' Kate said, 'It's all so overgrown.'

'I can't wait to start hacking down all that long grass and those nettles and brambles and what-have-you. I can see we shall have to buy a strimmer. Come on, let's go this way,' Nick said, heading off towards the tall trees that marked the beginning of the woodland more or less directly ahead of them.

They trudged carefully through the waist-high vegetation until they reached a small, broken-down, gate that led into the woodland.

'I haven't looked at the deeds all that carefully as yet, but I'm pretty sure the woodland is ours,' Nick said. 'I can't believe how lucky we are.'

Kate smiled. 'I grant you it's a wonderful setting, Nick, but I'm worried it'll be all a bit too much for us to manage. And how often do you think we'll come down here anyway, and who's going to look after it when we aren't down here?

'The trouble with you Kate is that you can't think beyond your immaculate London home. But, as I see it, all we really need to do is to decide which parts of the house we want to live in, and to make sure they're comfortable. As long as the rest of the house is sound and secure, we can just leave as it is. We've got water and we should be able to get some sort of electricity supply. It could all be rather fun, don't you think?'

'What about hot water? We can't live out of a kettle for ever!'

'Well, I've had a quick look at that range cooker. I think it's got a separate boiler for heating the water. Of course, we'll have to have all the pipes checked and the tank too, wherever it is. I'll need a bit of help with that, but I think we should be able to get it working. There's no central heating, but there's a fireplace in practically every room, so we never need to be cold.'

'Fires in every room? And who's going to keep those going? We don't have a maid you know! And where do you think we're going to get the fuel from? And how much do you think it's all going to cost?'

'You're always so negative Kate. With all this woodland we've got a permanent supply of free firewood on our doorstep. All we need is a chain saw and somewhere to store the logs. I'll be happy to put in the hard labour, and there are loads of outbuildings we haven't even looked at yet.

'Nick, oh Nick, I do love you so when you get carried away with your grand ideas. I don't know what to say, I really don't. I grant you this is a wonderful part of the country, and I can see how easy it would be to fall in love with it. If this was that little cottage we had imagined it to be then it might be a different matter. We could easily manage something on that scale. But this isn't at all what we expected. It's a huge project, well beyond anything we can manage or afford. When we wake up to reality, I think we'll be well advised to contact a local estate agent and ask for a valuation, and preferably not from those blighters Ratcliffe, Pullen and Jones who appear to have done sod all about the place for years. We need to get some idea of what the house is worth and of its saleability?'

Kate could saw the disappointment on her brother's face and her heart went out to him. She put a comforting arm round his shoulders.

'I don't know about you,' she said 'but I'm feeling cold and it's getting dark. Let's go in and prepare something for supper and then we can sit and talk things through. I can see you've fallen in love with the place and I promise to listen to how you see things.'

Chapter 6

NICK WAS THE first to wake the following morning. He was surprised at how well he had slept. They had been so tired they had rolled out their sleeping bags quite early the previous evening. He saw Kate was still fast asleep, with her head resting on her forearm. He felt a pang of emotion. He and Kate had always been close. She had been the one to stick up for him when he had decided to pursue a career writing music, much against the advice of their parents. Over supper they had discussed possible future plans for High House and had reached an amicable agreement about the way forward. Kate had insisted they should still go ahead with a valuation of the property for insurance purposes, if for no other reason. However, after Nick had said he wanted to move into the house over the summer, where he would divide his time between writing music and making the place more liveable, Kate had agreed to hold back on any plans to put the house up for sale, at least until the Autumn.

Nick crawled out of his sleeping bag and tiptoed over to the window. It was only six thirty but a pale, early morning sun was already blinking through the trees, the tops of which were swaying in a light breeze. He put a jacket on over his pyjamas and made his way through to the kitchen where he lit the burner on the primus stove and put the kettle on. The house was silent, the only sound coming from the gas hissing under the kettle. He opened the back door and looked out over the garden. The sun was still low in the sky and everything on that side of the house remained in shadow. High above a tall ash tree, a large dark-coloured bird was seesawing in the breeze. He had never been very good on birds and wondered what it was. It looked too big to be a blackbird but then was it a crow, a rook or even a raven? He would have time to read up on that sort of thing now. He felt a surge of joy at the thought of the months that lay ahead, the challenges, the delights, the opportunities. He was woken out of his day-dream by the sound of the kettle whistling on the stove. He made two mugs of tea and carried them through to where he had left Kate sleeping.

'Room service,' he called out, putting one of the mugs down on the floor next to Kate's sleeping bag. She sat up, yawned and then climbed out of her sleeping bag and made for the door. 'I'm bursting for the loo. I can't spend the rest of the weekend crouching in the bushes!' She called over her shoulder. 'Do you think you might be able to get that downstairs toilet working today?'

'I'll take a look at it right after breakfast,' he called after her as she grabbed a coat and hurried out into the garden. He returned to the kitchen, refilled the kettle and put it back on the stove. He soon had eggs boiling in a pan, made a jug of coffee and buttered two thick slices of wholemeal bread. While he was preparing breakfast Kate came into the kitchen, with a towel round her neck, and went through to the scullery to wash and brush her teeth.

'That's better,' she said returning to the kitchen. 'Such wonderful ice-cold water, so refreshing, I feel like a new woman. What's for breakfast then, master chef?'

'Nothing too ambitious I'm afraid, just boiled eggs, buttered bread and coffee.'

'Perfect. It's a lovely morning. Do you think we might do a bit more exploring outside? I know there's lots to do in the house, but it's such a huge task it's difficult to know where to begin. I can't help thinking it would be wiser to wait until we're armed with more effective cleaning materials. We've got to go back to town this evening. I'd like to spend what little time we have left getting a clearer picture of exactly what we've inherited.'

'My own thought entirely. I'd like to take a look at those outbuildings first and then, perhaps, we could explore the woodland. I want to find out where our land begins and ends. But, first of all, let me take a look at that downstairs toilet. With any luck it'll just be a matter of finding another stopcock.'

They didn't linger over breakfast and while Kate cleared things away and washed up, much to her delight, Nick managed to locate and turn on the stopcock that provided water for the downstairs toilet and washbasin. After spending half an hour scrubbing out the cloakroom they were ready to set out on a further exploration of their small estate.

The main outbuildings were attached to the back of the house. There was a large room, with shelves running from floor to ceiling, which they assumed had originally been used for storage. It was empty, apart from a rusty old hand-operated mangle and a chest of drawers with one of its legs missing. Next door there was a small empty room where it appeared that coal had originally been stored. Lastly, there was an outside toilet with a broken seat. Standing some twenty feet apart from these buildings was a taller, barn-like, structure with a stone roof, part of which had fallen-in. It looked to be considerably older than the house itself and the other outbuildings. The large wooden door was hanging off its hinges at a precarious angle. As they put their heads through the doorway to look inside, a large rat scurried past and Kate stepped back in alarm.

'Ugh, that's as far as I'm going, if you don't mind!'

'There's nothing much to see anyway,' Nick said, laughing out loud at his sister's discomfort. 'Half the roof's fallen in, but otherwise there doesn't appear to be anything much inside. Well, that's the last of the outbuildings, let's go to beat the bounds of our country estate!'

They set off down the path they had trodden the previous evening, passing through the gate into the adjacent woodland. It was heavily overgrown with wild grasses, brambles, nettles, bindweed, a host of wild flowers and patches of bracken. The trees were mainly deciduous and, in many cases, choked in ivy. But, despite nature's efforts to reclaim the land, the traces of a pathway were still plainly visible and they were able to make their way without too much difficulty. They came to a clearing in the wood where a fallen oak tree offered an inviting place to sit and take in their surroundings.

'What a magical place,' Kate said. 'Don't you just love the sweet smell of the earth?'

Nick closed his eyes and raised his head to the warmth of the sun which was now almost directly overhead, relishing the tranquillity of the woodland clearing. 'Just listen to the silence!' he said. 'Apart from the occasional burst of birdsong there's hardly a sound. Do you know what Kate? This is just what I've often dreamed of, somewhere where I can shut the world out and let the creative juices flow.'

'Yes, I can see that. It's a very special place and I understand how it appeals to your creative instincts. But, as I keep saying, it may just prove to be too much for us. Forget the house for a moment, just think how much effort will need to be put into reclaiming the garden and clearing the woodland, let alone making the driveway navigable.'

'Funnily enough I'm not so worried about the gardens and woodland. Apart from clearing up the area immediately around the house, I'm all for letting the rest of it grow wild. Isn't that what we're being encouraged to do these days, anyway?'

'There goes the romantic again! But seriously Nick, of course I get where you're coming from and I've agreed to give it a go. However, I hold on to the thought that it might make more sense to put this place up for sale and to invest in a more modest property round here, or somewhere equally appealing. Wouldn't we be better off with a two, or three, bedroom cottage with a small garden and good views. Somewhere you could open up whenever you want to with the minimum of effort, and leave feeling confident it'll be safe and secure.'

But from Nick's response, she could tell he wasn't really listening.

'What I love about this place is that it really is an escape. Once you turn in at the gate you leave the world behind. It's not that I'm particularly anti-social; you know I'm not. But I've been finding it increasingly difficult to write anything of consequence with all the distractions of living in central London. I know I'm being selfish and thinking of what I need, but I'm certain I could spend many truly productive months down here each year. It's the perfect place to find inspiration.'

'I understand that, of course I do. It's just the size and scale of it all.'

'I know but, as I keep saying, surely it's a matter of how much we decide we actually have to do. We probably only need to tackle one of those large downstairs rooms in addition to the room we're sleeping in. The kitchen is a bit of a challenge, but I'm game to take that on, and the upstairs bathroom too. I'm sure we'll be able to hire a bit of local professional help with them if we ask around, and that applies to the electrics too. The main bedrooms on the first floor only need a good coat or two of paint. That done, there'd be plenty of room here for us to come down to stay whenever we want, and I'm including Mother in that. Just think what a fantastic place it would be for us all to spend Christmas together.'

'Well, I've already agreed to give it a chance. Bill will think I'm an idiot, but there it is, a promise is a promise. I guess I shall just have to learn to live rough for a while when we come down here, and that's no bad thing. You said you're thinking of coming down over the summer.

What about your teaching commitments, aren't you tied down until the school holidays?'

'Actually no. All my lot are taking their exams in a couple of weeks and I can relinquish my teaching duties after that. I can be down here from the middle of June right through until mid-September and maybe for even longer than that. You see, we've been warned there are likely to be cuts to the music budget and I may not even have a job next year. Bloody Tories, they're cutting everything apart from the core curriculum. They don't seem to be interested in anything creative apart from making more money! I fear that music and drama will be for the chop!'

'I'm really sorry to hear that. I know Bill's been going on about the Government's lack of commitment to the arts and broadcasting, especially the BBC, which they seem to see as some kind of threat. But, if you lose your teaching role, how will you survive?'

'Well, there's great-aunt's £150,000 of course, but that won't last for ever, especially if we're going to spend money on this place. Frankly, I need to come up with an idea for a commission. Most of my work, so far, has been on a comparatively modest scale, you know, string and wind trios and quartets, and pieces for small ensembles and choral groups of one kind or another. I feel the time has come to write something more substantial, an orchestral work requiring larger forces, perhaps even on a symphonic scale. I'm well into my thirties, I've been lucky so far and had good support from the Arts Council, as well as a few nice little commissions from festivals and music societies. But your time runs out in this game. The world always seems to be searching for new talent, and you're lucky to remain anywhere near the limelight after you've hit forty. If I don't make it big soon with something impressive, I shall be destined to join the growing scrap-heap of fallen stars!'

Kate turned to him, smiled and put a reassuring hand on his knee. 'You know I'm on your side. Go for it young man, that's what I say. I believe in you and I'll give you all the support I can, even if it means tethering your feet to the ground from time to time! Anyway, enough of all that for now, we've more exploring to do and I'm getting hungry.'

They rejoined the path beyond the clearing and continued through the densely packed trees until they reached a fence at the edge of the wood which, they assumed, marked the boundary of their property.

In the adjoining field a herd of cattle was basking in the sun. From where they stood, they had an uninterrupted view of the Black Hill. It rose up steeply just a few hundred yards from where they were standing. It was shrouded in a thin layer of cloud, its lower levels heavily clad in bracken. Looking to their right and left they could follow the line of the fence marking the boundary of their property. They lingered there for a while, intoxicated by the splendour of the view and the warmth of the late afternoon sun. When they finally meandered their way back along the path they talked excitedly about future plans. They agreed to carry out a more detailed inspection of the house and grounds. Then they would draw up a plan of action to establish the order in which essential work needed to be carried out. Once back at the house they sat in the garden, and ate up the remains of the bread and cheese Kate had brought down from London.

'Kate, I know you're struggling with the idea of hanging onto this place. I can't thank you enough for agreeing to give me a chance to see what I can achieve here over the summer, before we finally decide what to do with it. I guess it's up to me to prove we can turn it into somewhere we can enjoy together without it becoming a millstone around our necks.'

'I do see how perfect it could be for you and, I must admit, I'm seriously taken with this lovely county. Bill and I have often talked about trying to find a bolt-hole where we can escape from everything and everyone. His life is very public and the demands on an MP are very considerable, particularly when it's someone as conscientious as he is.'

It was just after six o'clock when they set off back to London. They were exhausted after all their hard labour, but well satisfied with the achievements of the weekend.

Chapter 7

THE TWO WEEKS to the end of Nick's teaching commitment passed quickly. Relieved of the pressures of school life, he was able to concentrate his energies into preparing for an extended stay in Herefordshire over the summer months. Given his modest income, he had been fortunate to find a fellow teacher whose lease had expired and who was desperately seeking temporary accommodation while looking for somewhere new. Nick had been concerned about leaving his Crawford Street flat empty over such a lengthy period and they soon come to a satisfactory agreement. The following Friday evening Kate agreed to drive him and a car full of clothes, food and other essentials down to Hereford. His survival, out in the countryside, was dependent on his having some form of transport, so they spent the Saturday morning there looking for a cheap second-hand vehicle. They finally settled on a small van, ideal for carting around the various tools and materials he would need to purchase during the renovation of the house. While in Hereford they also found a hardware store with an impressive range of household goods, where they purchased half-a-dozen oil lamps and two portable gas heaters. As Kate had to return to London, they transferred Nick's belongings into his newly acquired van and he drove on down to Clodock on his own.

When he arrived at High House he found a note had been pushed under the front door. It was from Samuel Benjamin, welcoming him and his sister to the village, apologising for not having been there to greet them at the time of their first visit, giving details of where to find him at Juniper cottage, and inviting them to call round at any time. As there were a number of matters he wished to raise with Mr Benjamin he decided there was no time like the present and set off on foot in search of Juniper Cottage. He came across the retired parish clerk, leaning on a garden fork outside the front door of his attractive, whitewashed, cottage.

'Good afternoon Mr Benjamin. I'm Nick Mortimer from High House. Thank you so much for your note. I do hope this isn't an inconvenient time to call?'

'Good afternoon, young man. I'm so glad you got my note. I assumed you'd be down again soon. I'm sorry we weren't here to welcome you before but Mrs Benjamin and I were visiting my sister in Newport. I was just about to go in for a cup of tea, I do hope you'll join me.'

'Thank you, that's very kind.'

The Benjamin's sitting room was bright and cheery. The walls were covered with attractive watercolours of what, Nick assumed, were local scenes and, in a corner, there was a glass cabinet full of china figures. Mr Benjamin motioned to Nick to sit down in one of the two flowery chintz armchairs beside the fireplace.

'I see you have an artist in the family,' Nick said, admiring a watercolour of sheep grazing in front of a copse of tall trees.

'Yes, these are all Mrs Benjamin's work. She studied at the Hereford College of Art and Design you know. It's now called the Hereford College of Arts. She'd have liked to have worked professionally somewhere in the Art sector but there weren't so many opportunities in those days. She loves her painting and she's sold quite a few through local artists' exhibitions across the county. I'm sorry you won't meet her today as she's upstairs washing her hair.'

'I look forward to meeting her on another occasion.'

'All in good time. Now what can I do to help? I've done my best to keep an eye on High House, to make sure it's safely locked up and that there are no serious leaks or that kind of thing.'

'Yes, Mr Jones, up at the estate agents, said you'd sorted out a rat problem recently.'

'Indeed, I'm afraid it's a real issue in the countryside. Leave anywhere empty for a while and the blighters'll move in before you can say Jack Robinson. I hope we've solved the problem. Now, what else can I do for you.'

'Well, you can imagine that when my sister and I heard we'd been left High House it came as something of a surprise. You see, we hardly knew our great-aunt, and it had certainly never crossed our minds that she'd leave us anything, let alone a small estate here in Herefordshire.'

'I can see that must have been quite a shock. It's such a responsibility taking on a house like that, especially with so much land. Poor old house, it hasn't had a very happy history, being empty all these years. You know, nobody's actually lived there for, let me see now, yes, it must be over fifty years. When a house remains empty for such a long time people begin to ask questions, you know what they're like. They tend to jump to all sorts of conclusions and to assume there must be something wrong with the place, and that soon leads to all sorts of wild imaginings. I don't have time for such nonsense, but you know how people are, letting their imaginations run riot.'

Nick listened patiently while Samuel Benjamin chattered on. He had never, himself, had much time for people who talked about houses having an atmosphere, whether it be happy or unhappy, friendly or unfriendly, or any other such nonsense. As he saw it, a house could certainly have negative or positive aesthetic qualities, but beyond that it was just bricks and mortar to him. He couldn't help chuckling when the elderly gentleman went on to tell him that quite a few local villagers still clung to their old beliefs, with their heads full of stories of ghostly spirits and things that go bump in the night.

'Well, that's all very fascinating, but I've never taken such matters very seriously myself. All I can say is that in the short time we've spent at High House so far, neither Kate nor I have had any particularly negative feelings about the place. After being empty for so long, it's certainly in need of a bit of love and hard work but I can't see anything we shan't be able to put right.'

'I'm glad to hear you're planning to do the place up. Not that it's any of my business of course, but are you planning to get contractors in or looking for a local tradesman to take on the work for you? If it's the latter, I may be able to help. There are any number of such folk around hereabouts, plumbers, electricians, contract gardeners and pretty much any other service you may require. It's one of the joys of living out here; there's never been any shortage of those kind of skills.'

'That's really kind and helpful.' Nick said. 'The thing is, Kate and I haven't altogether decided what we're going to do with the place as yet. That being said, I've fallen in love with the house already and I want to keep it. You see, I write music and it's just the sort of place I've always wanted. It's somewhere to escape to, where I can concentrate on my work without being distracted. I can see myself living down here for much of the year. But it's different for Kate. She's married to an MP and their life is inevitably pretty much centred on London. I'm sure they'll want to come down here from time to time. After all, it provides a perfect bolt-hole for anyone wanting to escape the demands of Westminster. However, I think Kate's initial feeling is that the house is rather bigger than we need and can afford. As she sees it, it's likely to require too much work to make the place comfortable. I'm used to living a simpler life and don't have the same reservations about the place. Anyway, she's agreed to let me see what I can achieve over the summer, during which time I intend to do my best to make the house more habitable. But, coming back to your kind offer of help, I'm not looking for a builder, at this stage, but I could definitely do with an electrician. We need to get the house reconnected as soon as possible. I expect the whole place probably needs rewiring. However, for the present, all I need is a limited power supply so that I can run extension cables from the supply point to operate power tools, lighting and my computer.'

'I know just the man for that. He's called Bob Jenkins, and lives up the road in Longtown. I think you'll find him very helpful and efficient, although you may have to wait a week or two as he's much sought after. I can give him a call if you like?'

'That would be really helpful, especially as we don't yet have a landline and the mobile signal seems to be somewhat variable hereabouts. I can't get any signal at all at the house. The other thing is, do you know anyone who's good with old boilers? As you know there's a pretty ancient cooker and boiler in the kitchen. I'm not sure what it is – it could be an early Aga, or something like that – but there doesn't appear to be any branding on it. I'm not too concerned about the cooker, but if we could get the boiler going it would make all the difference. We can't get by for long without hot water.'

'I'm not sure who to recommend for that. But I'll ask Bob. If anyone knows he will. As you're incommunicado down at High House, are you happy for him to just call round when he's in the area?'

'Yes, that'll be fine. Apart from popping out to do the odd bit of shopping, I'm not planning on going anywhere.'

'By the way, in case you haven't yet discovered it, there's a well-stocked village shop up at Longtown where you should be able to get most things you need. For building materials and anything like that, you can get practically everything you want in Pontrilas. Otherwise, we tend to drive down to Abergavenny but there are good suppliers in Hereford, Hay, Ross and Monmouth.'

'Well, you've been wonderfully helpful, Mr Benjamin. I really am very grateful.'

'No trouble at all, young man. By the way, please do call me Sam, everyone does.'

Well then, thank you, Sam, and you must call me Nick. Now, if you'll excuse me, I'd best be on my way. I haven't unpacked the van yet.'

'Goodbye then and good luck.'

'Goodbye and thanks again.'

As Nick made his way back down the lane, Mrs Benjamin emerged through the front door with a towel wrapped round her head and stood next to her husband.

'I could hear you talking outside. He seems like a nice young man. Don't you think you should have warned him about the house?'

'Well, it did come up you know, in a round-about sort of way. But he made it pretty plain he doesn't take such matters seriously and I didn't want to alarm him. After all, we really don't know whether there's any substance behind the stories we've heard. If there is any truth in them, don't you think it best they find it out for themselves?'

The evening sun had begun to sink down towards the top of the Black Hill by the time Nick returned from the Benjamins, and the front of High house was cast in dark shadow. He quickly unpacked the van, carrying everything through to the study. He had already decided this was where he would continue to camp out for the time being. It was in the old drawing room, on the other side of the hall, where they had come across the furniture which had been abandoned by the antique dealer. And it was from amongst these items that Nick selected the least threadbare of the armchairs and a small table which he carried through to the study. It had been a long day and he was both tired and hungry. He prepared a simple meal which he ate at the kitchen table. After he had eaten he retired to the study where he wrapped himself in a thick woollen blanket and lay down on his sleeping bag.

He closed his eyes to absorb the tranquillity of the evening. What a contrast this offered to his noisy London flat. There, the daily hustle and bustle of life in the street below could be heard from the early morning milk deliveries through to the ripples of intoxicated laughter as the late diners set off on their way home. It was a still evening without a breath of wind. Apart from the occasional fluttering of wings, the birds too were silent. He took in a deep breath of satisfaction. 'This is what I've always wanted,' he whispered to the shadows. 'I know I shall be able to work here.' Accompanied by these comforting thoughts he fell into a deep sleep, and didn't wake until a shaft of early morning sun had already cast its light across the room.

Chapter 8

IN LESS THAN a week, Nick had washed down the walls of the old study, made good the rough patches and applied sealant and a first coat of white emulsion paint to both the walls and ceiling. He was pleased with how much lighter the room now looked. He was washing out the brushes in the scullery one morning when he heard a knock on the front door and someone call out his name. He went through to the hallway to discover that a young man, with a mass of dark wavy hair and a straggly beard, had already made his way in and was standing at the foot of the stairs looking up at the high ceiling,

'They don't build 'em like that these days, more's the pity. . . wonderful craftsmanship'. The young man paused and grinned at Nick. 'I hope you don't mind me coming right on in but I wasn't sure as you could hear me, this being such a big place. I'm Bob Jenkins by the way. Old Sam Benjamin said as you might have a job or two needs doing.'

'Thanks a million for calling round so soon. Mr Benjamin gave me the impression I might have to wait a while as you're always pretty busy.'

'It's your lucky day! You see, it just so happens that a job I was about to start has been delayed. Some argument with the Council which'll likely take a week or two to sort out. So, I thought I'd just pop by to see what you want doing.'

'That's very good of you. What I need help with, at this stage, is the power supply. It must be years since this place was last wired and goodness knows how long since it was last in use. I wouldn't want to risk using it without a thorough examination. To be honest, the whole place probably needs rewiring, and that's a big job, not something we want to take on at present. But all I actually need, right now, is a limited feed to somewhere from where I can run extension leads while I start to do the place up. I could also do with your advice before I talk to the power supplier. You see I'm not sure what we have to do to get reconnected.'

'That'll be Western Power in the first place; they provide the infrastructure and bring the power to the house. That shouldn't be too tricky as there's been a supply here before. When you've decided where you want it, I can provide the consumer box and some temporary wall sockets. All you have to do then is to decide which company you want to buy your energy from and they'll come and connect you up. If you like, I'll be more than happy to talk to a chap I know at Western Power to get things moving. It should only take them a few days.'

'That'd be great. Where do you suggest we put the consumer box?'

'Well, I'd like to take a look round to find the existing power supply point. Going by the siting of the external power cables, I'd say it's most likely to be in the kitchen, or somewhere at the back of the house. It'll probably be simplest if we replace what's already there rather than start from scratch somewhere else.'

'That makes sense. As it happens, I haven't actually come across anything resembling a consumer box as yet, so let's go and take a look.'

They went through to the kitchen and scullery where they searched in all the cupboards but to no avail. They eventually found what they were looking for in a wall cupboard in the storeroom, in the outbuildings at the back of the house. Bob Jenkins explained that if he set the consumer box up there he could easily run a cable through the wall into the scullery and bring a power supply into the house. Nick said it would also be useful if he could provide a couple of sockets in the storeroom itself, as it would be an ideal place to set up as his workshop. In the longer term, Nick had had his eye on the storeroom as a potential music studio from the moment he had first seen it.

'Well, I reckon we'll be able to get all that fixed pretty quick like. I'll call Western Power when I get back home and let you know what they have to say. I can pop back tomorrow to fix everything this end, if that's OK with you. Meantime you need to decide who you want to be your supplier.'

'I quite fancy one of the greener companies. I'm in favour of anything we can do to help save the planet.'

'That's up to you, of course, but make sure as you're not saving the planet at the expense of your own pocket!' Bob said with a wry smile on his face. 'Now, moving on, Sam said as you might want me to take a look at that old kitchen range.'

'Oh, I hadn't realised it was something you might be able to fix.'

'I can't say as I can until I take a proper look at it. But at least I can give it the once over to see if it's worth salvaging.'

'That would be fantastic. It's the boiler we're really interested in. We desperately need to have hot water. I don't care about the cooker at present, that can always come later,' Nick said.

'Well, let's see how I get on tomorrow. Perhaps there'll be time for me to take a look at it after I've finished with the electrics.'

'Sounds good to me. What time shall I expect you in the morning?'

'Eightish, if that's OK. I like to make an early start.'

'That's fine. I'll have the kettle on.'

'Milk and two sugars and builders' tea for me, if you don't mind. I can't stand that fancy stuff some of the posh folk round here give me.'

'Don't worry, builders tea it shall be, and thanks again.' Nick stepped forward to offer his hand but Bob Jenkins was already halfway towards the front door. 'Bye then and thanks again.'

'Cheerio, see you in the morning,' the departing figure called back over his shoulder.

Nick breathed a sigh of satisfaction at the successful outcome of the morning. Not only had he achieved the prospect of a limited, functioning, power supply within a few days, but it seemed he might have found just the man-of-all-works he was going to need, in the months ahead. He spent much of the afternoon cleaning the storeroom in preparation for the electrician's arrival the following morning. Apart from a small patch of damp, in one of the corners, the room was generally in a good state of repair. With some difficulty, he managed to manoeuvre the old mangle out through the door and into the neighbouring coal bunker and cleared away several boxes of rubbish. He spent the rest of the day running backwards and forwards to the scullery with bucketloads of water and washing up liquid to wash down the ceiling, walls, and finally the stone floor.

It was mid-afternoon by the time he had finished cleaning the storeroom. He had toiled away, without a break, for the best part of the day and only now realised how hungry he was. He lugged a kitchen chair out into the back garden and, armed with a thick crusted cheese sandwich and a mug of tea, he sat down to enjoy the sun. He breathed in the pleasant scent of a massive honeysuckle bush that had grown rampant over much of the rear of the house. High up above, two kites circled round, floating effortlessly on the warm air currents, in search of their prey. He closed his eyes and listened to the bees buzzing busily around the jungle of grasses and wild flowers. He would have fallen asleep had it not been for the raucous cawing of the crows, coming from the upper branches of the ash trees at the edge of the wood. Their strident clamour seemed to arouse all the birds of the forest and soon the air was full of a chorus of birdsong.

It was amidst this cacophony that Nick first heard the sweet sound of a distant human voice raised in song. He could not tell precisely from where it came but sensed it was from somewhere above where he was sitting, although that seemed unlikely. It was unmistakably the voice of a young woman. The song was unknown to him but the melancholic melody had an instant appeal. The voice was far enough away for him to have difficulty catching the words, save for the phrase 'do not grieve', or something like it. And then the voice was gone, and there was only the sound of the birds and of the breeze rustling the leaves on the nearby trees, and he wondered whether he might come to believe he had imagined it. There was certainly no sign of any other human presence. He had often been asked from where he found the inspiration to write his music but had never felt able to provide a satisfactory answer. Indeed, the whole business of trying to define the sources of inspiration had remained as much a mystery to him as to many other creative people. When challenged on the subject, all he ever said was that there were times when he struggled to find a voice, that musical ideas often came when least expected, and from where he usually didn't know. Nick found the melody he had just overheard to have been sufficiently compelling to hurry inside and write it down on a score sheet before he forgot it.

The rest of the day he spent compiling a list of essential items they needed to make living at High House more comfortable. He had already decided to redecorate the bedroom on the first floor that was still furnished. The mattress on the large oak bed had been covered with a dust sheet and was in good condition. The large, four-drawer chest of drawers and wardrobe were a little dated, but quite serviceable. Apart from new bedding, all the room needed was a thorough scrubbing down and a couple of coats of paint. Much of the rest of Nick's shopping list comprised cooking utensils, crockery and cutlery, large cans of brilliant white gloss and emulsion paint, which he intended to use throughout the house, a bucket and mop, dustpan and brush, bleach and disinfectant. Satisfied with his day's work, and in readiness for an early start the following morning, he ate a light supper and retired to his makeshift bed in the study where he was soon fast asleep.

Chapter 9

NICK WOKE THE next morning to the sound of the study window rattling in its frame, shaken by a sudden gust of wind. Looking at his watch, he saw that it was only six o' clock. Through the window he could see the tops of the trees swaying in the heavy breeze. Dark grey clouds were scudding across the sky and there was no sign of the sun. It was a cool morning and he dressed hurriedly, putting on a thick woollen sweater over his 'T' shirt. He was surprised at how quickly the weather had changed. He went through to the scullery to wash and then boiled the kettle to make tea. By the time Bob Jenkins arrived, dead on eight o'clock as he had promised, the sky was even darker and the first drops of rain had begun to fall.

'Rotten morning mate, especially after yesterday,' Bob said, as he and Nick went through to the kitchen. 'But that's how things are round here. Weather changes in the blink of an eye. You can blame it on the Welsh 'cos it's coming in from the West, off the mountains,' he added with a chuckle.

Nick laughed. 'Well it's good to be able to blame it on somebody, I suppose. Would you like some tea? We're a bit short of home comforts but the kettle's just boiled.'

'Perhaps a little later, if you don't mind. I've only just had my breakfast and I'd like to get on with looking at the electrics. I managed to get hold of Western Power by the way. I've got a contact number for you as you'll have to place the order. They say they can't do anything this week but can send somebody over early next, if you give them a call. It may take a little while 'cos they say they'll have to check the overhead cables as they haven't been used for so long.'

'I thought as much, but that's OK I can manage for a while.'

'At least I can get everything sorted this end ready for the connection. I don't suppose you've decided which supplier you're going with?'

'No, not yet. Frankly, I'm not sure it makes all that much difference. Whoever you go with seems to put their price up at the end of the first year, which is why everybody keeps switching. As I said before, my instinct is to go for one of the companies investing in renewables.'

'Well, that's up to you of course, I'm all for saving the planet providing, that is, they don't start putting those massive wind turbines down the Golden Valley and spoiling our landscape.'

'I should think we're pretty safe from that round here aren't we? After all tourism's a growing industry.'

'You may say that, but I don't trust any politicians, do you? Most of them don't put their heads outside Westminster so far as I can see!'

Nick couldn't help grinning but decided it was not the moment to inform the swarthy young electrician that his sister was married to a Labour MP. He quickly changed the subject. 'I want to do a bit of shopping. I need a decent supermarket and a hardware store. Any suggestions?'

'Well, a lot of folk go up to Hereford, but I prefer Abergavenny myself. It's, nearer, not quite so busy and much easier to park. There's a big new Morrisons in Park Road near the centre of town and you won't beat Bailey's DIY for your decorating materials, household goods and that sort of thing. If you fancy going a bit more up market, there's a big Waitrose just out of town.'

'Sounds good to me. I'll have to buy some gardening gear too before too long but that can wait until I've got things in the house a little more under control.'

'That'll be a job and a half, when you get round to it, and you'll need more than a fork and spade. If it's any good to you I've got an old strimmer you can have; bought myself a new one last year. The old one works OK. It's a bit temperamental but, once you've got it started, it runs well enough.'

'Yes, I shall definitely need a strimmer, but you must let me pay you something for it.'

'That really won't be necessary. It's no use to me now and it'll only end up on the rubbish tip if you don't have it. I'll bring it along next time I come. Anyway, it's time I got started. I'll just go and get my kit out of the van.'

'Can I do anything to help?'

'The occasional mug of tea'd come in handy, otherwise I'm best left to get on with it, thanks all the same.' Whistling away cheerfully, Bob made his way out to his van. He was still whistling when he passed back through the kitchen on his way to the storeroom, wheeling a heavy-duty workman's trolley. Nick spent the rest of the morning scraping off loose bits of yellowed paint from the shelves in the kitchen and scullery. Bob returned to the kitchen with his sandwich box soon after midday. Nick made himself a cheese and pickle sandwich and they sat down to lunch together. Bob talked of what it was like living in the sparsely populated borderlands and Nick asked whether he had ever been tempted to move away.

'It can be a bit of a struggle making a living out here, I grant you. But who would ever want to swap the wonder of these hills turning blue on a summer's evening, the majesty of an open sky and the sound of the brook bubbling over the stones, for a three-bedroom house on an overcrowded housing estate in the suburbs. My life is here and always will be here. This is where I belong.'

'Wow, quite a poet aren't you! I like your passion.'

'I suppose I am quite passionate about the life I lead; it brings me a great deal of happiness and I don't see any point in looking beyond what I already have.'

'A sentiment I very much respect and share. I can already sense how easy it must be to so fall in love with this corner of England that you'd never want to be anywhere else.

'But you must be used to very different kind of life.'

'That's true, and I suppose there are things I would miss if I were here all the time. It's a question of finding the right balance. What I do know is that it's not something I've been very good at so far. Part of me longs for peace and tranquillity to spur on my creative impulses, but there are times when I need to be part of a wider creative community.'

'If it's of any comfort, you'll find no end of creative people out here: poets, musicians, writers, artists not to mention all the potters, woodcarvers and weavers to name but few.'

'I've been hoping that would be the case and imagine I shall get to know some of them, if I make an effort to become involved with the community.'

'That you will! But look at the time, I must get on or you'll be destined to remain in the dark for ever!' Bob said with a grin. 'Look, I can fix myself the odd mug of tea when I want one, it's stopped raining and it's brightening up. Why don't you take that trip down to

Abergavenny to do your shopping. Unless you get lost, I'll likely still be here when you get back.'

'Well, if you're sure you don't need me?'

'Sure as buttons!' Bob said, putting his empty mug down and heading off back to the storeroom.

'What an interesting fellow,' Nick thought to himself. 'I can see myself enjoying his company up at the Cornewall Arms.'

Chapter 10

NICK ENJOYED THE drive down to Abergavenny with the Black Hill rising up steeply to his right. He passed through the small village of Waterstone and continued on until joining the main Hereford-Abergavenny road. When he reached Abergavenny he easily found the large Morrison's supermarket, where he stocked up with groceries. Bailey's DIY was bustling with activity and stocked a wide range of products and he found everything he was looking for. Before leaving the town he filled up at a petrol station where he also purchased a petrol can and fuel in readiness for the arrival of Bob's old strimmer.

When he arrived back at High House he was pleased to see Bob's van was still in the drive. He was beginning to enjoy his company. He found him in the storeroom, on his knees, fixing a length of cable to the wall just above floor level.

'How'd you get on with the shopping?' Bob asked.

'Pretty well thanks. I found just about everything I need, for the time being at least. I can't go too heavy on the food front as there's no fridge. There's always Hope's in Longtown and I'd like to give them my trade anyway.'

'You'll go down well in the village with that sort of attitude.'

'Talking about such matters, I rather thought I might pay my first visit to the Cornewall Arms this weekend. I'd like to begin to get to know some of the locals. Any chance you might join me for a pint or two on Saturday evening?'

'That sounds a great idea. How would around eight suit you?'

'That'll be fine. I reckon I'll have earned a break by then.'

'By the way, I've fixed the fuse box over there and I've run a cable to a double socket on the wall nearest to the kitchen. That'll get you started once you've got the supply. You should be able to run your extension leads from here into the house OK.'

'That's fantastic!' Nick said 'Thanks a million for doing it all so quickly. Kate and I'd like you to give the house wiring the once-over at some stage. It would be helpful to know how much needs to be done and what it's likely to cost. I suspect it'll mostly want to be replaced, but we can manage for now. I've got stacks of oil lamps and Kate won't be coming down all that often. Perhaps we can think about tackling any rewiring later in the Summer? It would be good to have it all up and running before the dark winter nights set in.'

'That suits me; I've got a load of work on over the summer. Now, do you want me to take a quick look at that old boiler before I go? I may not be able to fix it myself, but at least we can get some idea of whether there's any hope for it.'

'That would be great, if you've got time.'

They returned to the kitchen where Bob began a thorough examination of the boiler. He opened the door to the fuel compartment. 'Blimey!' he exclaimed,

whoever last used this never bothered to clean it out. It's full of crap.'

'Don't bother with that, I can clean it out later,' Nick said

'What's interesting is that it looks like it's a wood burner. I've never seen that in a cooker this old before. They were usually solid fuel. That's good news, given the price of coke and stuff these days. You've a ready supply of timber in your woodland, if you don't mind a bit of hard work that is! Now, as far as I can see, apart from wanting a thorough cleaning out, it should work fine. Frankly, built as they were in those days, there's not much could go wrong with it. The question is, what's the state of the flu and the water pipes. From what I can see, all the piping is galvanised. That means it will almost certainly contain some lead in it, and I expect you know about the dangers of lead poisoning.'

'Do you think we'll have to have it all replaced then?'

'Not necessarily, it's up to you really. You see the problem is that the pipes coming in from your natural spring are likely the same, so it would be a major job to have done and mighty expensive.'

'That's something I'll need to discuss with my sister.'

'Fair enough. In the meantime, if you like, I can check the pipes up to the tank which, I assume, is somewhere up in the roof. If that's OK, we should be able to get the hot water system working. I can't do that now, I'm afraid, it'll take too long. Where are we now, Tuesday isn't it? I've got a job on tomorrow, but I could make it back here again Thursday afternoon, if that suits?'

'Thanks, that will be fine. I'm not planning on going anywhere this week. Look, before you go, could you do me a favour? I'm fed up with sleeping on the floor. Could you give me a hand to move a chaise longue through from the drawing room into the study? I can't manage it on my own.'

'No problem.' Bob said, and the job was soon done.

'Well, I'd best be on my way, see you Thursday then.'

It was approaching seven o'clock when Bob Jenkins left. The sky had brightened after a day of mixed weather and Nick went outside for some fresh air. He took the path to the wood and, after passing through the gate, continued on towards the clearing where he and Kate had sat on the fallen oak tree on their first visit. He was startled by a sudden frantic fluttering in the branches of a broad-girthed oak tree from which an angry-looking black crow flew off, disturbed by his presence.

He walked on, savouring the intoxicating scent of wild garlic. He was nearing the clearing in the middle of the wood when he first heard the sound of laughter and, directly ahead, saw a young couple standing with their arms tightly wrapped around one other. They were no more than fifty yards from where he was standing. The young man, who was considerably taller than the girl, had long, thick, black hair and heavy sideburns. His russet-coloured shirt hung down untidily over his breeches. By contrast, the girl's hair was the colour of burnished gold and hung in loose tresses halfway down her back. She was wearing a long, flowing, white summer dress that glistened in the sunlight.

Not wishing to disturb them, Nick stepped off the path to conceal himself amongst the trees. He was unable to take his eyes off the couple. He watched the girl reach up and begin to unbutton the young man's shirt. He, meanwhile, continued to hold her by her slender waist. He must have whispered something in her ear because she suddenly burst out laughing. She reached up to put her hands round his neck and gently pulled his head down so she could kiss him on the lips. Leaning forward he raised her off the ground, kissing her with renewed passion. Nick looked away, embarrassed. Although he realised the young lovers were trespassing on his land, he really didn't care. High House had been unoccupied for years and local people would, doubtless, have felt free to wander at leisure through its woods. The tall grasses and clumps of bracken, dampened by the early morning rain, were now vaporising in the warmth of the evening sun. Nick couldn't resist taking another look. The young couple were being slowly enveloped in a thickening mist that was swirling towards him through the trees. Their features grew less distinct and the sound of their voices faded away until it was as if they had never been there. Nick thought they must have wandered off further into the woods. He returned to the path and entered the clearing, making his way to the place where he had seen them. The mist was much denser now, adding an ethereal quality to his surroundings. He stood by the fallen oak tree. There was a strong scent of a perfume and, although he could neither see nor hear anything, he felt he was not alone. A sudden blast of ice-cold air surged around him, creating a vortex that scattered the fallen leaves and bent the bracken and tall grasses to the ground. Nick stood, frozen to the spot, unable to move. And then, just as suddenly, all was still again, the mist began to clear and he felt the warmth of the sun on his back.

Severely shaken, Nick sat down on the fallen oak tree. What on earth had he just witnessed? He couldn't imagine how but was it, in some inexplicable way, related to the young couple he had just seen? Or was it just a bizarre coincidental happening, some freak of nature? The young couple had seemed real enough and there was that strong scent of perfume. But then where had they gone. It was as if, somehow, they had been swept up and carried away. And now, looking up at the evening sun blinking through the tall trees, and listening to the last calls of the birds before sundown, it was already difficult to believe what he had seen, or at least, thought he had seen. Once back at the house, he found comfort in a plate of bread and cheese and several glasses of Rioja.

Chapter 11

NICK WOKE IN the middle of the night with a crick in his neck. He'd drunk a glass or two too many the night before, had a raging thirst and felt very much the worse for wear. He went through to the scullery, downed two mugs of water and doused his head under the tap. He returned to the study hoping to gain a few hours more sleep, but he couldn't stop thinking about the young couple in the wood and the mysterious occurrence that had ensued. He finally fell asleep just as dawn was breaking and didn't wake again until brilliant sunshine was pouring in through the window. The nightmare memories of the previous day no longer seemed so tangible. The more he thought about it, the more real the young couple became, and the more likely it seemed that what had followed was nothing more than a weird freak of nature.

He turned his mind to the tasks that lay ahead. There was so much in the house requiring his attention. He needed to win Kate over so he decided to start with the upstairs bedroom. He laboured tirelessly throughout the day, missing out lunch altogether, and hardly stopping for anything other than the occasional hot drink. By the time the light was beginning to fade and it was too dark to continue, he had made good the walls and ceiling, sanded the door and window frames and applied a coat of primer. He looked forward to being able to apply the first coat of emulsion the following day. He had purchased good quality paint and was optimistic that it would need no more than two coats. With any luck he would have finished painting the room by the end of the week, and would be able to relax and enjoy his Saturday evening with Bob, up at the pub.

The following day he woke much refreshed after a good night's sleep. He remembered Bob had promised to call that afternoon to take a further look at the boiler and water pipes, so he set about clearing the ash out of the stove. He had only just finished when Bob arrived, earlier than expected.

'Hope you don't mind my coming so early, but I've finished the job up at Mrs Watkins and thought I'd come right on over.'

'No problem at all. In fact, I've just emptied out the ash.'

'You've made a pretty fair job of it by the looks. Now the trouble with these pipes is they've been painted and it's not too easy to see what lies underneath,' He took a penknife out of his pocket and scratched away at one of the pipes. 'Ah, you're lucky, they're copper. Mind you, they were probably installed before the use of lead in copper pipes was banned, but I doubt you'll come to much harm with them. They seem solid enough,' he said, giving them a good shake. 'Now I need to follow them upstairs to the bathroom and then up to the tank, wherever it is. I need to give it the once over to make sure there aren't any leaks. It's probably been drained, so we'll have to locate the stop cock and run some water up there to test it. You don't want to get flooded out.'

Water systems and the like had always been something of a mystery to Nick who nodded sagely in a vain attempt to conceal his ignorance. 'Is there anything I can do to help' he asked.

'Not just yet. There'll be another stopcock somewhere around that lets the water through to the system. Once we've checked the tank, we can come back down to look for it.'

Nick nodded his consent and they went upstairs to the bathroom where Bob made a further inspection of the pipes. They then went on up to the attic where they found a hatch above the landing giving access to the loft. Armed with a torch and standing on a rickety chair, found abandoned in one of the bedrooms, Bob managed to hoist himself up through the hatch. 'The tank looks in remarkably good condition,' he called down, after a few minutes. 'But . . hang on . . . now there's a surprise. It's your lucky day, young man. The copper piping up here's all relatively new. I'd say it's definitely been put in since the regulations banning lead. I wonder if the whole house has been replumbed at some time?'

'Well, I know my great-aunt had some work carried out a good few years ago. They did some work on the roof and most of the windows were replaced as well as the outside guttering. Perhaps they did the pipe-work at the same time.'

'Do you happen to know when that was?'

'I'm pretty sure the solicitor said it was in 1986.'

Bob climbed back down, dusting off some cobwebs from his head and shoulders. 'That explains it then. You see the regulations banning lead were introduced in 1970.'

'What about the main water pipe from the spring? Do you think they might have done that at the same time?'

'Very unlikely I'd say. That'd be a very big and expensive job, depending of course on how far it runs underground. But I wouldn't worry too much about that. It seems that most of your pipe-work is OK and I doubt you'll get lead poisoning.'

'Well, that's a relief. One less expensive job to have to worry about.'

'Now the next thing we need to do is to find the hot water cistern which must be somewhere up here. That door over there looks like a likely candidate,' Bob said, opening a narrow door between the two bedrooms. It opened into a large cupboard with floor to ceiling shelves down one side, and a sizeable copper cistern with flaps of lagging hanging down in tatters from its sides. 'Looks like the mice have got at it,' Bob said. 'You'll need a new jacket but that won't set you back too much. The cistern itself looks OK too.'

'What a relief,' Nick said.

'What's behind there?' Bob asked, pointing at the door Nick and Kate had found to be locked on their first exploration of the upper floor.

'We don't know. It's the only door in the house for which we don't seem to be able to find a key.' I haven't been back up here since we first came down.

'It'll likely be another bedroom,' Bob said, leaning heavily on the door. 'Ah, there's no give and it's pretty solid. You'll need to find a locksmith if you want to get in there.'

'Well, one day perhaps, but it's hardly top of our list as there's so much else to do.'

'Nothing like a little mystery,' Bob said grinning. 'Who knows, it may be hiding all sorts of secrets.'

Nick laughed. 'Like what? A hidden horde of treasure? A heap of gold nuggets? A couple of rotting corpses? More likely another pile of broken furniture, knowing our luck!'

'Now let's go and find that stopcock and see what happens if we run some water through the system.'

They found the second stopcock low down on the floor, just to the left of the cooker. It was similar to the other one only it was stuck fast after years of not being used. Bob finally managed to free it with the help of a small block of wood and a hammer. They immediately heard the welcome sound of water gushing through the pipes.

'That wasn't so difficult, was it?' Bob said. 'Now, if you stay down here, I'll go back up to make sure the ballcock's still working. I'll shout down if there's a problem and you can turn the water off. It's a pretty big tank so it'll take a while to fill. Why don't you put the kettle on while you're waiting, I could murder a cuppa!'

When Bob came back down again he was grinning. 'Tell you what,' he said. 'That was one of the easiest jobs I've ever done. The tank's full and, after a bit of greasing, the ball cock's working fine. I reckon you great-aunt must have replaced the system. I've tested the taps in the bathroom, and in the washbasins in the first-floor bedrooms, and they're all working just fine.'

'That's great,' Nick said. 'You've sure earned your cuppa.'

They sat down together at the kitchen table.

'You know what comes next, don't you?' Bob said. 'Unless you're one of those odd types who takes a cold bath in the morning, We need to light the boiler fire. There's a knob that lets you isolate the boiler from the rest of the cooker. So, are you up for giving it a try?'

'I sure am,' said Nick. 'There's a pile of chopped wood outside in the coal bunker. It must have been there for years, so should be nice and dry.'

In no time at all they had a bright fire burning behind the panelled glass door and soon the pipe leading up to the cistern was warm to the touch.

'All good so far,' Bob said. 'As long as you keep the fire well fed you should have plenty of hot water by the time you go to bed.'

'You mean I may actually be able to have a bath tonight.'

'Cleanliness is next to godliness my grandmother always says.'

'Mind you, I shan't be doing this every day, it's far too much like hard work. But once or twice a week it'll be good to be able to have a hot dip, and Kate will be overjoyed, I can tell you.'

'Once we've fixed the electrics, what you really need is an immersion heater in that cistern. I'll be able to fix that for you too, if you want.'

'Yes, that'll be a real necessity, especially when Kate comes down. She'll want a constant supply of hot water. She's not used to the simple life and nor is her husband.'

'Well, there's not much more I can do now, not until Western Power have provided the connection. I hope they show up when they said they will and don't run into any difficulties.'

'I've always thought it best to expect the worst, then there are less disappointments in life.'

'Anyway, let me know when it's sorted, and you've signed up with a supplier, and I'll come back and do my bit. I'd better not hang around. I've promised my girlfriend a night out at the Courtyard in Hereford to see one of those tribute bands, Bowie, I think it is this time. She loves that kind of thing. I'm more into folk myself, but I don't suppose you're into in that kind of music.'

'Actually, you couldn't be more wrong. It's a common misconception that classical composers are only interested in the sort of stuff they write themselves. As far as I'm concerned, there's good music and there's bad music and you can find that in every genre. Bowie definitely goes down as good music in my book.'

'I can see we shall have plenty to talk about on Saturday night. Anyway, I'd better be off. Enjoy your bath.' And, with a cheery wave, Bob strolled out through the front door.

Nick sat at the kitchen table, well pleased with the day's achievements. What a find was Bob Jenkins, a true man of many parts. With any luck he'd be able to finish painting the upstairs bedroom tomorrow. After that he'd tackle the storeroom in readiness for when he could set up his computer in there. He couldn't wait for the day when he would be able to get back to writing. The storeroom was a decent size and he wondered whether he might eventually be able to move the baby grand in there. He enjoyed using the Sibelius programme on his computer but preferred to develop his initial ideas on the piano. With this thought in mind, he went through to the drawing room. The piano stood in the corner, covered in many layers of dust. There didn't appear to be a piano stool so he selected a wooden chair from amongst the discarded furniture and sat down at the piano. The maker's name ROGERS was inscribed in gold, just above the keyboard lid. It was no Steinway or Bösendorfer, but it would do. He knew 'Rogers' to be one of a number of London based British piano manufacturers that had flourished for much of the twentieth century, before being overtaken in the popular market by the likes of 'Yamaha' and other successful Japanese, American and European brands. He lifted the piano lid and tentatively played a few chords. Apart from needing to be tuned it was in good working order.

He spent much of the rest of the late afternoon and evening keeping the boiler fire stoked up. However, he found time to take a short stroll around the garden and began to plan where he would start strimming. That evening he took his first bath. The water was so hot he couldn't hold his hand under it. It had been hard work, but he was thoroughly enjoying the fruits of his labours.

Chapter 12

FRIDAY WAS A day of slow but steady progress in the house and garden. Bob called round first thing in the morning to drop off the strimmer and Nick managed to get it going, but not without a struggle. He attacked the heavily overgrown back garden with a vengeance and cleared the whole area leading to the wood. He left the front garden untouched, knowing that Kate would have very definite views about what needed to be done there. He would have liked to call her to tell her how much he had achieved but didn't feel like driving up the lane in search of a signal. He went to bed that night tired and frustrated. There was so much more he could do if only he had electricity. He chuckled when he thought of the old campaign slogan 'Power to the People'. 'Too damned right,' he said out loud, raising a clenched fist to the heavens.

Nick was more cheerful when he woke on Saturday morning. The sun was out,
the birds were in full song, the bedroom was ready for a final coat of paint, and there was his visit to the Cornewell Arms and the good company of Bob Jenkins to look forward to. The day seemed to whistle by and by seven o'clock he was ready to lay down his tools, wash, and get ready to walk up to the inn. He hoped there might be somewhere there where he could recharge his 'phone. He was on his way out when he saw the envelope, lying on the floor inside the front door, with 'Western Power' boldly printed on the front. His hopes were dashed when he opened it and read the contents of the enclosed letter. 'Following an initial inspection of the site, we are sorry to inform you that the amount of work required to provide you with a safe supply of electricity is considerably greater than we had anticipated. We regret to advise you that, this being the case, and due to current demands elsewhere in our area, we are unlikely to be able to commence work on your supply until late September. We shall write to you again nearer to the time . . .'

'Damn, damn, damn!' Nick shouted out loud, banging his clenched fist furiously against his thigh. 'Just what I don't need! Oh bugger!' He folded the letter and put it into his back pocket. He would show it to Bob, but feared even he wouldn't be able to do anything about it.

By the time he had reached the end of the drive, and turned into the lane, he was feeling a little less angry. It was such a magnificent evening. As it sank slowly towards the Black Hill, the sun wore a crown of gold surrounded by ripples of bright orange, turning to scarlet and mauve. There was hardly a breath of wind. It was so intensely still it was as though the surrounding countryside had fallen asleep. He passed the Benjamins' cottage. The elderly couple were sitting in the back garden soaking up the last of the evening sun. A little further on he crossed the old bridge over the brook that joins the Monnow further down the valley. The water was flowing slowly and was crystal clear. He passed a cluster of houses to his right and there was the Cornewell Arms, next to St Clydog's churchyard, doubtless happy to serve the dead as well as the living.

He was early for his meeting with Bob and so decided to take a wander around the graveyard. He had always been fascinated by the more bizarre epitaphs that appear on headstones by which the living choose to remember their loved ones. When he and Kate were children, out on a drive, their parents had often stopped to look at the more interesting historic churches. Bored with their father's enthusiasm for Norman arches, lancet windows and ancient brasses, he and his sister had ventured out into the graveyards to see who could find the oldest person to have been buried there.

He was nearing the far end of the graveyard when he first saw the young woman. She was kneeling on the grass in front of a tall grey headstone. In her hand she held a glass jar full of wild flowers. She looked up as he approached and he was struck by how remarkably pretty she was. Her long green dress was open at the neck. Her hair was neatly tied back, the colour of the summer harvest. Her features were soft and delicate and there was a slight pout to her lips. Nick smiled and said a cheery 'Hello'. She returned his smile and then turned away as if too shy to respond further. He walked on, every now and then stopping to look back until the girl was no longer in view. He didn't know why, but there had been something slightly disturbing about his encounter with the young woman. It wasn't until he had almost reached the lychgate that he realised what had unsettled him. The girl bore a remarkable resemblance to that other young woman, the one he had chanced upon with her lover in the woodland. He felt compelled to go back to where he had seen her, kneeling by the grave. However, when he got there she had gone but the jar of wild flowers was still there, propped up against the headstone. So, whoever she was, she was certainly no figment of his imagination. He examined the headstone. The bold letters of the inscription had been finely carved into the granite:

TO OUR BELOVED DAUGHTER
AND SISTER

FRANCES WHITMORE

BORN 16TH MARCH 1908

DIED 17TH DECEMBER 1929

MAY THE HOLY ANGELS
WATCH OVER HER

He stood there for a while thinking how sad it was that a young woman should have died so young, just twenty-one. It was nearly a hundred years since she had died and he couldn't help wondering why the young girl would place flowers at this particular graveside.

When he entered the Cornewell Arms, Nick found himself in a long room with a stone floor and low-beamed ceiling. There was a scattering of wooden tables and chairs and two fine, high-backed, oak settles on either side of the open fireplace. There were traditional pub games too, table skittles, quoits and a dartboard. It was just as he imagined pubs used to be between the World Wars. Indeed, if it had been part of a film set the designer might well have been accused of gross exaggeration in his search for authenticity. The walls were littered with paintings, drawings, cartoons and photographs, many of them recording historic moments in village life. The only other customers were an elderly gentleman, sitting on one of the settles by the fireplace, and a middle-aged couple occupying a table at the far end of the room. On checking his watch, Nick noted it was already ten minutes after 8 o'clock and he assumed Bob was probably not the best of timekeepers. There being no bar as such, he saw that drinks were served through a side hatch and went over to order himself a beer. The young girl who served him explained that they didn't normally serve draft beer, but that he could choose from a variety of local bottled ales. He decided on a bottle of Butty Bach from the Wye Valley Brewery in Bromyard.

He was examining some of the pictures when he heard the inn door open and was pleased to see Bob Jenkins had just walked in. He had never enjoyed drinking on his own. Bob gave a friendly nod to the old man on the settle, who was busy rolling himself a cigarette, and came over to join Nick.

'Welcome to the Cornewell Arms,' he said. 'How do you like our little watering hole? A bit different to the sort of places you're used to, I imagine?'

'And thank God for it. There's hardly a pub left in London that hasn't had a ghastly makeover. These days it's all about serving over-priced beers, wines, smart cocktails, flavoured gins and classy food. I suppose they've got to make a living and it's hard to do so without moving with the times, but I miss the good old English pub.'

'Thank the Lord for the Real Ale revival.'

'Yes, that's the one saving grace. You can get good beer in town at a price, even if you're not always so keen on the surroundings. Anyway Bob, what are you drinking?

'I see you're on the Butty. I'm a cider man myself. Stowford Press is my poison. I see you've brought your mobile. Plug it in over there, I'm sure the landlady won't mind.'

Nick bought Bob's cider and they sat down at a table on the opposite side of the room. He noticed the elderly gentleman was no longer sitting by the fire.

'Who was the old boy, the one who was sitting over there?' he asked.

'Oh, that's Harry Williams, lives in a cottage across the way. He'll only have gone out for a smoke.'

'I saw him rolling a fag. I thought he was going to light up inside.'

'He would if he thought he could get away with it. Get him on the wrong day and he's a cantankerous old sod. Used to be caretaker up at the school in Longtown but had to retire early because of his rheumatism. Does a few odd jobs round the village to keep the wolf from the door. Look, I know we've just sat down, but how about we take our drinks out into the garden? We don't get many evening's like this. We might as well enjoy the sun while we can.' Bob said, gesturing towards the door.

'Good idea. Do you think the fine weather will hold for long?' Nick asked as they made their way out into the small garden overlooking the churchyard.

'You never can tell round here but I've got my fingers crossed. Mind you the farmers could do with a bit of rain but then they're always complaining about something. They moan when the sun's out and they moan when it's raining, they're never happy as far as I can see.' They both laughed.

Nick remembered the letter from Western Power which he'd tucked in his back pocket. 'Talking about moaning, I've got something to moan about. This came today and I'm pretty pissed off.'

Bob read the letter and shook his head. 'Uhm, that isn't so good. I thought there might be a problem, but not as serious as they're making out.'

'It's a pain and it's going to hold us up with work on the house. What's more, there go my plans to indulge my creative skills over the summer. I'm desperate to get back on my computer, not to mention my mobile phone. I'm really at a loss.'

'Well, I may have a solution. You see I've got a small petrol generator. It won't provide you with all that much power but enough at least to run your computer, an electric drill and a light bulb or two. The thing is, I lent it to Dave Wilmott, lives down the lane a mile or so past your place. He wanted to keep his chickens warm during the winter. I've been meaning to go to pick it up this last week or two. I'll call round there tomorrow and see if he's done with it.'

Nick heaved a sigh of relief. 'You're a mate, you really are. You keep coming to my rescue and I don't know how I shall ever pay you back!'

'Well, I'm trusting you'll know where to come if you finally get round to rewiring the house. In the mean-time you can buy me another pint of Stowford.'

After Nick had refilled their glasses he asked Bob if he'd always lived in the village.

'Oh no, only for the last three years. Mind you, I don't come from that far away. I was born and brought up in Hay. My dad's an accountant and wanted me to join the family business, still does as it happens, but he must be near to giving up on me by now. You see I went to Hereford Sixth Form College, did well with my A's and was all set to go off to Uni to do Business Studies when I got cold feet. I've always been a country lad and the thought of setting off for the smoke never appealed to me. My dad thinks I'm a drop out although I'm pretty sure my mum get's it. Anyway, I've a friend who's a builder and he kept telling me there's a real shortage of skilled plumbers and electricians in these parts. I took the hint, apprenticed myself to a local electrician, learned the trade and got my diplomas. It was a bit of a slog, but I didn't mind because it meant that, in the end, I'd be able to work for myself, something I've always wanted to do.'

'Do you get on all right with your parents now?'

'Pretty much so. Dad and I are like chalk and cheese but my mum's a softie. All she ever wanted was for me to be happy.'

'And are you?'

'Happy? I should say so. I work whatever hours I want. I'm in love with the girl of my dreams. We've found ourselves a pretty little cottage just this side of Longtown and we're about to move in together. You can't ask for much more!'

'No wonder you're so bloody cheerful. I'm sure you deserve it.'

'That's as may be, but what about you. Tell me honestly, if you're not planning to sell High House are you intending to come to live here permanently? There's plenty of folk who've bought places down here who only come down for the occasional weekend. But I don't see you as a part-timer somehow.'

'The honest answer to your question is that nothing's yet been finally decided. If it was left to me, then I'd be moving in permanently alright. But I've got a sister to work on who owns an equal share in the property. She's yet to be convinced that we should hang onto the place. It's not that she needs the money. Her husband's an up-and-coming Labour MP and she earns well making films for TV. No, it's definitely not the money. I think she's daunted by the size of the house and all the land that goes with it. She's afraid of taking on so much responsibility. I'm sure she's loves it down here just as much as I do but she reckons we'd be better off with a small cottage where I can spend what time I like writing my music, and where the rest of the family can come when they need a break. But I'm working on her and I'm determined to win.'

'Well, I hope you do. It's a great part of the world for anyone looking for inspiration. If you don't mind me asking, is there anything you're working on at the moment?'

'Not really. I've got a few ideas but nothing I'm too sure about as yet. I've composed lots of small-scale stuff. Frankly it makes sense these days if you want to get your work performed. However, I feel the challenge to put my pen to something more substantial but don't yet know what it is.'

'So do you actually earn a living writing music?'

'The short answer is no. I've been lucky. I'm doing a good deal better than many of my contemporaries, but only a handful of composers make a living, solely by writing. I supplement my earnings by teaching in a North London Secondary School. It's tough going but I've had a few successes.'

They talked on until it was nearly dark. Finally, Bob apologised and said he really ought to get back home as his girlfriend was due to finish her nursing shift at Hereford Hospital.

'I'll call on Dave Wilmott in the morning to see if he's finished with that generator. If so, I'll pop by and drop it off in the morning. By the way, don't forget your 'phone,' he said as he climbed into his van and drove off.

'I don't suppose there's much chance of being stopped by the police round here,' Nick chuckled to himself as he went back inside to unplug his 'phone before setting off on the short walk back to High House.

Chapter 13

AS PROMISED, BOB called round the following morning to drop off the generator. He soon had it set up and showed Nick how it operated. 'You'll find it's quite greedy on fuel so I would only run it when you really need to,' he said as he climbed back into his van and drove off.

By mid-afternoon Nick had had enough of decorating for the day. He'd finished the bedroom and there wasn't much more he could do until he moved his belongings out of the study. It was another fine afternoon so he decided to go for a walk. He took his mobile with him in the hope of finding somewhere with a signal. He was keen to catch up with Kate.

He passed through the village and headed for Longtown. He had just passed the Crown Inn, and was proceeding up the hill, when he heard his mobile 'ping'. The signal got stronger as he climbed the hill and, by the time he had reached the ruins of the castle, he had three bars on his screen. He 'phoned Kate who picked up almost immediately.

'I was wondering when you were going to bother to call,' she said. 'Bill thinks you must have gone completely native. You're all right, aren't you?'

'Yes, I'm fine thanks. There's bucketloads of work to do but I'm making good progress.' He told Kate about how they'd managed to get the boiler working and could now get hot water, with a bit of an effort. He shared his disappointment about the electricity supply but told her about Bob's small generator. 'But the best news is that I've finished decorating that upstairs bedroom and I've bought some new bed-linen. I shall sleep up there myself, but it's all yours when you come down.'

'I'm impressed.'

'Well, don't be too impressed. Much of the credit for all this goes to a chap called Bob Jenkins, he's been a huge help. It's him who lent us the generator. I found him through Sam Benjamin. He's a local electrician, jack of all trades, and one of the nicest blokes you could meet.'

'Do you want me to come down again soon?'

'You bet I do. I want to show off my handiwork.'

'You mean Bob's, by the sound of it.'

'Yes, but he hasn't done the decorating!'

'Look, as it happens, Bill's going away again on Thursday, another of his Parliamentary gigs. I was thinking I might come down on Saturday and stay over for a few days.'

'Oh Kate, that would be wonderful. I'm longing to see you and show you around. I had a drink with Bob in the Cornewell Arms last night, you know, the pub in the village. It's a real time-warp, you'll love it.'

'Perhaps we could eat there one evening?'

'No such luck, I'm afraid, they don't do food. But there's 'The Crown' in Longtown and I'm told 'The Bridge' at a place called Michaelchurch Escley is rather good.'

'OK, you've persuaded me; I'm coming down. Is there anything you need me to bring with me?'

'Not really Kate. I'm pretty organised. You can bring some eats if you like. But bear in mind we've only got the camping cooker and there's no fridge.'

'Yes, we need to improve on that. We can't be eating out all the time. Look, I'm sorry Nick, I'm afraid I'll have to go. Bill's calling me from the hall. We're late for another of those wretched receptions. He sends his greetings, by the way.'

'And mine to him. Goodbye Kate. I can't wait to see you.'

'Goodbye Nick, love you!'

Nick was determined to impress his sister and applied the paintbrush with renewed energy. By mid-week he had finished painting the study and storeroom and was able to begin work on the bathroom. He felt it was time for a dash of colour and, after a further trip to Abergavenny, returned with two cans of paint with the exotic names of 'Blissful Blue Silk' for the walls and 'Saphire Salute' for the window frame and woodwork. He also bought two tripod twin work lights which meant he could work later into the evenings. He had finished painting by lunchtime on Friday and spent the rest of the day tidying up the bedroom in readiness for Kate's arrival. He made the bed and filled a glass jug from the scullery with wild flowers which he placed on the chest of drawers. He retired to his makeshift bed in the study, exhausted but more than satisfied with his achievements.

Kate hadn't said what time she expected to arrive but he assumed it wouldn't be until lunchtime at the earliest. He decided the best way to spend the morning would be to attack the overgrown front garden. He only intended to clear it enough to provide Kate with a clean canvass for whatever she might decide she wanted to do there. After a couple of hours strimming he was surprised how much of the layout of the original garden began to emerge. He had uncovered the remains of a sizeable circular bed, in the centre of the drive, and a low stone border wall encircling the parking area. Most of the once plentiful shrubs behind the wall had either long since died, or lost any semblance of their original shapes. One plant that had survived and flourished was a magnificent fragrant rose covering much of the frontage of the ground and first floors of the house to the left of the porch. Its outer petals were a delicate shade of pink while the inner petals were of a much darker hue.

He was sitting out on the terrace to the rear of the house when he heard the voice again. This time it sounded closer and was more distinct but, as before, he couldn't make out the words at all clearly. It was unmistakably the same voice, singing the same melody. He listened intently, trying to determine from where it was coming. It wasn't from higher up this time, of that he was certain. No, it sounded as though it was coming from somewhere round the rear of the outbuildings, where the vegetable garden used to be. He called out 'Hello, where are you, can I help you?' But the singing continued, undisturbed by his intervention. He stood up and made his way round the back of the outbuildings. On reaching the vegetable garden, now a tangled mass of overgrown grasses and weeds, he stood rooted to the spot. What he saw he could only describe as a brief shimmering of something white and insubstantial which slowly dissolved into the air around it before he could fully take it in. The disappearance of the mysterious phenomenon was followed by an intense silence. It was as though all living creatures looked on in stunned disbelief. When he had recovered from the shock of what he had just seen, his mind wandered back to the image of the young couple in the wood.

Although substantial enough beings at first, they too had suddenly seemed to evaporate into the air around them. For a moment it occurred to him that someone was playing tricks on him, was trying to spook him, but he soon realised how unlikely that was. It was odd, but somehow, he wasn't over-disturbed by what had occurred. There was something so enchanting about the voice, something so beguiling. He wondered what Kate would make of it. He decided it would be wise not to mention it to her, not for the time being anyway. The last thing he wanted was to provide her with any further reason for not keeping the house. With such thoughts running through his head he returned to the front garden where he worked on until lunchtime, raking up into neat piles the grass and weeds from his morning's strimming.

After lunch, as Kate hadn't yet arrived, Nick began to clear the drive. It was around 3 o'clock when he heard the sound of a car engine and saw Kate's car cautiously heading down the drive towards him. With a welcoming smile, he stepped back to let her pass, downed tools and hurried back to where she had parked in front of the house.

'You've made it,' he said, as she climbed out of the car and greeted him with a warm hug.

'I intended to set off earlier,' she said. 'I wanted to avoid the Saturday morning shoppers. But, what with one thing and another, you know what it's like. The M4 was pretty busy, otherwise I've not had too bad a journey. I left the motorway near Swindon and came across country via Cirencester, Gloucester and Ross. I didn't fancy taking the motorway all the way through to Newport. Such a pretty run, that last part from Ross through Garway and Ewyas Harold. Anyway, enough of that, how are you, little brother? You've picked up a bit of a tan and you're looking quite the country boy in those old jeans and checked shirt.'

'I'm pretty good thanks. All this hard work rather suits me and the weather's been fantastic. But you must be dying for a drink after your journey. Let me put the kettle on and then I'll give you a guided tour.'

'Thanks, I could certainly do with a drink and I can't wait to see what you've been up to.'

Kate followed Nick round the side of the house and they entered the kitchen via the back door.

'It doesn't look very different in here,' she said. 'So where've you been practising your decorator's skills.'

'You'll see in a minute, but let's have that cup of tea first. Things worth seeing are worth waiting for!'

They sat at the kitchen table where Nick told Kate about what he and Bob had had to do to get the boiler working and of the joys of having hot water. 'Mind you it's quite a business getting it fired up and keeping it going, not something you'd want to do every day,' he said. 'Bob suggests we install an immersion heater when we have a proper source of electricity.'

'That makes sense,' Kate said, standing up. 'Come on then, show me your handiwork.'

'OK then, let's start with the old storeroom soon to become my work space, follow me.'

'Goodness, that's amazing. It's so much bigger than I remember and I can see your friend Bob's been busy in here.'

'Yes, that's where the feed will come in. Once we have a supply, Bob says he can provide us with a few power points straight away. However, as we thought, he reckons the whole house needs rewiring before we can have power throughout the house, that's excluding the attic floor of course.'

'And how much will all that cost?'

'Well, the honest answer is we don't know. Bob's happy to take a thorough look at the existing system and to give us a quote. I didn't want to give him the go-ahead until I'd spoken to you. I doubt whether it will come cheap.'

'Um, I'm not all that happy about committing ourselves to too much expenditure just yet. On the other hand, I suppose that whatever we eventually decide to do with the house, we're going to have to sort out the electrics. I think you should go ahead and ask Bob for that quote. Do you think we should get someone else to quote as well, to make sure we're getting a good deal?'

'Frankly, no I don't. I know Bob and I trust him. I'm sure he's not after making a huge profit and I'd rather go with the man I know.'

'OK then, I'll leave it in your capable hands. You seem to have got this room sorted, so where to now?'

Nick showed Kate the study next, where she was impressed by how much lighter the white painted walls now made it. They then went upstairs to the bathroom.

'I hope you like the colour-scheme,' Nick said.

'Oh, I do, its lovely. And you've polished up the brass taps, they're just like new, and you've found a mirror to put over the washbasin. It's perfect. I can see myself spending lots of time in here.'

'As you are wont!' Nick said, with a broad grin. 'And now for *la pièce de resistance*, the boudoir. I hope it is to madame's satisfaction.' He threw open the bedroom door and Kate uttered an exclamation of genuine delight.

'Wow, that's amazing. I love the bed linen and look, you sweetie, you've even provided me with a lovely bunch of wild flowers. Are they all from the garden?'

'They certainly are. So, do you think you'll sleep all right in here.'

'I can't imagine why not. It's such a lovely room now, so light and airy. All it needs is a colourful rug on the floor, and some pretty curtains, and it'll be home from home.'

'So, how many marks out of ten do I get?'

'Er . . . let me see now, how about nine and a half?'

'That's a bit mean isn't it, after all my hours of slavery?'

'There's always room for improvement.'

'So I keep telling myself. What do you think I should tackle next?'

'We should tackle next', Kate corrected Nick. 'I've come down expecting to work, you know.'

When they had gone back downstairs, Kate suggested they might sit in the garden while they discussed what should be their next project. It was so hot outside they chose to sit in a shady corner under one of the tall ash trees.

'You know you've done an incredible amount already, and I'm so pleased you've started on the garden, it was such a jungle.' Kate said. 'Being practical, I suggest the one room that does need our attention is the kitchen. We're likely to be spending a fair amount of time in there and it desperately needs some loving TLC. If you've any more of that white emulsion, I'll put on some old clothes and we can bash on with it together.'

'It just so happens I picked up several more cans on my last visit to Abergavenny.'

'Welsh paint, you mean you had to go abroad to buy paint!' Kate said grinning. 'I hope you had your passport with you.'

'You probably didn't know this, but where we are now, and much of this side of Herefordshire, used to be in Wales,' Nick said. 'Hence all the Welsh village names hereabouts, Llandinabo, Llanwarne, LLanvenoe, Llangrove, LLangarron, not to mention Ewyas Harold, the village at the centre of the ancient kingdom of Ewyas.'

'You've been reading up your history' Kate said, impressed.

'Not really, just putting two and two together, supported by a wee bit of advanced research before we came down here.'

Kate couldn't remember when she had last seen her brother looking so content and full of enthusiasm. She could see his new life was suiting him well. He'd had a tough few years and deserved a break. The unexpected generosity of Great-aunt Emmeline could not have come at a better time for him. She decided, there and then, that she would try hard to help his dream come true.

By half past six they had washed down the kitchen walls and ceiling. Nick had made good the cracks and crevices, while Kate had got down on her hands and knees to wash and scrub the tiled floor.

'I think that'll do for today,' Nick said. 'How about we wash up and I'll see what I can dig out for supper.'

'Actually, I've got a little surprise for you Nick. You'll find it in the boot of my car.' She threw him the keys.

He returned with a happy smile on his face, carrying a large cardboard box.

'Kate, this looks incredible, it must have cost you a fortune,' he said, cutting the tape that bound the box and easing out a large stainless steel camping stove with an oven, grill and a twin-burner gas hob.

'Actually, it wasn't as expensive as you might think and I couldn't bear the thought of you struggling away any longer with that tiny little primus. You can't live on baked beans and boiled eggs for ever. There's a large gas cylinder on the back seat of the car. I suggest you pick up a spare before too long.'

'I love you Kate, you're the best sister in the world.'

'In that case, what are you cooking me for supper?' she asked, squeezing his arm affectionately.

'It depends on whether you'll settle for *table d'hote* or want to go *à la carte*.'

'Well, despite the fact you're now equipped with a brand-new cooker, I'm happy to settle for *table d'hote*. Do you know what I really fancy?' she said, taking the lid off a picnic box she'd brought with her, 'My local baker's crusty French bread, with brie and tomatoes and a slice of paté accompanied, of course, by a glass or two of Bill's best Mouton Cadet.'

'You think of everything! It'll be dark soon. Shall I get the generator going or would you prefer to dine by candlelight.'

'It's a jolly good thing you're my brother or I'd think you were trying to chat me up. But, jesting apart, let's eat by candlelight. It's so peaceful here, I don't think I could stand the noise of that old generator.'

They passed a pleasant hour together over their supper until Kate yawned, said she was exhausted after such a long and busy day, and suggested they took an early night as there was much to do the following day. Nick boiled a kettle and carried it upstairs to fill the bathroom washbasin so that his sister could wash before going to bed. He kissed her goodnight, washed in cold water in the scullery sink and retired to the study where he soon fell into a deep and contented sleep.

Chapter 14

IT WAS SOMETIME during the early hours of the morning that Nick was woken by a strange and unfamiliar sound. At first, he couldn't make out what it was or from where it came. He sat up and listened. It was silent now and he began to think he must have been dreaming. But then, there it was again, a muffled, whimpering sound that seemed to be coming from somewhere upstairs.

There was no-one else in the house apart from Kate, so it had to be her. It was such a doleful sound. What could possibly be the cause of such despair. Was she crying in her sleep, tortured by some horrible nightmare? By now the whimpering had turned into a long, low series of moans interspersed with heavy sobbing. He had never heard Kate cry like that before. What on earth could be the cause of such unhappiness. Something had seriously upset her and he needed to find out what it was. He grabbed a torch and crept out into the hallway where he stopped to listen. There it was again but this time much louder and unmistakeably coming from upstairs. He had just passed the first turn in the stairs when it stopped. He reached the landing and put his ear to Kate's bedroom door, not a sound. He couldn't even hear her breathing. He tapped gently on the door but there was no response. He turned the handle, gently pushed the door open and shone the torch round the room and then towards the bed. Kate was lying with her head nestled in her arms in what appeared to be a deep and undisturbed sleep.

He shone the torch round the bedroom again. Everything appeared to be normal. He stood in the doorway trying to make sense of what he had heard. And then, there it was again, the same long, low, moaning sound, but definitely not coming from Kate's bedroom. A shiver ran down his spine. He had never heard anything so harrowing or unearthly before. He shone his torch towards his sister's bed again and saw that she was now awake, sitting up with a startled look on her face.

'What is it Nick? what's that awful moaning? . . . where's it coming from?'

'I don't know Kate,' he whispered. 'I . . . I thought it was coming from in here. I thought you were having a nightmare or something.'

He sat next to her on the bed and they huddled together, listening in horror and disbelief to the relentless wailing and sobbing coming from somewhere beyond the bedroom. She clutched his arm and he could feel her quivering with fear.

'I'm so frightened Nick. What in heaven's name is it?'

'I don't know Kate, but we need to find out. There may be a perfectly straightforward explanation . . .'

'But how can there be? Have you ever heard anyone cry in such desperation? It's almost as if ... as if it isn't of this world.'

'Shhh, there it is again. We've got to find out where it's coming from.' Nick crept over to the bedroom door and peered out. He shone the torch along the landing but there was nothing to be seen. He turned to look back at Kate. 'I think it's coming from the attic. I'm going to take a look. Are you coming with me or do you want to stay here?'

'I'm coming with you!' Kate said, hurrying across the room to take hold of her brother's hand. 'There's no way I'm staying here on my own, thank you very much.'

With Nick shining the torch ahead of them, they cautiously climbed the narrow staircase up to the attic. The sobbing grew steadily louder until they reached the top of the stairs, and then it stopped. The only sound was of the floorboards creaking under their feet. Kate crouched back against the landing wall while Nick moved stealthily forward until he reached the first of the bedroom doors. He turned the handle, held his breath and tentatively pushed the door open. When he shone the torch round the room it was just as they had last seen it, an empty space, devoid of all furniture. He edged his way further along the narrow corridor towards the second bedroom to which the door had been left open. Apart from the pile of abandoned furniture, nothing appeared to be out of place. Kate followed Nick along the corridor, gripping his free hand, terrified of what they might encounter. They stood with their backs pressed firmly against the wall of the corridor, waiting in fearful anticipation of what they might be about to hear or see. Nick shone the torch up and down the corridor and along the wall on the opposite side. The light came to rest on the door they had been unable to unlock. Apart from the cupboard, it was the only remaining door on the attic floor. And then, there it was again, unmistakably the sound of a woman weeping in the utmost despair.

'It's coming from in there,' Nick whispered, gingerly stepping forward towards the door. Kate clung onto his arm and tried to pull him back.

'For God's sake don't try to open it Nick, please don't . . . I can't bear it.' But it was too late, his hand was already on the doorhandle. But the door wouldn't budge, even when he tried putting his shoulder to it, so he called out 'Who are you? Why are you crying? What do you want?' It was at this moment that they heard a wild hammering from down below and the sound of men's raised voices, shouting angrily at each other. THorrified, hey froze with their backs against the wall of the corridor, too terrified to move. The sobbing from behind the locked door stopped and then a sudden rush of ice-cold air passed by them. This was followed by an ear-piercing scream and a crashing sound as if someone or something had fallen down the stairs. And then there was absolute silence. Nick was so shaken he dropped the torch, the light went out and they stood, huddled together, in the intense darkness. They were too frightened to move.

'In God's name Nick, what was that?' Kate whispered.

'I don't know, but whoever or whatever it was, I don't think it's up here anymore and whatever all that commotion was downstairs seems to have gone now. We can't stay up here all night. Let's go down and take a look. I've had enough of this ghastly corridor and its dark secrets.'

He bent down to pick up the torch and managed to turn it on again. The little light it gave shone on nothing other than the uncarpeted boards of the staircase and the bare walls and closed doors of the first-floor landing. There was nothing to be seen when they reached the ground floor so they headed cautiously for the kitchen. Nick lit two large oil lamps which filled the room with a warm and reassuring light. They were severely shaken by what they had just witnessed. Kate sat slumped over the kitchen table, nervously playing with strands of her hair while Nick put the kettle on. It was only after they were each clasping a mug of hot tea that they felt able to discuss what they had just experienced.

'You know how sceptical I am of anything to do with the paranormal but, against my better judgement, I think I've just become a believer.'

'The thing is, Nick, if you tried to describe to someone what we've just witnessed, they'd have every right to look at you in disbelief.'

'But, whatever it is or was up there in the attic, we both heard it. We know there was something up there, even if we can't explain it.'

'But what was it, Nick? That weeping and wailing was so intense, so utterly heart-rending, you could swear it came from a living being.'

'That's just what I thought, even when I realised it wasn't you. I imagined some poor, grief-stricken girl had made her way up to the attic for goodness knows what reason. After all, this place has been empty for years. Who knows who may have been using it as a secret meeting place or even as somewhere to hide. But then, when we found where the weeping was coming from . . . well then, I think we both knew it had to be something else, something I'd rather not contemplate.'

'Whoever or whatever it was came out of that room and passed right by us, of that I'm certain. The corridor was freezing. You must have felt it.'

'Oh yes, I felt it all right!'

'And then there was those angry voices we heard shouting at each other downstairs, that violent hammering on the front door, that awful scream and the crashing sound that sounded like someone had fallen down the stairs, what was all that about?'

'I honestly don't know, but I think that whoever it was we heard crying up in the attack was drawn by all the commotion going on downstairs. Whether we like it or not, there's something going on here we can't explain. It looks like our dear great-aunt has left us a house where not all the spirits are at rest.' Nick paused for a moment. 'Kate, I haven't mentioned this before, but I've had one or two other weird experiences since I've been down here. Until now I'd rather passed them off as figments of my imagination, but not now, not after tonight.'

Nick told Kate about the voice he had overheard singing on two separate occasions.

'What did you actually hear? Could you make out any of the words?'

'Well yes, there were words but they were all so indistinct. It is the melody that sticks in my mind it was so . . . I don't know, it was so beautiful, so magical, so perfect. The only words I could make out were something like 'do not grieve', but I can't be sure.

'Oh my God!' Kate exclaimed. 'What if that voice you heard belongs to the same being we've just heard crying her heart out in the attic?'

'Yes, of course, that's just what I'm thinking. But it's all beyond me. We've no idea what we're dealing with. If it is some kind of supernatural happening, then who or what is it?'

'More to the point, what are we going to do about it?' Kate said earnestly. 'I don't see how we shall ever be able to sleep in this house with some broken-hearted spirit wandering the corridors.'

'Well, the first thing we need to do is to find out what's behind that locked door, not now of course, but in the morning when it's light.'

Kate leaned forward to put her hand on her brother's arm. 'I'm not sure I'm up for that,' she said. 'I'm really scared Nick.'

'But, don't you see, we have to find out, otherwise we'll never feel at ease. You know, ever since we came here I've had a feeling there's something odd about this house, something I can't put my finger on. Don't get me wrong, I love the place but I want to find out what it is. I rather think our friendly electrician Bob Jenkins may know something and Sam Benjamin too for that matter. If you think about it, isn't it rather odd that nobody wanted to buy High House when they put it on the market? I mean it may need a lot doing to it, but, with all this land it's a pretty desirable property for somebody with plenty of dosh. Places like this were selling like hot cakes in the 1980's and 90's.'

'I can see all that, but I'm not sure we should interfere with something we don't understand.'

'I don't think we have any alternative, Kate. You see there's more. I've had a couple of other rather weird experiences.' He went on to tell his sister about the strange incident with the young couple in the wood, and of his subsequent encounter with the young woman in the churchyard, who he thought might be the same girl. 'I can't swear that these occurrences was supernatural but I certainly can't find any other explanation for either of them.'

'You should have told me all this before, Nick. This is getting more and more bizarre.'

'And that's why we've got to find out everything we can. I'm beginning to believe these events may be connected in some way. We need to find out what's behind that locked door. Look, I'll see if I can get hold of Bob in the morning. Let's see if he knows anything about this place. In any case, there's nobody I'd rather have to help us force open that door. It all seems pretty scary now but I'm sure we'll both feel better about it when it's daylight.'

'OK, I suppose you're right. But what are we going to do now? There's no way I'm going back upstairs to my bedroom. Heaven alone knows what may be up there.'

'Of course not. I was going to suggest you sleep in the study. You can have the chaise longue and I'll go back to my sleeping bag on the floor.'

Thankfully, the house appeared to be at rest again when they went through to the study. Whatever disturbed beings had crossed their paths troubled them no further that night.

Chapter 15

AS IT TURNED out, Nick didn't have to call Bob the following morning as the young electrician called round himself, just as he and Kate were finishing their breakfast.

'Hope I'm not intruding. I've brought you a new spark plug for the generator. I thought it was sounding a bit rough when we started it up the other day.'

'That's really thoughtful, Bob. As it happens, we've hardly used it as yet but I'll need it next week, when I'm hoping to get back onto my computer.'

'You do know you won't get a signal round here, don't you? At least not until you get a telephone line.'

'That's not a problem at present as I won't be needing the internet for a while. I've spoken to BT Open Reach and they're coming round next week to reconnect the telephone line and, fingers crossed, to provide us with high speed broadband.'

'Well good luck with that!'

By the way, you haven't met my sister Kate; she's down for the weekend. Kate, this is Bob, who I've been telling you about.'

'It's good to meet you Bob. I've heard such good things about you. I gather you are a man of many talents.'

'You have to be if you're going to survive in these parts. It's nice to meet you too. As you will no doubt have noticed, your brother's taken to rural living like a duck to water.'

'Yes, he fell in love with this place from the moment we first came down, although I'm not so sure he's feeling quite the same way about it this morning.' Kate said with a meaningful expression on her face.

'Oh', Bob said, looking surprised 'what's up then? I hope it's nothing I've done!'

'No, nothing like that.' Nick said. 'The thing is, we had a very unpleasant experience last night. It was genuinely scary and, whoever or whatever it was, it was definitely not of this world. I've had my doubts about the paranormal, until last night that is. But we can't see there's any other possible explanation. There's something very strange going on in this house.' He went on to describe what had happened during the early hours of the morning and his other unaccountable experiences since moving into the house. Bob listened, with a look of disbelief on his face. He watched Kate nervously picking at a loose thread on her jumper. Nick concluded by asking Bob if he had ever heard any talk of unusual happenings at High House.

Looking noticeably uncomfortable, Bob folded his arms and leaned back against the kitchen table. 'Well, I suppose I have heard the odd story. But you know what folk are like, with their wild imaginings. I don't set much store by such talk. If you listened to some of the gossip round here you'd think there was a ghoul hiding behind every tree!'

'I'm still surprised you didn't say anything to Nick,' Kate said sounding rather cross. 'Don't you think you might at least have warned him?'

'Hold on a minute, warned him of what? I never said I believed any of these tales,' Bob said, clearly disgruntled. 'I take most of what I hear about such nonsense with a pinch of salt. I certainly wouldn't want to go round putting the wind up people.'

'That's fair enough, Kate,' Nick said. 'Don't forget that until last night I too was a confirmed sceptic. The big question is, what do we do now?'

'One thing's for sure: I have no intention of spending another night in this house with some forlorn spirit wailing away in the attic. It was absolutely terrifying.'

'I know Kate, I was scared too, bloody scared. But I don't think that whatever it was means us any harm. Let's face it, we weren't threatened or attacked and we didn't even see anything. In the full light of day, with the sun shining, I don't feel half so scared anymore. But we do need to see if we can find out what we're dealing with.'

'It sounds like whatever secrets this house may hold lie behind that locked door up in the attic,' Bob said. 'I've got a sledgehammer in the van. How about we have a go at smashing the lock? Then, at least, we can see what's in that room'

'I'm up for that. What about you Kate?'

'I suppose so, as long as we all stay together. There's no way I'd go up there on my own, even in the full light of day.'

A shaft of bright sunlight was shining through the open door of one of the attic bedrooms, casting a warm yellow light across the narrow corridor. Gone was the oppressive pitch-black corridor of the previous night. They stood at the top of the stairs to listen. The only sound was of a house-martin flapping against one of the bedroom windows. Kate hung back watching while Nick and Bob moved forward towards the locked door. Bob tried turning the handle with his shoulder pressed against the door, but it didn't budge.

'Are you sure you don't mind me attacking the lock with my sledgehammer?' he asked. 'I can't guarantee not to cause some serious damage to the door.'

'Swing away,' Nick said. 'Frankly, I don't care about the door, I just want to see what's on the other side.'

'Right, here goes,' Bob said, raising the sledgehammer to waist height, stepping back, and taking careful aim. It took just one well-directed blow and the door flew open. Nick and Bob peered cautiously into the room. Kate continued to hang back.

'How very odd,' Nick said, stepping inside the room, 'it's still fully furnished. Come and look Kate, there's nothing to be scared about in here, not now anyway.'

'There's a touch of the Miss Havisham's about it, don't you think? Nick said, opening the window. 'What with the cobwebs and years of dust it's so musty I can hardly breathe in here, let's have a bit of fresh air.'

Kate had now plucked up enough courage to join them and was standing, open-mouthed, just inside the door. 'I don't understand it,' she said. 'I never thought we'd find a fully furnished room, not with fine furniture like this anyway. Look at that bureau, it has quality written all over it. The wardrobe and chest of drawers are fine pieces of furniture too. You'd never have expected this, not on the servants' floor.'

'I don't get it. Look, the bed's even made up and there's a towel hanging on that bar under the washbasin,' Nick said, scratching his chin in disbelief.

'It's a very girlie sort of room, if you ask me,' Bob observed. What with those flowery curtains and the embroidered bed spread.'

'I think we'd already guessed that, hadn't we Nick? It ties in with your account of the girl's voice you think you heard singing from up here and with that awful sobbing and moaning coming from in here last night. That was definitely a young woman, Kate said.'

'Actually, it's a rather a pleasant room. It's quite a bit bigger than the other two bedrooms up here, and it looks out over the front of the house rather than the vegetable garden at the back.' Nick said.

'It feels like this room has remained locked and undisturbed ever since this ceased to be a family home,' Nick said. 'I wonder why? We don't know quite when the family moved out and the house was put up for rent but, by all appearances, none of the subsequent tenants ever bothered to try to get in here. From what Mr Prendergast told us, the first occupant was a market gardener who only really used the outbuildings. After he left, the place remained empty for several years and was only re-let to an antique dealer after a considerable amount of repair work had been carried out on the house. He didn't live in the house either. In fact, nobody's actually lived in the house for the best part of seventy or eighty years.'

'That means the last people to make it their home were the family of the Hereford businessman who went bust and sold his business, including the house, to our grandfather,' Kate said.

'That's right,' Nick said, 'and we don't know anything else about him or his family. We don't even know his name. But whoever he was, why was this room locked and left as it is? It's almost as if it's some kind of shrine.'

'Maybe that's just what it is,' Bob said. 'You know how some people can't accept it when a loved one dies, especially if it's a child or a young person.'

'Yes, I think you may be onto something. It certainly feels like that in here.' Kate said, picking up a pretty little silver-handled mirror, inlaid with tortoiseshell, from off the top of the chest of drawers. 'I wonder who last looked in this mirror? If only it could talk. You know, the furniture and fabrics in here are definitely far too good quality for this to have been one of the servant's rooms. Whoever the young woman was, I wonder why she chose to sleep up here?'

'Well, although it's quite a big house, there are only three bedrooms on the first floor.'

'Whoever she was, she certainly enjoyed reading. Just look at these books,' Kate was, kneeling down in front of a small bookcase next to the bureau. 'Austen, Bronte, Dickens, Trollope and she must have been especially fond of Hardy. There's a copy of almost everything he wrote here. Looks like she was pretty keen on poetry too, not just the classics either. There's a fair bit of early twentieth century stuff, Wallace Stevens, Wilfrid Owen and, Good Lord! this look like a first edition of Elliott's 'The Wasteland'.

'Look what I've found!' Nick exclaimed, excitedly. He'd been examining the contents of the bureau and stood clutching a small leather-bound book in his right hand. 'If I'm not mistaken, this may hold the key to whoever it was who occupied this bedroom.'

'Why, what is it?' Bob asked.

'I think it's a diary,' Nic said, unfastening the metal clasp that bound the covers together. 'Yes, just as I thought,' he said, reading from the title page. '*This is the diary of Frances Whitmore, given to me by my Mother in celebration of my twenty first birthday, Saturday, March 16th 1929."*

'1929, that's not far short of 100 years ago!' Kate exclaimed.

'But hang on a minute, Frances Whitmore,' Nick said. 'I'm pretty sure that was the name on the grave in the churchyard where I saw the young woman leaving those wild flowers in a glass jar. And, you know what, the inscription on her headstone said that she died aged twenty-one. If this diary was given to her for her twenty-first birthday, it must record the last few months of her life. I can't wait to read it. Who knows, it may even reveal what happened to her. Just look at the neat handwriting. There seems to be an entry for most days. So, Frances Whitmore, who were you? Was this little bureau where you wrote this diary? Why are you not at rest? What is it that causes you to sing by day and to weep at night?'

'Hang on a minute, Nick,' Kate said disturbed by her brother's invocation. 'Don't you think it's a bit dangerous to start communing with the dead.'

'I think she's right, Nick. We don't know what we're dealing with?' Bob said looking equally concerned.

'I know, I know,' Nick said, smiling. 'I'm not sure why, but since we came in here I don't feel scared anymore. I don't sense the presence of anything evil or malevolent. If I had to describe what I feel it's an overwhelming atmosphere of sadness. I don't know why, but there's something about the room that speaks of unhappiness, a lack of fulfilment, of tragedy even.'

'You were scared enough up here last night,' Kate retorted

'I know, but it was dark then, and we didn't know what was in here. Don't get me wrong, I still believe we're dealing with the paranormal but, somehow, it doesn't feel so threatening anymore.'

'What are you trying to say? That it's some kind of friendly spirit or something?' Kate said, looking increasingly uneasy.

'No, nothing like that. It's difficult to describe, but it's rather as though what we experienced last night is something that happened in the past that's simply repeating itself.'

'What, like some kind of imprint in time?' Bob conjectured.

'Yes, something like that. You know, things are only really frightening when you don't understand what they are. I don't deny, for one moment, that I was spooked by that young couple in the wood, and last night I was as scared as you were, Kate. But the other experiences, the singing and the girl in the graveyard, they didn't frighten me at all. All I want to do now is to get to the bottom of all this. I'm sure there's an explanation and it may well lie in this diary.'

'Didn't you say you'd heard bits of odd gossip about this place, Bob? Is there anything you've heard that might help us to understand what's going on here?' Kate asked.

'Frankly, as I've already said, I haven't taken anything I've heard very seriously, not until now anyway. The only thing that does ring a bell is Nick's description of the voice singing from high up in the house. That's something I have heard talk about.'

'We need to find out more about the family who lived here,' Kate said.

'Well,' Bob said, 'the person most likely to be able to help you is old Sam Benjamin.'

'Yes, that seems like the obvious place to start, especially as he's been keeping an eye on the house for so many years. Kate, I know you have to get back to London today. I'd like us both to talk to Sam. When can you next come down?'

'I can't do next weekend, Bill's home. But I could get away next Tuesday for a couple of nights. Bill will be away again and there's not much on at work at the moment. But how do you feel about staying on here, all on your own, after everything that's happened?'

'Oh, I'll be fine. As I said, I don't think we're dealing with anything at all threatening. I'll start on the diary to see what we can find out about Frances Whitmore.'

Satisfied that there was little else to discover in the attic bedroom they made their way back downstairs. Bob apologised but said he had to leave as he was late for his first call. Nick and Kate sat out in the garden until it was time for her to set off back to London. After she had gone, Nick opened the diary and sat out in the garden. He was still there that evening when the sun began to sink over the Black Hill.

EXTRACTS FROM THE DIARY OF FRANCES WHITMORE

Saturday March 16ᵗʰ 1929

Goodness knows how long I have sat staring at the blank pages of my new diary. I cannot help feeling daunted by the challenge of filling all these spotless white pages. It is such a pretty little diary, such a sweet gift from dear Mother. She has always kept a diary herself and insists that every young woman of our social standing should do so, to record her thoughts and observations at the passing of each day. It is rather an old-fashioned obligation, but I shall try to rise to the challenge.

But of what shall I write? So little of consequence occurs in our daily lives. When Father is not attending to his business affairs in Hereford, he mostly confines himself to his study and will tolerate no disturbance. As for poor Mother, she suffers so much from her asthma that she is obliged to take to her bed for much of the day.

If it wasn't for my dear sister Charlotte I fear I should die of boredom. Since taking up a position as a part-time teacher-come-nursemaid to the younger children at the Junior School in Longtown, she has become a source of endless amusing tales of the children and their many misdeeds. How she brightens our otherwise dull lives. If only I too could escape from this dreary house but Father insists that I remain here to care for Mother and to oversee the running of the house.

O joy of joys! This evening Mother was sufficiently recovered to join us for high tea in celebration of my birthday. Mary had laid out such an impressive array of cold meats to be served with her delicious home-made chutneys and onion pickle. What a dear woman she is. She had also baked my favourite almond sponge cake, topped with sugar icing. Where would we be without our devoted cook who has been with us for so many years?

To my surprise, Father was unusually jocular. He presided over the occasion with a benign smile. He is so rarely in such a good mood these days. I can only assume that he was heartened by the fact that Mother was well enough to join us. After I had blown out the candles and the cake had been served, he stood up and made a little speech, thanking Mother for having provided him with two daughters of whom he could be so proud. After these unusually generous words, he turned to me with a smile and took from his pocket a small, red-leather, jewel box which he invited me to open. Inside was a solid gold bracelet with my initials beautifully engraved upon it. I was so delighted I stood to embrace him but, not given to demonstrations of physical affection, he simply responded by patting me on the top of my head as though I were a pet dog. I could not help noticing the look of anguish on Mother's face. She is of such a sweet and gentle disposition that I cannot imagine how distressing she must find Father's unnatural physical reserve.

After Mother had retired to bed and Father to his study, Charlotte and I went through to the sitting room where a bright fire was burning in the grate. We played a long hand of canasta before we too retired to our rooms and I to making this first entry in my diary..

Tuesday March 19th 1929

It was such a fine afternoon that Charlotte and I decided to walk up the lane to the cottages above St Michael's church, where we called on Mrs Edwards. The poor woman recently gave birth to her fifth child, but sadly the baby girl had barely survived three days. We did what we could to comfort her. I can only imagine how difficult it must be for her with two small children still at home, not yet old enough to attend school, and with her husband Tom out all day, labouring in the fields. On our way back home we found ourselves discussing how regrettable it is that there is such a high mortality rate amongst the children of the poor. Charlotte, who has always been outspoken, said she believed that little would change until there were more women's voices in Parliament raised up on behalf of the working poor. While, of course, I must agree with her, I was intent on discovering who might have influenced her thinking on this matter as most of those with whom we regularly engage are of strong Conservative opinions.

Father is a governor of Longtown school and it was he who arranged for Charlotte to help out there with some of the younger children. She told me of a recent conversation she had had with Mr Cuddington, the newly appointed assistant schoolmaster. It seems that he is a committed advocate of the need for political reform. He had told Charlotte that, while welcoming the previous year's Act of Parliament, which had given all women over the age of twenty-one the right to vote, he deeply regretted that, as yet, so few women were represented in Parliament. He also shared with Charlotte his anger over the prejudice against women's rights that still exists amongst the majority of voters of all classes. He is of the opinion that most men still identify with the 1868 ruling by the Court of Common Pleas which states that 'every woman is personally incapable of voting'. I was not in the least surprised when Charlotte told me she had heard it said that Father had voted against Mr Cuddington's appointment. A man with such strong radical political views was hardly likely to have gained his favour.

I am devoted to my sister and admire her commitment to these new ideals. However, I am concerned that she may fall too much under the spell of Mr Cuddington. She speaks with such passion. I fear for the consequences should she ever be so bold as to openly express her views in front of Father. As a leading figure amongst the Herefordshire

Conservatives, I am sure he would see this as a betrayal of everything for which he stands.

Sunday March 24ᵗʰ 1929

I woke up early this morning to the sound of rain beating against my bedroom window. I had not slept well, my head being full of the radical ideals Charlotte shared with me yesterday afternoon. I am not without sympathy for her beliefs, but I do hope she has the good sense to keep them to herself.

By the time I had dressed and gone down to breakfast, the rain clouds had passed over, and the sun was battling hard to penetrate the thin layer of cloud that lay over the valley. Mother, Charlotte and I felt able to walk to church without the risk of being caught in a further shower of rain. Father had declined to join us on this occasion, as he had an important business matter to attend to. As we walked along the lane to St Clydog's, the upper reaches of the Black Hill were heavily veiled in cloud. It was one of Mother's better days and she chatted away cheerfully to the other parishioners we met on the way. It was a joy to see her in such good spirits.

It being Palm Sunday, the church was full. As we walked down the aisle to our customary pew, Mother received welcoming smiles from everyone. They were clearly pleased to see her up and about again after having been confined to her bed for much of the winter. Although her illness has prevented her from taking an active part in parish activities of late, she has, in the past, been a stalwart member of the Mother's Union, and is known and loved for her kind and generous acts of charity. After the reading of the second lesson, the vicar solemnly ascended the steps to the pulpit from where he preached a long and gloomy sermon about Judas Iscariot and the act of betrayal. Our beloved vicar is never short of words. I only wish he could learn to be more observant of his captive audience, many of whom had either fallen asleep or were thinking of their Sunday lunch while he droned on.

After the service, we were standing outside the porch, talking to the vicar, when Charlotte pointed to a good-looking young man who was engaged in earnest conversation with a young couple. 'You must come and meet Mr Cuddington,' she said. 'I'm sure you will find him engaging.' Charlotte managed to catch his eye and beckoned us to follow her to where he was standing, just inside the lychgate. He welcomed us with a hearty smile, politely asking after Father, whom he had met but once when being interviewed for his new position. In a strong northern accent, he spoke about his new role at the school and said how much he was looking forward to becoming familiar with village life. He went on to speak of how different he expected his new life would be to the life to which he was accustomed back home in Lancashire. He talks about everything with such enthusiasm that I readily understand why Charlotte finds him so engaging. He has such natural charm, and I could see that this was working its magic on Mother, who has clearly taken a liking to him. He informed us that he is organising a school outing to visit Hereford Cathedral, the Saturday after Easter. It seems that Charlotte had already agreed to help to look after the children and he wondered whether I might like to join them. With upwards of twenty excitable youngsters in the party, they were likely to be a bit of a handful. He said they were hiring a charabanc from Yeoman's Coach Company and would be leaving from outside the school at 10.00am. Mother said it would do me the world of good to get out of the house for a day, and so I willingly agreed.

I can see that Charlotte is more than a little attracted to him. Throughout our conversation she seemed to hang on every word that passed his lips. I can readily understand why. He must be all of six feet tall and is very handsome with his long dark wavy hair, broad features and a ruddy complexion. I find his Lancashire accent most appealing. Somehow it seems to enhance his undoubted sincerity.

Saturday April 6th 1929

After breakfast, Charlotte and I went through to the kitchen to help Mary prepare the picnic for today's school outing. In addition to salad sandwiches, hard-boiled eggs and generous slices of homemade veal and ham pie she had prepared for the two of us, she had thoughtfully also baked ginger biscuits and a large fruit cake for the children.

It being too far to walk for us to arrive at the school on time, Mother persuaded Father to drive us up to Longtown in the car. He was due to attend a meeting of fellow committee members in Ross-on-Wye later in the morning, and was not over-pleased at having to set off earlier than he had originally planned.

The morning was still quite chilly when we left home. The heavy, overnight dew, sparkled in the morning sun. The white and pink hawthorn in the roadside hedges was beginning to bud and the intoxicating scent of early spring was in the air. How I love this time of year when the countryside reawakens after its winter slumber and the air is full of the sound of birdsong. As we were nearing the schoolhouse Charlotte squeezed my arm. I knew how much she was looking forward to our day out and I shared her excitement at the prospect.

When we arrived, most of the children were already gathered outside. They were clustered around Mr Cuddington and an attractive, if rather stout, young woman who he introduced to us as Mrs Elizabeth Powell, the mother of Peter and Rosie, two of the children who were coming on the outing. Before we could engage in further conversation, to the delight of the children, we spotted our Yeoman's charabanc coming down the hill. I realised that for many of the children this would probably be their first ride in a coach.

We all climbed in and took our seats. The charabanc struggled a little up the hill to the Llanveynoe turning, but after that we motored comfortably enough through Michaelchurch, Vowchurch and Clehonger. The children were surprisingly quiet and well-behaved until we reached the outskirts of the city. However, once we began to drive up St Martin's Street towards the river bridge, they became very excited and had to be told firmly to remain in their seats. Finally, we pulled up outside the Cathedral at the top end of King Street. After disembarking, the children were ordered to stand in a long line, two by two, with Mr Cuddington leading at the front, Mrs Powell and Charlotte taking up positions halfway along the line with me bringing up the rear. The cathedral rose majestically in front of us, its grey-pink sandstone basking in the bright Spring sunshine. We filed across Broad Street into the cathedral close and entered the cathedral by the north door.

I have visited the cathedral on many previous occasions and consider myself to have a reasonable knowledge of its history and fabric. As Mr Cuddington is such a newcomer to the county, it came as something of a surprise and a delight to discover that his knowledge far exceeds my own. I was especially impressed by how well he was able to retain the attention of the children. He was forever pointing out interesting features, such as the fourteen figures of Knights Templars in chainmail armour on the shrine of St Thomas Cantilupe, the strange mix of carvings of mythological beasts and grotesques supported by the choir stalls, and the exquisite sculpture on the reredos representing Our Lord's Passion. He enthralled the children with tales of St Thomas Cantilupe who, as Bishop of Hereford, had condemned the proud Lord Clifford to walk barefoot through the cathedral where he had personally beaten him with rods, in front of the high altar, as penance for assaulting a number of his episcopal tenants.

Another highlight of the children's visit was Mr Cuddington's exposition of the quite remarkable Mappa Mundi. He told them that it was nearly seven-hundred years old and was believed to be the work of a priest called Richard de la Battayle. During the period of the

Reformation it had been hidden under the floor of one of the cathedral's chantry chapels, where it had remained for some years. The youngsters were especially fascinated by the depiction of the expulsion of Adam and Eve after eating the forbidden fruit.

Our tour of the cathedral completed, we emerged from the dark interior into a blaze of sunshine. It being such a fine day, we made our way across Castle Green and over the Victoria Bridge to Bishop's Meadow, where we found a sheltered spot with a fine view of the river and settled down for our picnic. After we had finished, the children were encouraged to run off the considerable quantity of sandwiches, biscuits and cakes they had consumed, and Mr Cuddington, Mrs Powell, Charlotte and I enjoyed a pleasant conversation under the shelter of a large ash tree that was just coming into leaf. When I complimented Mr Cuddington on his knowledge of the cathedral and its history, he said that his interest in historic buildings had been largely fostered by his father. He told us that, as a child, he had been introduced to many of the more important historic sites in his native Lancashire and up as far north as Westmoreland and Cumbria. Charlotte said he would find there were plenty of places of historic interest worth visiting in Herefordshire and over the border into Wales. I could not but notice how delighted she looked when he suggested that perhaps she might like to drive out with him to explore some of these sites. I am not at all surprised that my dear little sister is so smitten by the charms of our handsome young schoolteacher and I think that I am, perhaps, just a little jealous.

The children were quiet on the way home, tired after their day's excursion, and the journey back to Longtown was uneventful. After they had been collected by their parents or made their own way home, Mr Cuddington insisted on driving us back to High House in his little Austin 7. We found Father in a foul mood. It appears there has been a disagreement between some of his fellow Conservatives, but he didn't wish to talk about it further. Charlotte and

I went upstairs to see Mother. She had spent much of the day in bed after yet another asthma attack. I do worry about her. We can only hope that the warmer Spring and Summer weather will bring some relief to her suffering.

Tuesday April 16th 1929

There was a loud knock on the front door this morning, while we were taking our breakfast, and I was surprised to open it to a young lad who cannot have been more than ten years old. Following a late frost, it was a severely cold morning and the poor lad, with his bright, ruddy, farmer-boys' cheeks, must have been frozen stiff, standing there in his shorts and threadbare winter coat. When I smiled at him he managed a shy grin. He hovered on the doorstep for a moment or two, standing first on one leg and then on the other in obvious embarrassment. Then, digging deep into his coat pocket, he withdrew a crumpled white envelope which he handed to me. He said he was calling on behalf of Mr Cuddington, touched his cap politely, and then scurried off down the driveway.

The envelope was addressed to Mr and Mrs Charles Whitmore and the Misses Charlotte and Frances. I was dying to know the contents of the envelope and hurried back to the dining room where I handed it to Father who, to my disappointment, grunted, put it aside and continued with his breakfast. Charlotte wanted to know who it was who had called at the house so early in the morning. When I told her it was a young lad with a letter addressed to us all from Mr Cuddington, her eyes lit up at the very mention of his name. We were obliged to wait patiently until Father finally laid down his knife and fork before we were able to persuade him to open the envelope. To our delight, it contained an invitation to attend a piano recital in St Peter's church in Longtown, the following Saturday. Father passed the invitation to me and I read that the recital will largely comprise pieces by Mozart, Beethoven and Schumann, and is to be performed by Miss Ursula Blake, a young teacher at The Royal Academy of Music, whose parents live in nearby Ewyas Harold. I said it was a great pity that Mother was so unwell as I felt sure she would have wished to attend the recital. Father grunted again and made it clear that he would not be joining us as he would be attending a meeting of the Conservative Party Divisional Executive that same afternoon, in preparation for a likely General Election in the late Spring or early Summer. However, he had no objection to Charlotte and I attending the recital, provided that Mother was well enough to be left on her own for the afternoon. I think Father was relieved to have an excuse not to attend the recital. I am not quite sure why, but I sense he has taken a dislike to Mr Cuddington. I suspect the rumours that have reached Charlotte's ears are true, and that Father did vote against his appointment. Mr Cuddington's plain manner of speaking would have been quite enough to have persuaded him to do so. How odd it is that the very things about Mr Cuddington that Father finds distasteful, Charlotte and I should find so appealing.

Saturday 20th April 1929

We took an early lunch today and, after attending to Mother's needs, Charlotte and I set off on the pleasant walk up to Longtown parish church. We were blessed with another fine afternoon, with a pale blue sky, and a thin band of wispy cloud running along the top of the Black Mountains rising majestically to our left. Charlotte talked incessantly all the way which I put down to the prospect of seeing Mr Cuddington again. However, I am sure she would have denied this had I so challenged her.

When we arrived, a large number of people had already gathered outside the church. Judging by the number of children present, I imagine that many of those who had come for the recital were school parents, although I recognised a number of other families with whom we are acquainted. Charlotte and I had just fallen into conversation with our neighbours, the Aldingtons, when I spotted Mr Cuddington heading in our direction. He greeted us most warmly and said how grateful he was that we had come to the recital. He informed us that the ticket sales had already raised over twenty pounds and there was still the raffle to come. The money raised was to go towards the provision of some much-needed playground equipment for the school yard. During our conversation we could hear the sound of a piano from within the church. It was evident that our guest recitalist was in the final stages of rehearsal. Mr Cuddington said how grateful he was to Mrs Barraclough who had kindly agreed to lend her fine grand piano for the occasion. It had been carefully carried the hundred or so yards down the lane on the blacksmith's cart and ceremoniously borne into the church by four lusty farmworkers. There it had been reassembled and handed over to the attentions of a local piano tuner. Mr Cuddington made us laugh when he said the piano had been carried into the church with such pomp and ceremony that one could have been forgiven for thinking it was a state funeral. I could not help noticing how Charlotte hung on to his every word. I sensed too that he was anxious to impress her.

St Peter's Church is of a much later construction and is nothing like so fine, or historically interesting, as our lovely St Clydog's. The recital was most enjoyable, although I suspect the church acoustic was not altogether kind to the piano. Miss Blake, who is but a wisp of a young woman, attacked the keyboard with surprising force during her playing of Beethoven's 'Appassionata' Sonata and displayed a considerable degree of sensitivity when it came to Mozart's Adagio for Piano. She opened the second part of her recital with selections from Schumann's 'Scenes from Childhood', a work I have not come across before but which I very much enjoyed, so much so, indeed, that I must see if I can obtain a copy of the score, as I believe I may be able to manage to play some of the pieces myself. Miss Blake concluded the official part of her programme with a performance of Beethoven's seven variations on 'God Save the King' which was greeted with rapturous applause.

At this point, Mr Cuddington rose and walked down the aisle to join Miss Blake by the piano. We were all rather taken by surprise, but delighted, when he announced that, in place of the usual encore, she had kindly agreed to accompany him in a song he had written himself, set to a poem by Christina Rossetti. It was an exquisite performance. Mr Cuddington has a fine baritone voice and the beautifully crafted melody so perfectly captured the melancholic passion of the poet. Charlotte and I were both in tears by the end of the performance.

After the recital, Charlotte and I were amongst the many who wished to congratulate Mr Cuddington, or William, as he insists we must now call him, on his elevating performance. It was a glorious late-spring afternoon and we were overjoyed when he asked if he might walk with us back down the lane to Clodock, his cottage lying but a short distance from the village centre. On the way we stopped by a field gate from where there is a particularly fine view. The sun would soon sink below the top of the Black Hill and the upper slopes were turning a deep misty blue. William told us how enchanted he was by the Golden Valley, set, as it is, against the dramatic backdrop of the Black Mountains. He said how much he was looking forward to exploring this magical stretch of the Welsh border and to learning more about its often-troubled history. He went on to talk, with equal enthusiasm, of his own native Lancashire, of the village near Rochdale where he was born, of Pendle Hill, famed for its witches, and of the miles of open moorland stretching across Lancashire, over the Pennines, and into the neighbouring county of Yorkshire.

On nearing the village, we stopped by the pathway that leads to a small cottage which has lain empty since the death of old Mr Watson, last spring. I was surprised to discover that it is where William has taken up his lodging, as I understood it to be in a state of considerable disrepair. We could see that William was tired after his busy day and so declined his kind offer to accompany us the rest of the way back to High House. We arrived back home to find Father had not yet returned and that Mother was asleep upstairs. We sat down to a light supper that Mary had kindly prepared for us. After we had eaten we were both happy to opt for an early night. To be honest, I think Charlotte sought some time on her own to reflect on the events of the day and on our exchanges with William Cuddington. As for me, well I shall go to bed unable to get that delightful song out of my head.

Monday April 29th 1929

Charlotte has been helping out at the school again today and returned home far from her usual cheery self. Indeed, she seems to be in very low spirits and unusually uncommunicative. I fear her reluctance to talk to me must be related to something I have said or done although I cannot, for the life of me, imagine what it can be. This has led to there being a decidedly sombre atmosphere in the house, especially as Father is as ill-tempered as ever, which always casts such a dark shadow over everything. If only Mother was well enough to be up and about more often. She is the only one who knows how to deal with Father at such times. But, sadly, her condition seems to worsen by the week. When Dr Hudson called today the only comfort he could bring us was the likelihood of there being some improvement in her condition once the warmer summer weather is upon us. I dread to think how unbearable life in this house would be if she were no longer with us.

Tuesday April 30th 1929

When I came down this morning Charlotte was in the hall putting on her hat and coat. I asked where she was going, so early in the morning. She said she was setting off to the May Fair in Hereford with William and some of the children. She was in a hurry as he had offered to pick her up from the end of our drive at 8.30am. I had quite forgotten it was May Day and could not but help feeling a little disappointed that I had not been invited to join them. The last time I was taken up to Hereford for the celebrations was when I was ten years old, just before I was sent away to boarding school. My life is so uneventful nowadays that I often feel like a prisoner in this house. I know that dear Mother wishes it were not so, but her poor health lays a very heavy burden upon Charlotte and me. At least Charlotte has been permitted to help out with the children up at Longtown, but I must remain here, bound to my domestic responsibilities. Charlotte appeared to be more cheerful this morning, as well she might. The prospect of a further day in William's company has clearly raised her spirits. I wish her well, of course, but I cannot help feeling a little resentful. This is the day when the ancient Celts called on Bel, the god of fire and sun, to shine upon their newly sown seedlings. If only he would shine a little light on my dreary life!

Wednesday May 1st 1929

Charlotte didn't appear at breakfast this morning so Mother sent me upstairs to see if she was unwell. There was no answer when I knocked on her bedroom door. All I could hear was a muffled sob. When I put my head round the door I saw my sister lying, face down on the bed, with her head buried in a pillow. Her shoulders were shaking as she wept her heart out. I was quite taken aback. She is normally such a cheerful soul. I sat down on the bed and put my arms around her, hoping to bring her some comfort. When she looked up I was shocked to see her tear-stained face and the woeful look she gave me. I pleaded with her to tell me what had upset her so, but she turned her head away and begged me to leave her alone. I went back downstairs and, not wishing to alarm Mother or Father, I simply told them that Charlotte was not feeling well.

I did not see Charlotte again until just after midday. I was in the vegetable garden at the time, planting out some beans. As she approached I could see her cheeks were still wet with tears and she was deathly pale. In a tremulous voice she begged me to forgive her for so rudely rejecting me when I had visited her bedroom earlier that morning. I could see that she now wanted to open her heart to me, so I hooked my arm through hers and suggested we might take a walk in the woodland where we could be sure of not being overheard. She nodded her agreement and we set off down the path. We walked in silence until we reached the clearing in the middle of the wood. We sat down on the fallen ash tree where we have so often sat before. I could see my poor sister was struggling to summon up the courage to tell me what was troubling her. As I thought it likely it had something to do with her attachment to William Cuddington, I broke the silence by asking her whether she had enjoyed yesterday's visit to the May Fair.

'Oh Frances,' she said, 'I so wish I could say that I had.' She went on to tell me that, of course, the fair itself had been wonderful, the streets had been full of stalls and rides and people selling all kinds of delicious things to eat, and the children had enjoyed a most wonderful time. However, William had offered her so little attention all day that, for some unknown reason, she felt he must have taken against her. I did what I could to reassure her. I said I was sure she must be mistaken. Was it not more likely that he had been preoccupied, keeping an eye on the children? But she remained adamant that there must be more to it than that. If not, how had he managed to find the time to engage with the children's parents, while almost totally ignoring her. She then began to cry again. I put my arms around her and hugged her tight until she had regained her composure. I am not sure whether it was right to do so, especially as we had never discussed the matter before, but I felt I had to ask her if her feelings for William went beyond those of friendship. I could tell at once, by the look on her face, that this must indeed be the case. How deeply I feel for dear Charlotte. Of course, I understand the attraction. William is such a good-looking young man and so highly principled and he expresses himself with such passion and sincerity. I tried to console her by saying I felt certain she was reading too much into his apparent neglect of her; that he must have been distracted by the burden of his responsibilities; and that she would surely find him in a more amiable mood when she went to help out at the school again on Friday. This appeared to reassure her. I certainly hope so. I only wish her well in her relationship with William but, if Father should ever find out, I fear for the consequences.

Friday May 3rd 1929

Father went up to town early this morning. Happily, it was one of Mother's better days and, it being such a pleasant morning, she said she felt well enough to venture outside. We chose to sit in the rose garden where we would be protected from the stiff breeze blowing down the valley. I wrapped a rug round her knees. Mary carried out a tray of tea and some of her delicious homemade scones. Mother chatted away excitedly about her plans for planting out the border beyond the rose garden. She is always so much more relaxed when Father is out of the house. I hate to speak of him thus but he is so stern and without humour these days that his very presence weighs upon us all. Mother expressed her concern over Charlotte who she observed had been rather out of sorts of late. She asked whether I had any sense of what might be the matter. Bound, as I am, not to betray the confidences Charlotte has shared with me, I confined myself to saying that she had seemed cheerful enough when she had set off for the school this morning. Mother expressed her concern about Charlotte's decision to help out up at the school. She told me Father had been very much against it as he didn't want her to come under the influence of Mr Cuddington, of whom he has a very low opinion. I must pass on to Charlotte what Mother has told me. As I feared, she needs to be fully aware of the dangers of pursuing her friendship with William.

Saturday May 4th 1929

As I was unable to find a suitable opportunity to talk to Charlotte yesterday evening, I felt compelled to do so today, before it is too late. The government has called a general election for the 29th May, so Father went out early to attend an emergency meeting of the local Conservatives. As Mary had taken a breakfast tray up to Mother we had the dining room to ourselves. I was anxious to learn how things had passed between Charlotte and William. I suppose it is inevitable that I should have felt a little apprehensive about raising the subject, especially as I feared that things might not have gone well. I also felt I must tell her of the conversation I had had with Mother and warn her of the extent of Father's disapproval.

I was prepared for the worst but I could not have been more surprised or shocked by Charlotte's response. 'It's you,' she said, 'It's all because of you, although I don't suppose for one moment you are aware of it'. I stared at her in disbelief. What in heaven's name was she was referring to. Then she burst into tears and it all came pouring out in a torrent of anguished words. I can hardly credit it but apparently, although William had been cordial enough to her, he had enquired after me with such a fond look in his eye that it had become evident to her where his heart really lay. Over the weeks that have passed since she had first introduced him to us she told me he had enquired after me on several occasions. What she had initially taken to be polite enquiries after my general well-being she now understood to be a clear indication that I was the one to whom he was really attracted.

I was so shocked by this unexpected revelation that I sat at the breakfast table unable to speak or fully take in the import of what Charlotte had just said. I was, and still am, utterly dumbfounded by this news. I hardly know the dear man and am quite certain I have given him no reason to entertain such feelings for me. Of course, I only have Charlotte's word for this and, in the hope of reassuring her, I told her quite firmly that I was sure that she must be mistaken. However, there was nothing I could say that would alter her conviction and she rushed out of the room in floods of tears, leaving me to ponder the magnitude of this wholly unexpected turn of events.

As I sit at my bureau, looking out through the window at the mighty ash tree swaying in the wind, I am deeply unsettled by the inference of Charlotte's assertion. What shall I do if it turns out to be true? I am so inexperienced in such matters. I admit my heart missed a beat when she told me of William's feelings for me, although I had not entertained any serious thoughts for him until that moment. But perhaps that isn't entirely true, for have I not been a little envious of what I believed to be his attachment to my sister. Whatever Father may think of him, I must admit that I find William Cuddington to be a most attractive and intriguing young man. He is so much more entertaining than anyone I have met amongst our local acquaintances. I have suffered enough from the tedium of living in this dreary place. Here, so little ever changes and so rarely is there anything to look forward to. How often I have dreamed of the possibility of escaping to a new life, a life so very different to that of nurse and housekeeper. Yet, shall I ever have sufficient courage?

Tuesday May 7th 1929

My heart goes out to Charlotte. She returned home early from the school this evening and I immediately sensed that something untoward must have occurred. I challenged her in the hallway but she turned her back on me and headed directly upstairs to her bedroom. Of course, I had little doubt it must have something to do with her relationship with William but decided it best not to pursue her. It wasn't until she came down to dinner that we learned the true cause of her distress. She announced that she had decided her assistance was no longer required up at the school. I refrained from making any comment. It was evident she wished to avoid having to explain further the reason for her decision.

Unfortunately, Charlotte's unexpected announcement provided Father with an unwelcome opportunity for a further angry outburst about her decision to take on her role at the school in the first place. He said he had considered it to be a most unsuitable occupation for any daughter of his, the more so since the appointment of 'that troublemaker Cuddington'. He was unspeakably vitriolic, describing William as 'a dangerous radical, with a head-full of disturbing ideals' and said that, in his opinion, 'he should never be allowed anywhere near children.' I could see that Charlotte was struggling to contain herself. Indeed, I wasn't in the least surprised when she informed us she had a headache and retired to her bedroom. I could see that Mother was finding the whole matter extremely distressing. However, cowed as she is by Father's domineering manner, she refrained from saying anything until he had stormed out of the room. It was only after he had slammed the study door behind him that she turned to me, with tears in her eyes, and asked if I knew what lay behind Charlotte's decision. I denied having any explanation, as I felt I must. Mother said she was dismayed by Father's unkind attack on Mr Cuddington as she had found him to be a most polite and agreeable young man.

I wonder, must I always lack the courage to voice my opinion when Father is so unreasonable. His outdated political ideals and moral values are certainly not suited to this post Edwardian age. It is so typical that he should have been the only one to speak out against William's appointment. I am sure he still believes that young village boys and girls would be better employed working in the fields than gaining an education..

On my way up to bed, I put my head round Charlotte's door, but she was already asleep. I straightened out her eiderdown and kissed her lightly on the cheek. I feel so sorry for her. But I cannot feel guilty. If William has feelings for me, and I do question whether this can actually be so, it is certainly not anything I have encouraged. My head is so full of unanswered questions I doubt I shall sleep tonight.

I was woken early this morning by the sound of Mother coughing and choking in her bedroom down below. I hurried downstairs to find she had collapsed on the landing outside the bathroom. Father was standing over her, apparently quite helpless, not knowing what to do. I knelt down beside her and helped her to sit up, propping her back against the wall. Charlotte had also appeared by now, so I sent her to fetch a glass of water while Father went off in search of Mother's spray. Once she had recovered sufficiently to inhale we were able to help her back to bed where she lay, deathly pale, leaning back against the pillows. I could see that Father was beside himself with worry. For all his faults, he is devoted to Mother and would be utterly lost without her. Thankfully, after a while, Mother drifted off to sleep and, there being little point in our returning to our beds as we were now all wide awake, we went downstairs where Father and Charlotte sat round the kitchen table while I brewed a pot of tea. It was clear that Mother is very unwell and Father said he would send for the doctor as soon as it was light.

Dr Hutton kindly made us the first call on his rounds, after completing his morning surgery up at Longtown. He must have been with Mother for a good half hour before emerging from her bedroom looking deeply concerned. Father invited him into the sitting room where he confirmed that Mother's condition had worsened considerably since he had last seen her, in the early New Year. He told us that from a medical point of view there is little else he can do to help. However, he felt confident she would benefit from spending the summer months somewhere by the sea, where there would be an abundance of fresh sea air. I could see Father was far from happy at this suggestion. It was later, when we were sitting down to dinner, that he told us he had managed to secure two room reservations at the Palace Hotel in Torquay, for an indefinite period, from this coming weekend. He said his business commitments and the forthcoming General Election will prevent him from staying there with Mother, and so had decided she should be accompanied by Charlotte, now that she is no longer working up at the school. He insists that my principal responsibility must be to stay at home to look after him and the management of the house. When I suggested that Charlotte and I might take it in turns to stay with Mother he would have none of it. It would seem that I am forever to be the Cinderella of this house!

Saturday May 11th 1929

I hardly slept at all last night. I could not stop thinking about poor Mother and how she will cope with being away from home. Of course, she will have Charlotte to keep her company but then Charlotte, much though I love her, is hardly the most dependable of people. We had already packed everything they will need for their lengthy stay in Torquay, so there was little left to do this morning before setting off for Hereford station. Our last breakfast together was a sombre occasion during which none of us seemed to know quite what to say. I shall miss Mother and Charlotte so much. I cannot imagine how lonely I shall be with only Father in the house. It took me all my time to hold back my tears. At least I shall be able to go through to the kitchen to chat to Mary. She is such a ray of sunshine and always ready to entertain me with the latest titbits of village gossip.

We left for the station around mid-morning. The platforms were very crowded when we arrived but, fortunately, it transpired that most of the people were waiting for the London train. With the help of a porter, we made our way over the footbridge to the far platform where the train for Newport was due to come in. Mother and Charlotte had so many suitcases and other items of hand luggage that the porter had to make two journeys. When the train finally came chugging into sight we embraced and shed a good many tears, except for Father, of course, who never shows his emotions in public. I felt utterly forlorn as we waived them goodbye and watched the train labour its way down the track towards Newport, where Mother and Charlotte would have to change train for the last part of their journey down to the south coast.

Father told me he had business to attend to at his office in King Street that afternoon and suggested we took a light lunch at the Green Dragon. He was unusually cheerful and talkative. This I found difficult to comprehend as I was still feeling so forlorn after Mother and Charlotte's departure. He spoke enthusiastically about the forthcoming General Election which, despite the current unpopularity of the Unionist Government, he is confident they will win. He said that although the current Unionist MP for Hereford. Samuel Roberts. is standing down, the seat has been won by the party in successive elections in 1922, 1923 and 1924 with a comfortable majority, and there was no reason to believe that their new candidate, Frederick Romilly, would fail to hold onto it. Politics is the only subject that seems to excite Father these days. He was soon at full throttle, moving on to last year's Representation of the People Act which gave women over the age of twenty-one the right to vote. Although he had been strongly opposed to its introduction, he said that, now it was law, it was incumbent upon educated women, like myself, to use their vote wisely. In his opinion there could be absolutely no doubt that the Unionists were the only party worthy of governing the country. As he is never interested in discussing any opinions other than those he so firmly embraces himself, I let him ramble on.

After luncheon he left for his office and I spent a rather tedious afternoon looking at the shops, as there was nothing I needed to buy. I was feeling immensely depressed at the thought of the months ahead alone with Father.

As I write down my thoughts now, in the peace and solitude of the late evening, I cannot help wondering what William Cuddington might have had to say, had he been a party to our lunchtime conversation.

Sunday 12ᵗʰ May 1929

Father never has much to say over breakfast, preferring to bury his head in *The Times*. This morning was no exception. Apart from the occasional grunt when he read something to which he took exception, he hardly spoke. Although I was missing the bright and amusing breakfast conversation I so often share with Charlotte, on this occasion I was grateful for the opportunity to allow my mind to wander freely without interruption. I was, in truth, still recovering from a weird and upsetting dream I had last night, in which a heart-broken Charlotte floated slowly away into the distance, with her hands held out imploringly towards me, while a seemingly unconcerned William Cuddington looked on.

Once Father had retired to his study and I had discussed the arrangements for lunch with Mary, I set off to attend morning service at St Clydog's. If I am to be honest, I was excited at the thought that I might bump into William again but, to my disappointment, he was not amongst this Sunday's small number of worshippers.

When I returned home after the service, Father was in his study. I went through to the kitchen to help Mary with the lunch. Earlier this morning she had asked if she could take the afternoon off to visit her sister in Garway. I insisted she should leave as soon as we had been served and said that I would clear everything away afterwards. Father chose not to linger over lunch as he had a number of calls to make on local party helpers in preparation for the election. He asked how I intended to occupy myself and I said I thought I might walk up to Tanhouse Farm to collect next week's supply of eggs. But I doubt I would have chosen to undertake this errand if I hadn't known it would take me past the pathway leading to William Cuddington's cottage.

I was in two minds as I closed the front door behind me and set off down the lane. While I hoped I might come upon William as I passed by his cottage, there was another part of me that was apprehensive at the thought of such an encounter. I am so unsure of my true feelings towards him. My sense of unease grew as I drew nearer to his cottage. I began to wish I had never set out in the first place. But, sometimes, things occur over which we have no control and which, on reflection, seem as though they were intended. I had passed his cottage and was approaching the entrance to the farm when an all too familiar voice hailed me from behind, the voice of the one person I was not sure I was ready to encounter.

My heart missed a beat. I managed a flustered response and waited for William to catch me up. I informed him I was on the way to collect eggs from the farm. He smiled and asked if I minded if he joined me as he was going there to buy eggs himself. I wondered if he had just made this up as an excuse for accompanying me, but how could I refuse him. As we walked along the lane he asked politely after Charlotte. He told me how disappointed they all were she was no longer helping out at the school as her work had been very much appreciated, and the children were missing her already. He appeared to be genuinely surprised she had decided to leave so I thought it best to tell him about Mother's worsening health, the doctor's advice that she would benefit from spending the summer near the sea and that Charlotte had chosen to go to the south coast with her. He said how sorry he was to hear about Mother's poor health and that he was sure she would benefit from the sea air. He asked me to be sure to pass on his very best wishes to them both. After we had collected our eggs we stopped close to the 'mound' from where there is such a good view across the valley and up towards Black Daren. William asked how I would get by without the company of Mother and Charlotte. He must have seen my eyes were watering, because he took hold of my hand and apologised profusely for his impertinence in having asked such a question. I assured him that I didn't mind in the least, but that I was missing them a great deal already.

We walked on in silence for a while and then he asked me, in a very blunt manner, if I shared Father's political views.

I was a little taken aback. I told him that I had not really given politics much thought. He said that coming from a part of the North of England where the Labour Party is in the ascendancy, he is finding it difficult to adjust to moving into such a strong Tory area. I told him the Labour Party has never had much support in Herefordshire and often didn't even field a candidate. He smiled and said he understood the Liberals had quite a following in the county, and asked if I knew anything about Frank Owen, their new parliamentary candidate. I said Father had mentioned his name once or twice but that the Tories were confident they would see him off. William said he thought Mr Owen's cause could only benefit from his having been born locally. He was impressed by the number of people to whom he had spoken who had told him they intended to vote for him. I said I was not altogether surprised, as there is a good following for the Liberals amongst the nonconformists down the Golden Valley. Our conversation drew to a close when we reached the path to his cottage. He told me how much he enjoyed my company. He said he was planning to arrange a picnic for the following Saturday. He said he intended to invite Elizabeth Powell, whom I had met on the school outing to the cathedral, and her husband John, and asked whether I would care to join them. I so wish I could have said yes, for I had enjoyed his company every bit as much as he said he had enjoyed mine. But I knew, only too well, what Father would say and had no choice but to decline his kind invitation. I made up some feeble excuse about being required to stay home on Saturday to cook Father's lunch as it was the cook's day off.

Father was in his study when I returned home so I came straight up to my bedroom. I needed some time alone to reflect on my meeting with William. He is so very likeable. The passion with which he expresses his opinions is irresistible, and his delightful Lancashire accent seems to contribute to the sincerity of his convictions. The pain Charlotte is enduring must be even more difficult to bear knowing, as she does, that his affections lie in my direction.

Oh, what am I to do and why is life so difficult? I hardly know this young man and yet I have never felt so instantly attracted to anyone before. Of course, it is hopeless. William will never be welcomed as a guest in our house, let alone to be my suitor. Father intends that I should marry the son of a wealthy farmer or one of his young business colleagues. But they are all so tedious and small-minded. Surely there is more to life than living out one's days in such dull company.

Monday 13th May 1929

When I came in from the garden this afternoon Father informed me that Charlotte had telephoned from Torquay. The good news is that Mother appears to be benefitting from the warmer climate and fresh air although she continues to wake up during the night, when her asthma is at its worst and she has difficulty with her breathing. Charlotte is sufficiently concerned to have arranged with the hotel for them to give up their separate rooms in exchange for a larger double with a sitting room. This will enable her to keep a closer eye on Mother and be there to help her whenever necessary. Father told me Charlotte has promised to write to me before the end of the week. When I asked him how soon he thought we might be able to drive down to Torquay to visit them, he said, hopefully, before the end of the month, depending on how well the Election campaign is going. I am so down-hearted. I miss Mother and Charlotte so much.

Wednesday 15th May 1929

I cannot help asking myself: am I a dreadful daughter? Sometimes I have such unkind thoughts about Father. It took me all my time to conceal my delight when he announced, at breakfast this morning, that he will be going up to Hereford tomorrow afternoon and will most likely remain there until the early part of next week. Of course, my immediate thought was that I may, after all, be able to join William and the Powells for the picnic on Saturday. It is odd how quickly one's mood can change. I can hardly believe it, but Father actually apologised for giving me so little notice of his intentions. It is so out of character for him to apologise for anything. Apparently, the election campaign is not going so well as he had expected. It would appear that not everyone has taken to Mr Romilly, the new candidate. A number of senior members of the constituency Conservative Party are most unhappy about our former MP's decision to stand down in order to return to his native Sheffield to contest the safe seat of Eccleshall. What a smile this will bring to William's face. Father has been asked to escort Mr Romilly on a number of daytime and evening rallies around the constituency. He maintains that it will be more convenient for him to put up at the Green Dragon, rather than to motor up and down to Hereford each day. He said he regretted leaving me on my own, but said Mary would be on hand should I need any help.

Thursday 16ᵗʰ May 1929

I have never known a morning pass so slowly. Father went directly to his study after breakfast. There being little else to occupy me, I endeavoured to speed the morning on by planting cabbage and broccoli seeds in the greenhouse. I did not see Father again until Mary sounded the lunchtime gong. Although he was preoccupied with his plans for the election, he did, at least, show some concern for my well-being during his absence. He had stowed his suitcase in the boot of the Daimler before lunch and, as soon as we had finished our dessert, he put on his hat and overcoat, kissed me lightly on the top of my head and drove off to Hereford.

As soon as the Daimler had disappeared round the bend in the drive, I felt a thrill of excitement such as I have rarely experienced before. For the first time in my life I had some time to myself during which I was free to do as I chose. My first thoughts were of the picnic. Was it too late for me to tell William that I was now able to join them? What if he had already invited someone else in my stead? There was nothing for it. I would have to call round at his cottage as soon as I possibly could.

I told Mary I was going out for a walk and set off down the lane towards the village. There was no-one about save for a couple of farmworkers clearing a ditch by the lane-side. The church clock struck 3 o'clock as I passed through the village. I wondered whether William would be back from school as yet. As soon as I reached the path leading to his cottage, my heart began to beat faster and, if truth be told, I felt slightly sick with apprehension. The cottage stands rather further back from the lane than I had remembered, and the path leading to it was very overgrown. When the cottage came into view, I was surprised to see how much it was in need of repair. Several stone tiles were missing off the roof and the front door and window frames looked in need of a coat of paint. I took a deep breath and knocked on the front door. But it soon became evident that William had not yet returned. In anticipation of this eventuality I had prepared a written note explaining my changed situation. There being no letter-box, I placed it between two empty milk bottles under the wooden porch. I had no wish to be observed by any passer-by, so I hurried back out to the lane. I felt like an errant schoolchild sneaking out of school before the end of the day.

I have not yet received a word from William. Of course, should he intend to respond to my note, he will have to call round in person as I am sure he does not have a telephone. It is now so near to the weekend, I fear I may be too late.

Friday 17th May 1929

It was early this morning, while I was brushing my hair in front of the mirror, that I heard the sound of the front door bell. Mary was downstairs in the kitchen preparing breakfast. I listened intently, knowing she would answer the door. I held my breath and strained my ears hoping, with all my heart, that it was William's voice I could hear down below. But the exchange between Mary and the caller was so brief I was unable to discern who it was. I looked out of the bedroom window but, whoever had called must have left in a hurry, or taken the path to the side of the house, as there was not a soul to be seen.

I hurried downstairs where I spotted a white envelope on the silver tray in the hall, where Mary puts our morning post. I could see the envelope had been used before as the original address had been crossed out. Written below, in a bold, italic hand, I read 'To Miss Frances Whitmore', and then, in large bold letters, 'URGENT'. My heart was racing. It must surely be a message from William. I was about to open the envelope when I heard Mary's footsteps approaching from the kitchen. I did not wish to draw her attention to my excitement at the arrival of the letter, so I put it back on the tray and retreated into the dining room. I had hardly sat down at the table when Mary came in with the breakfast trolley. She greeted me in her usual hearty manner, laid the hot dishes on the sideboard and, with a knowing smile, handed me the envelope. 'I don't know whether you were expecting this Miss Frances,' she said, 'but it was delivered by that nice Mr Cuddington just before you came down.' I thanked her and put the envelope down on the table, feigning a lack of interest in its contents.

As soon as Mary had returned to the kitchen, I tore the envelope open. Inside there was a single sheet of notepaper on which William had written 'I am so pleased you are now able to join us. I shall call round for you at 11 o'clock tomorrow morning. There is no need for you to bring anything as I have everything in hand. My warmest good wishes, William.'

In a vain attempt to distract myself, I passed the morning trying to read my copy of Elliot's fine new poem 'The Wasteland', but I found it almost impossible to concentrate. During the afternoon, I sat out in the garden thinking of Saturday and of what I would say to Mary. I would have to tell her that I would be out for luncheon and much of the afternoon. And what if Father telephones while I am out? Mary would need to be able to explain my absence. But how much should I tell her? that was the question. I thought about the situation from every possible angle and finally decided I must tell her the truth. What point was there in trying to deceive her with some cock-and-bull story she probably wouldn't believe any way. Dear Mary, she's loved and cared for us since we were little children. Why did I ever doubt her loyalty. She has taken a liking to William and I should have known how pleased she would be for me. I told her of Father's low opinion of William and begged her to be discreet. Bless her, she said I need have no fears on that front as she had only heard good things about Mr Cuddington from her friends in the village. She said it was such a shame that Father had taken against him but felt sure he would come round eventually. I only wish I could share her optimism.

I am so excited, I can't wait for tomorrow. But I must remain calm. I am inexperienced when it comes to relationships and lack Charlotte's open and gregarious personality. I cannot imagine of what joys or disappointments I shall be writing when I next return to my diary.

Saturday 18th May 1929

I could not have been more delighted when I woke this morning, Bright sunlight was pouring in through the bedroom window. It seemed we were to be blessed with a perfect day for our picnic. After breakfast, Mary handed me a large brown paper bag full of buttered scones, embraced me and wished me the happiest of days. She is such a dear. I heard the sound of William's car approaching just as the hall clock struck 11 o'clock. By the time I had put on my coat and opened the front door, William had already pulled up outside. He asked if I minded if we had the roof down, it being such a fine morning. I said I was sure I would enjoy the feeling of the wind blowing through my hair. He apologised for his small car as he feared I might find it rather uncomfortable, compared to riding in Father's Daimler. I said I was certain I would be perfectly comfortable, especially as I imagined we would not be driving all that far. I was enchanted by the way he smiled and said he intended to keep our destination a secret. As we drove through the village and up the lane towards Longtown, I felt so comfortable in his company and found him so easy to talk to. He has that gift of putting everyone at their ease. Soon after passing *The Crown Inn* we pulled up outside a small cottage where the Powells were waiting for us. We were obliged to climb out of the car to put our seats forward so that they could scramble into the back. Elizabeth introduced me to her husband John, whom I judge to be a good deal older than his wife. He is short and swarthy and has the rough well-worked hands you would expect of a carpenter. We set off in low gear, crawling up the steep hill towards the castle. There was little point in endeavouring to engage in conversation until we reached the top, as every sound was blocked out by the noisy whine of the engine. After passing the castle ruins, William took the left turn down the lane that leads to Llanveynoe and to the Olchon Valley beyond. The road surface was extremely uneven and we were only able to make slow progress. The little car lurched and reared awkwardly like a seal out of water.

When we reached the tiny church of St Beuno and St Peter, William pulled up by the side of the road. He said he hoped we wouldn't mind stopping for a while as he had not yet had an opportunity to visit the church, which he understood stands on the site of the original church established by St Beuno, in the early seventh century. I knew nothing of St Beuno, but William, as ever, was a fount of information. He told us that the saint was of royal descent, the grandson of King Brychan of Brecknock and is credited with performing a number of miracles. Not the least of these was restoring the life of his niece St Winifred, who's head had been cut off by an angry suitor when he heard she was betrothed to another. Elizabeth was highly amused by this tale. She laughed so much that it fell to John to explain to us that she may well, herself, have narrowly avoided a similar fate, having been engaged to a local farmworker before taking up with him. I continue to be amazed by the extent of William's knowledge of our local history. It is quite remarkable that he is already so much better informed than those of us who have lived here all our lives.

After we had spent a while exploring the Victorian church and wandering about the graveyard, examining some of the older and more interesting gravestones, we climbed back into the car and drove on down the Olchon Valley. Before long the lane turned into little more than a farm track, and the going became even more difficult. William had to drop down into low gear to negotiate the many potholes. I can only imagine that the lane must be well-nigh impassable after a heavy fall of rain or snow.

We had not travelled much further before William pulled off the track by a gateway at the side of the road. He pointed to a well-worn pathway leading up-hill through a clump of trees. He told us it led to a perfect place for our picnic, not far from the top of the Black Hill. From there, he said, we would enjoy a panoramic view of Herefordshire, on the one side, and of Wales and the Black Mountains on the other. We set off up the path with William and John walking ahead, carrying the picnic hampers, while Elizabeth and I followed on behind with the rugs. It was quite a long and stiff walk up the hillside and, as we neared the top, the path became more difficult to negotiate. However, once we had reached the spot where we were to sit down for our picnic, it was plain to see why William had chosen it. It was a crystal-clear day and there was a magnificent view in every direction. Most of all I liked the view over the Vale of Ewyas with the Black Mountains providing a dramatic backcloth, such a contrast to the soft, undulating, Herefordshire countryside in the opposite direction..

Our picnic was a simple affair comprising cheese and chutney sandwiches, hard-boiled eggs, thick slices of cold ham and, of course, the delicious scones that Mary had freshly baked for us that morning. We washed this down with a mug of Herefordshire cider. We chatted away merrily while we ate. I had taken a liking to Elizabeth when we first met and I soon found myself warming equally to her husband John. He has a captivating sense of humour, and turned out to be something of a tease, especially where Elizabeth is concerned, all of which she seems to take in good part.

For my part, I was determined to find out more about William. I began by asking him why he had chosen to come to teach in Herefordshire. We were all a little surprised when he told us that his real ambition is to be a professional artist. He said that after gaining a scholarship to Manchester Grammar School, he had gone on to study at the Manchester School of Art, where he had gained a diploma with distinction. However, unlike most of his contemporaries who preferred painting urban and industrial scenes, he had always yearned for the opportunity to capture the many aspects of rural life. The teaching position at Longtown had appealed to him for this very reason. As it was part-time, he hoped to be able to develop his skills as an artist. He said he couldn't think of anywhere more idyllic to practice his art than the beautiful Herefordshire countryside

Our conversation soon moved on to politics and the forthcoming Election which is scheduled to take place on the thirtieth of May. I said my sister Charlotte believed William to be something of a political radical. He laughed out loud and said that everyone seemed to have got it into their heads that he was some kind of left-wing revolutionary. He assured us he was no Socialist, but the nation was moving into a new era, and people were no longer willing to put up with the old politics. He said 'The Roaring Twenties' may have been agreeable enough for the wealthy, but that the amount of government borrowing that had been required to sustain their good lives was bound to lead to economic difficulties in the future. He insisted that there had to be a major change in government policy if we were to avoid putting thousands of people out of work. When John asked who he would be voting for he said he was encouraged by the Liberals' campaign slogan 'We Can Conquer Unemployment' and their proposed programme of public works. He told us about a public meeting he had recently attended in Hereford where he had been impressed by the new Liberal Candidate, the young journalist Frank Owen, who had spoken with passion and conviction. He believed the present Government to be so unpopular that Owen had a reasonable chance of taking the seat, the more so since the new Tory candidate was a landed gentleman of the old school. Elizabeth said she too had heard good things about Mr Owen and that his being the son of a well-respected Hereford innkeeper, would surely help his cause.

I soon gathered that both John and Elizabeth are of very much of the same opinion as William and that they too will be voting for Mr Owen. I find their arguments very compelling. I am not well versed in the many and complex political issues that face the country, nor have I ever been encouraged to become so. However, if I am to be honest, I have always felt uncomfortable when political matters have been discussed within the narrow company we normally keep. The policies put forth have been so uncompromising that there are times when I cannot but feel that very little has changed in Herefordshire since feudal times. How furious Father would be if he knew I hold such opinions. He will take it for granted that I shall be voting for Mr Romilly and the Unionist Government. Thank goodness for the secret ballot. Father would throw me out of the house if he thought I was even considering supporting the Liberals. I am quite proud of myself. There are undoubtedly merits in a little deceit now and then.

We moved on to discussing some of the principal problems that would face whichever Party wins the election. I found this particularly informative and stimulating as I am so ignorant of many of the issues we discussed. We continued happily in conversation until we saw it was time to pack up our picnic and return home. We dropped John and Elizabeth off outside their cottage. William offered to drive me home but I said I would prefer to walk the last part of the way from his cottage, it being such a fine evening. He clasped my hands and said he had known we would become friends from the moment we had first met. I was so overcome I wanted to embrace him, but my modesty held me back from doing so. I thanked him for a truly delightful afternoon and set off on my way home. When I reached the bend in the lane I could not resist turning to look back. He was still standing in the lane, watching my progress. He waved and I waved back. My heart was beating so fast I thought I might faint.

I shall never forget this day. I feel positively liberated. Until now, I have never questioned Father's uncompromising opinions. I discover that I have a mind of my own and all it has taken is but a few hours in the company of the captivating William Cuddington.

Sunday 19th May 1929

I had just sat down to lunch when there was the sound of a car pulling up outside the front door. A few moments later I heard Father's heavy footsteps crossing the hallway. The moment he entered the dining room it was clear that all was far from well. After the most perfunctory of greetings, he sat down and waited in silence until Mary had served lunch. As soon as she had left the room, I tentatively asked him how the election campaign was proceeding. Such was the nature of his explosive response that you would think I had set light to a barrel of gunpowder. It seems that, after a promising start in which the general view was that another Unionist victory was as good as a certainty, the heat has gone out of the Tory campaign and it is beginning to falter. Father is furious with the election agent whom he describes as a numbskull. He said he has told him, time after time, not to underestimate the opposition. A thrill ran through my veins when he told me that 'that young upstart' Frank Owen's radical views and oratorical gifts are drawing a considerable amount of support. I can picture with joy the look on William's face when he hears that there is despair in the Unionist camp. Father continued to roar and expostulate throughout our lunch. It was with considerable difficulty that I managed to conceal my pleasure at his discomfort. It seems I have become an over-night convert to radical ideas!

Before leaving the table, Father told me he had spoken to Mother again, over the telephone, and that she and Charlotte were thankful for the fine weather. I am so happy to hear they have managed to take a short walk along the promenade each day to take the fresh sea air. It seemed, almost as an afterthought, that Father then asked how Mary and I have been managing in his absence. I was able to reply, with the utmost sincerity, that we had been so occupied we had hardly missed him at all. He said this was just as well as, counter to his original intentions, he had to return to Hereford later that afternoon and was unlikely to return until the coming weekend. He said it was a case of all hands to the pump if a further collapse in support for Mr Romilly was to be averted. Father is not used to matters not going his way and I couldn't help feeling a little sorry for him. However, as I sit at my bureau reflecting on the events of the day, I don't believe I have ever felt so happy. Ahead of me there lies a whole week in which I shall be free to go where I wish and to do what I want. I only hope I can trust what my heart is telling me. William, my dear William, I hardly believe it possible, but I think I am falling in love with you.

Monday 20ᵗʰ May 1929

Mary was all smiles when I came down to breakfast this morning. Due to Father's unexpected return I hadn't had an opportunity to talk to her since the picnic. I could see she was bursting to know how it had all gone, but was too aware of her position to enquire. I so very much needed someone I could trust, someone sympathetic to my situation and so, after breakfast, I went through to the kitchen to find her. She is so easy to talk to and I was able to open my heart to her without hesitation. I would trust her with my life and know she will never betray my confidences. When I told her of the strength of my feelings for William she was not in the least taken aback. I suppose I feared she would challenge the likelihood of my having fallen in love so instantly, or might think I was too inexperienced in such matters to be certain of how I really feel. I also expected her to caution me against pursuing the relationship because of the difference in our social standing. I should have known better, for Mary is kindness itself and full of understanding. She chuckled when I said I did not know whether William feels the same way and told me there is only one way to find out. I said that was all very well but how could I possibly ask him. The truth is I was terrified of being humiliated. By now, Mary was laughing at my timidity. She told me I must have the courage of my convictions. While convention might say otherwise, she believes there are occasions when it is the woman who has to make the first move.

I am so grateful to her. I am sure she is right. I must take the bull by the horns. While Father is away I am at liberty to do as I wish. William's school day finishes at three o'clock tomorrow afternoon. I know he prefers to walk rather than drive to school during the Spring and Summer months. I shall take a walk myself, through the village, and hope that I may meet him on his way home.

Tuesday 21st May 1929

My head is so full of the joy of yesterday's meeting with William that I can hardly put pen to paper. I have never felt so happy. I think he was rather taken aback when he found me waiting for him by the path leading to his cottage. However, his welcoming smile immediately filled me with confidence. He said he had quite a thirst after walking back from the school and asked if I would care to join him for a glass of cider. My heart was thumping madly as I followed him down the narrow path. His cottage is tiny, a simple little two-up, two-down affair, with a single storey extension out to one-side, under a sloping tin roof. I noticed he had left the front door unlocked. When I challenged him about this, he said that nobody back home in Lancashire ever locks their front door. He apologised for the musty smell in the small front room. He said it was not as unpleasant as it had been when he first moved in and was only due to the cottage having been empty for so many months.

He invited me to sit down on an old sofa that was much the worse for wear, while he went through to the kitchen to fetch the cider and some glasses. Looking around the room, I noticed how barely furnished it is. The walls are covered with a faded, flowery, wallpaper. In places, the cream paint on the ceiling has turned a deep ochre, doubtless due to many winters of smoking fires and pipes enjoyed by the fireside after a hard day's labour. There is but one picture hanging on the wall, taking pride of place above the fireplace. It is a compelling watercolour depicting an expanse of dark blue hillside beneath a purple sky. In truth, it is the only appealing object in the otherwise dreary room. I wondered if it was one of William's paintings. When he returned with the cider, he suggested we went out into the garden to find somewhere to sit in the shade. He led the way around the side of the cottage into a sizeable rear garden, with a fine view of the neighbouring pastures. We sat down on the grass under a large hazelnut tree, which William told me was a tree sacred to poets in both Welsh and Irish mythology. He said the Celts considered it to be a source of wisdom. It must have been the way I was looking at him because he suddenly burst out laughing and apologised for being 'a mine of useless information'. I said that, on the contrary, I was impressed by the breadth of his knowledge, and was more than happy to be schooled by him on subjects of which I have so little knowledge.

We chatted on merrily without a care in the world until, looking at my watch, I saw it was approaching dinner time.

I could tell he was disappointed when I told him I would soon have to be on my way. He took my hand as we walked back down the path to the lane. When we reached the lane he said how delighted he was I had called to see him and thanked me for the stimulating conversation we had shared. How much I desired to reach up and kiss him on those well-formed lips. It was then, to my delight, that he told me he would be finishing school early tomorrow and wondered whether I would allow him to cook supper for me at the cottage. I was sure Mary would not disapprove and, with Father away, I felt free to do as I wish. I have never felt so willing to say 'yes' but, in confirming my acceptance of his invitation, I found myself trying to conceal the true extent of my enthusiasm. How odd it is that when one has been conditioned to behave in a particular manner something holds one back, even when one's heart is pulling in a different direction.

It has been an extraordinary day. I can hardly believe it could end with so much happiness. I have never quite known what people mean when they talk about falling in love. But now, I think I am beginning to understand. William is such a new friend and yet, in so many ways, I feel I already know him through and through. He is so open and honest, so passionate about his beliefs, so full of compassion for others. He is, dare I think it, he is everything that Father is not. Poor dear Charlotte, how distraught you were when you discovered it was to me and not to you to whom he is drawn. And how noble and generous you were to tell me so. Why do I not feel more guilty? You have sacrificed your freedom to look after Mother while I am free to indulge my passion? And what of Father? He left me with the responsibility of looking after this house. Am I not deceitfully neglecting my duties?

But I must be true to myself. If my feelings for William are true, I shall need the strength to endure, for I know Father will do everything within his power to come between us.

'Whether we be young or old
Our destiny, our being's heart and home,
Is with infinitude, and only there:
With hope it is, hope that can never die,
Effort, and expectation, and desire,
And something evermore about to be.'

Thursday 23rd May 1929

The house is so quiet this morning. It is Mary's day off. She has gone to visit her sister and left before I had risen. Although I know she will be longing to hear all about my supper with William, I don't believe I am yet able to put my emotions into words. It is just as well I have the house to myself.

It was well after midnight when I slipped back into the house last night. Thoughtful as ever, Mary had left a light on in the hall. I made as little noise as possible as I did not wish to wake her. As I walked back home under a starlit sky, I grew increasingly fearful lest Father should have returned unexpectedly. However, as soon as I opened the front door, I saw the morning's mail remained undisturbed and breathed a sigh of relief.

I lay awake into the small hours, my head awhirl with thoughts of the wonderful evening I had shared with William. And now, I have the whole day ahead of me to think of nothing else. I can remember every word that passed between us, the excitement of our first kiss and the softness of his touch upon my all too eager body. My hand is trembling so much I can hardly write.

How strange it is that my thoughts were so troubled when I set off to walk over to William's cottage. Although I had no doubts as to my own feelings for him, I remained, as yet, uncertain as to whether he had similar feelings for me. Was it not possible that, as a newcomer to our village, he sought nothing more than friendship? There was another possibility too that lurked at the back of my mind. What if his intentions were not entirely honourable? However, he was waiting for me outside the front door of the cottage and gave me such a welcoming smile that all such fears instantly evaporated. Once we had gone inside he offered me a glass of sparkling elderflower champagne, which he said he had acquired from an elderly farm labourer. I was surprised to discover how delightfully dry it was compared to most of the country wines I have previously tasted. He asked after Mother and said how kind it was of Charlotte to have agreed to accompany her, as she would doubtless find life rather dull down in Torquay. He said she had a remarkable gift with young children, that he had found her to be the best of company and had grown very fond of her. I wondered to what extent he had any understanding of Charlotte's feelings for him. Did he realise that he was the reason why she had quit her job at the school? Of course, I made no mention of any of this to him and was pleased to change the subject.

When I asked him to tell me about his childhood and upbringing, he said he would be happy to do so, but not before he had served up our supper. We sat down at a small oak table. He dished up generous helpings of a steaming hot stew, accompanied by thick slices of crusty bread he had baked that same morning. He poured me a glass of cider and then began, as he had promised, to tell me about his family and childhood. He told me he had been brought up in Rochdale, an industrial town just north of Manchester, where his father still works as a clerk for the Borough Council. He said his mother used to work in one of the many local textile mills, but had been forced to give up her job due to ill health. She suffers from severe rheumatism, probably brought on by the exacting nature of her former employment. He told me about how, as a young boy, he had loved to walk to the end of their cobbled street and out onto a country lane which led up the valley, through the village of Green Booth and beyond, until it opened out onto the wild beauty of the windswept moorland.

After we had finished eating and were sitting together on a low sofa under the window, I asked him how he had managed to secure a place at Manchester Grammar School. He said he owed an enormous debt to the headmaster of his local primary school, an exceptional teacher, who had encouraged him to apply for a scholarship, as otherwise his parents would never have been able to afford the fees. It was through Mr Grimsby, the same inspirational teacher, that he had first been exposed to politics, learning about the origins of the Co-operative Movement with its deep roots in Rochdale. He talked excitedly about the Rochdale Pioneers, a small group of men who, in the middle of last century, had set up the first co-operative store, where food and other goods could be purchased at prices even the poorest could afford. He said it was from these modest beginnings that the modern Co-operative movement has grown and flourished. He went on to declare his deep commitment to political reform, to a society in which every man and woman would have a right to employment and to receive a fair reward for their labours. He said it was the existing injustices in our society that had led to the recent General Strike and that the time had come for action. This was why he found the Liberals' campaign for a comprehensive programme of public works to be so appealing.

I sensed he was watching me closely all the while, no doubt wondering how the daughter of a prominent Herefordshire Tory would react to his strongly-held beliefs. I was so aroused by the earnest expression on his face and the troubled look in his dark brown eyes, that I was quite overcome and found myself reaching forward to take hold of his hands. For a moment I think he was taken aback, but then his face lit up and he raised my hand to his lips and kissed my fingers. We sat looking into each other's eyes for what seemed an eternity. My heart was pounding. Then, he reached forward and gently pulled me towards him. I shall never forget the sheer joy of that first embrace. I think he must have guessed that this was the first time I had kissed a man out of pure desire. Dear, dear William, I felt such love for you that I would have done anything to please you. How I longed to stay the night and how willingly I would have given myself to you. But you are all that is kind and perceptive and understanding. Whatever the strength of my desire, you knew it was too soon.

Friday 24th May 1929

I have done little else all morning other than think of William, He is up at the school today and will be in Hereford tomorrow in support of Mr Owen. How much I would have liked to go with him, but dare not take the risk of being seen campaigning for the Liberals. It is just as well I made no such commitment as Father telephoned mid-morning to say he is returning home later today.

I must be patient. Sunday will soon be here and William has suggested we drive down to Pandy and then up the Vale of Ewyas to the remains of Llanthony Priory. I can only hope and pray that, with the election campaign moving into its last week, Father's return home will be a brief one. I am so unpracticed in the art of deception that I fear he may detect I am concealing something from him.

This morning's post brought a long and heart-warming letter from Charlotte. How relieved I am to learn that Mother is benefitting from the fine weather and their daily walks along the front. Charlotte tells me that the other hotel residents provide a constant source of amusement. Most of them are elderly and devote much of their time to telling of their recent operations! However, she says she is missing the company of younger people and is much looking forward to returning home and seeing me. She says that when she thinks about the future, she cannot see herself settling down to life in the depths of the countryside. She is considering looking for an occupation which will offer her a greater level of social activity. I cannot say I blame her. Although she did not refer to it, I suspect she is still bruised by William's rejection. At least I believe she accepts that he has, in no way, misled her.

Goodness knows what she would say if she knew that I have fallen headlong in love with him?

There are so many confusing thoughts flying around in my head that I do not think I shall write any more today. Father will soon be home and I can only pray he is in good humour.

Saturday 25ᵗʰ May 1929

I hardly saw Father yesterday. After the briefest of enquiries after my well-being, he asked for supper to be taken to his study, where he spent the remainder of the evening on the telephone. I frequently heard his raised voice from across the hall. Even during the succession of elections that have taken place over recent years, I have never known him quite so agitated and short-tempered. He was in no better mood this morning. Over breakfast he sat with his head buried in a large folder of papers and hardly spoke a word. I told him I had heard from Charlotte and suggested we might telephone Mother at their hotel. To my dismay, his only mumbled response was to say he had no time for such matters at present, and could I not see he was far too busy. As we were leaving the dining room he apologised for his ill humour. He said he did not understand what was wrong with the country as it seems that everyone is turning to Ramsay MacDonald's Labour Party, while in places like Hereford, Lloyd George's Liberals are gaining ground. Under the circumstances, he hoped I would understand that he must return to Hereford before luncheon and would be obliged to remain there until the vote has been declared the following Friday. I can hardly believe my good fortune.

Sunday 26ᵗʰ May 1929

The day I have spent with William has surpassed my wildest hopes and expectations. I cannot believe there is a finer man on this earth.

It is quite a while since I last visited the priory at Llanthony and I had forgotten how splendid are the remains. The site is overgrown and not well cared for but the fine high arch, that separates the choir from the nave, is truly magnificent, and enough of the priory still stands for one to get a real sense of what it must have been like in its heyday. As I might have expected, William had done his homework and wanted to share with me everything he had found out about the history of the priory. He told me it had been constructed on the site of an earlier chapel dedicated to St David. This had later become a place of prayer and contemplation for a pious Norman nobleman called Walter de Lacey. De Lacey was joined by others who set about building the priory which they dedicated to St John the Baptist. It soon became home to some forty Augustinian monks. I was not in the least bit surprised to learn that, as was the case with so many historic sites on the borders, the priory was regularly under attack from the Welsh and, from time to time, the monks were forced to retreat to a secondary home in Gloucester. I was particularly fascinated by some extracts William read to me from the medieval historian Gerald of Wales' description of the priory, which he visited on his 'Journey through Wales' in 1188. It seems that by then, what he described as once having been 'a happy, a delightful spot, most suited to the life of contemplation', had been debased by the English monks who lived far too well and were 'extravagant, ambitious and ungrateful'!

After we had finished our little picnic in the ruins of the priory, William suggested we might drive further up Hatterrall Ridge, through Capel y Ffyn and up towards the Gospel Pass where, he suggested, we could park the car and walk along the top to enjoy a fine view of the Welsh countryside. We left the car by the side of the road and walked some distance down the slope of Darren Llwyd Ridge. I was grateful for my pair of sensible shoes without which I would have struggled to make my way through the dense patches of gorse. We were surrounded by sheep, still dressed in their heavy winter coats. Seemingly, undisturbed by our presence, they carried on grazing peacefully..

When we had walked for half an hour or so, William suggested we stop to take in the view. Down below, shrouded in a white haze, were the villages that border the Wye and the small township of Hay. Above us was the splendour of Hay Bluff and, running all the way along the top of the ridge, the remains of Offa's Dyke marking the historic border between England and Wales. Apart from the wind and the occasional bleating of the sheep, the only sound was the shrill cry of a pair of kites circling above the hillside.

We had not seen a single soul since we set out on our walk and so we had the glory of this wonderful landscape all to ourselves. At first we were so intoxicated by the exceptional views that neither of us spoke. After a while, William slipped his arm through mine. He spoke, almost in a whisper as if humbled by the majesty of our surroundings. 'Don't you just love all this?' he said, 'the wildness, these stark hills, the harsh valley down there, and the wonderful folk who live in this place.' He spoke of how the people of these hills had been hardened against poverty, the weather, and the effort of trying to eke out a simple living, with the odds so heavily stacked against them.'

I was moved by his enthusiasm and sensitivity and felt completely at one with the thoughts he had just shared. My natural inhibitions melted away and, grasping him round the waist, I pulled him towards me and closed my eyes. I felt his arms slip down my back until they encircled my waist. Then, laughing, he raised me off the ground and swirled me wildly round in crazy circles, and I was laughing too until all the breath had gone out of my body. He put me back down and clung on to me with my head buried against his chest. He ran his fingers through my hair. I raised my head to look up and saw there were tears in his eyes. A shiver of excitement ran through me. He bent forward and kissed the top of my head while his fingers caressed my lips. I opened my mouth to kiss his fingers and then I felt his lips against mine and, from that moment, I was lost in a sea of exhilaration.

What happened after that I cannot find adequate words to describe. The wave of physical and emotional pleasure that swept through me was such as I never dreamed possible. It was the moment for which I have waited all my life. Even in my wildest imaginings, I never knew that love-making could be so absolute a coming together of two beings. I have looked in the mirror every day since I was a small child and have never, never until this day, seen who I really am. I have discovered a passion within me I did not know I possessed.

I can hardly bear it but I shall see little of William this week as he will be campaigning for Mr Owen, when he isn't up at the school. He is full of excitement at the enthusiastic response the Liberals are receiving at their rallies and on the doorstep. He tells me that from Longtown to Peterchurch, and throughout the Golden Valley, all but the most hardened Tories are turning to the Liberals and there is talk of a thrilling victory for Mr Owen, come polling day.

Thursday 30ᵗʰ May 1929

It has been such an odd day. I walked up to Longtown this morning to cast my first vote. I was greeted outside the polling station by two elderly gentlemen wearing their respective Party colours, one for the Unionists and one for the Liberals. I recognised the Unionist as Harold Pugh, one of Father's cronies, a neighbouring farmer and treasurer of the local party. He greeted me heartily and said how delighted he was to see I had taken the trouble to walk all the way up to Longtown to vote for Mr Romilly. I responded with what little enthusiasm I could muster and went inside to vote. I felt a wonderful sense of exhilaration as I stood in the little cubicle with my ballot paper in front of me. It was as if this was the first time in my life I had the power to do something I really wanted to do, without regard to Father. I was so certain that what I was doing was the right thing to do that I winked at the gentleman wearing the Liberal Party colours as I left.

I passed the rest of the day able to think of little else other than William. How fortunate I am to have found him and how I long to be held once more in his loving arms. But there is a dark cloud on the horizon for Father will return tomorrow evening

Friday 31ˢᵗ May 1929

It is now five whole days since I last saw William. He does not teach on Fridays so he will have gone up to the Hereford to join the crowds outside the Shirehall, waiting for the result of the Election to be declared. How I long to be there with him. Is it really possible that Mr Owen will take the seat? William seemed so confident but he must be on tenterhooks. What excitement there will be if he wins, and how I wish I could be at the count to see the look on Father's face! However, I am not sure I shall be able to cope with his fury should the Tories have lost the seat. I have told Mary everything. She says that since I may find it impossible to communicate with William once Father returns, she is willing to act as our go-between. I shall write him a note this very evening and ask her to take it to him tomorrow.

Saturday 1ˢᵗ June 1929

Father returned home this morning. From the moment I heard the front door slam and his angrily raised voice in the hallway demanding to know what had happened to the post, I knew the Liberals must have taken the seat. My joy at the thought of Mr Owen's victory was somewhat tempered by my fear of Father when he is so enraged. He shouted at Mary to bring him a jug of coffee and stormed into the drawing room. He was wringing his hands in such a terrible rage that I decided it wisest to remain silent. It wasn't until after Mary had brought in the coffee that he finally mumbled, under his breath, 'It's all over, it's all over. All that time and effort down the drain! We're done for now, take it from me, we're truly done for!' All his pent-up anger burst forth as he poured scorn on that 'illegitimate son of a Scottish farm labourer' and that 'garrulous braying Welsh scoundrel' who, he said, were on the point of climbing into bed together. I realised, at once, that he was referring to Ramsay MacDonald and Lloyd-George and to the likelihood of a Socialist-Liberal coalition. I was desperate to find out what had happened in the Hereford seat and did not have to wait long. 'And, do you know what?' Father exclaimed, 'That young upstart, son of a publican, has taken Hereford.' He rambled on about how those who had voted for him should be ashamed and how the country is heading for ruination. But even father's anger cannot stifle my delight in knowing how exalted William will be. I shall write to him this evening.

Tuesday 4th June 1929

I sneaked into the kitchen this morning to hand Mary the note I had penned to William. She promised to call by his cottage this very afternoon as she has to pass that way to pick up some sewing from Mrs Saunders.

In my note I explained that, once again, since Father's return, I had become a virtual prisoner in the house. However, I said the one way we could continue to see each other, without raising Father's suspicion, would be if we were to meet in the woods to the rear of our house, where I am free to wander whenever I wish. I told him he could access the wood through a small gate in the wall, a short way beyond the main entrance to the house. I promised to wait for him by the fallen ash tree, in the clearing in the middle of the wood, at three o'clock every afternoon until such time as he was able to join me.

When Mary returned she told me that William had not been in when she called by his cottage, so she had pushed my note under the front door where he was bound to discover it on his return home. When I kissed her and thanked her for her trouble, there were tears in her eyes.

I wonder how long I shall have to wait until I see William again. I do not expect it will be before Friday at the earliest because of his teaching commitments. But I shall wait for him every day until he comes.

Thursday June 6ᵗʰ 1929

There was another letter from Charlotte this morning. I was relieved Father was out when the post arrived for this would allow me time to linger over her letter without him standing over me, impatiently demanding to know what she had to say. Although the weather has largely remained fine, a cold south-westerly wind has kept the two of them indoors. Sadly, there has been no sign of any further improvement in Mother's health, but Charlotte is hopeful that things will improve when they are able to get out in the fresh air again. She says that when Mother isn't resting, they spend much of their time playing cards. Mother normally retires to bed after dinner leaving Charlotte to spend her evenings reading in the drawing room. She is putting a brave face on it, but I am sure she must be bored and dreading the long weeks ahead. She is such a bundle of life and must be missing the company of other young people.

I walked to the clearing again this afternoon, but there was no sign of William.

Friday June 7ᵗʰ 1929

Another day has passed and still William has not come. I feel so dejected. What if he never comes? What if I have been fooling myself into believing his affection for me is greater than it really is? My biggest fear is that he has been put off by the complexity of our situation. What if he is unwilling to engage with the constant need for secrecy and deception? What if, knowing how much Father detests him, he can see no future in our relationship?

Saturday June 8ᵗʰ 1929

At last, I have seen William. I was so overjoyed when I came upon him sitting, waiting for me on the fallen branch of the old ash tree. He threw his arms around me and all my fears melted away. I could tell, at once, that he had missed me as much as I have missed him. We made love in the long grass in the shadow of a tall Oak tree, surrounded by a sea of red campion where, but a few weeks ago, the bluebells had heralded the spring. We lay in each other's arms, intoxicated by the scent of wild garlic and our love for each other. I lost all sense of time and place as we gave way to our passion. Nothing existed, nothing mattered outside or beyond where we lay together.

After we had made love, William lit his pipe and we sat and talked for a while. As we had not met since the election, William took pleasure in describing the latter stages of the campaign, the joy at Frank Owen's victory, the celebrations that had followed and the prospects for the new coalition Government. I told him how angry Father is at the Unionist defeat and at Frank Own's local victory, and of how I had contrived to keep well out of his way. I told him I had heard from Charlotte again and of my concern that Mother's condition is showing little, if any, sign of improvement. We discussed the future of our relationship. I told him I could not bear for us not to be able to meet whenever we wished and that I was in despair at knowing what best to do. William said that he too had spent many hours considering the difficulties of our situation. He said he had recently joined a newly established choral group, 'The Golden Valley Chorale'. He told me that they meet for rehearsals every Thursday evening in St Peter's Church in Longtown, in preparation for a summer concert to be given in Dore Abbey. He said 'The Chorale' is still looking to recruit new members and, knowing of my love of choral music, he hoped I might consider joining them. He said it would provide us with a perfect opportunity to continue to see each other and that we could drive up to Longtown together, providing that Father had no objection. Of course, I leaped at the idea and said I would raise it with Father in the morning. We agreed to meet in the wood again at the same time tomorrow afternoon.

Sunday June 9ᵗʰ 1929

I lay awake much of last night worrying about how Father was likely to respond to my request to join the Chorale. Of course, he would want to know how I intended to travel to Longtown, especially in the winter months when it is dark so early. Although it was a falsehood, I decided I would tell him that Mr Cuddington was already providing a lift to two other members of the choir who live in the village and had kindly offered to take me along too.

As luck would have it, Father was in an affable mood when I raised the matter with him this morning and, to my surprise and delight, raised no objection. Indeed, he said he thought it would be good for me to get out of the house for a change. His willing consent is so out of character that I believe his mind must have been elsewhere at the time. He didn't even ask how I intended to travel up and down to Longtown. This was an unexpected relief as I so much prefer not to dissemble.

William was over the moon when I conveyed the good news to him when we met in the wood this afternoon. He suggested I wait for him by the entrance to the drive at seven o'clock on Thursday evening.

Thursday June 13ᵗʰ 1929

Mary provided me with an early supper this evening so that I could be ready for when William came to collect me. I was thrilled at the thought of being with him again, but a little apprehensive about meeting so many new people. We did not have much time to talk on the drive up to Longtown as we were running late. When we arrived at the church the other members of the Chorale had already assembled, and I was surprised to see how many there were, at least thirty men and women of all ages and, as I had suspected, very few were known to me.

William introduced me to Miss Standish, a handsome woman in her mid-thirties, who serves as both organiser and choir-mistress. She, in turn, introduced me to the other members of the Chorale and to Mr Windrush, an elderly gentleman with long, flowing white hair and dark bushy eyebrows, who was to accompany us on the piano.

One of the choir members passed round the sheet music for the first of the pieces we were to rehearse, 'Five English Folk Songs' by Vaughan Williams, a delightful piece I have not come across before. I was grateful for my musical education at school which enabled me to master the soprano part without too much difficulty. It soon became evident that none of my fellow singers were strangers to sight reading. I was pleased to have joined such a talented group. Miss Standish is an inspiring influence and led us through the more difficult parts with authority and a true understanding of the composers' intentions. After we had run through the Vaughan Williams a couple of times, we moved on to an old favourite, the Orlando Gibbons madrigal 'The Silver Swan', which the Chorale had been working on for some weeks. Scored, as it is, for five voices rather than the usual four, it provides quite a few challenges, even to accomplished singers. I love the narrative of this work that swans only sing when they are close to death. After we had spent a good half hour on the Gibbons, Miss Standish said she thought we had sung enough for one evening and suggested we repair to 'The Crown'. I was concerned not to be too late home because of Father, but William persuaded me to join the others for just one glass of cider before he drove me home, which I gladly accepted.

Although I wanted to spend more time with William, I thoroughly enjoyed the evening and am so glad he suggested I join the Chorale. As I said to him on the way home, there will surely be occasions in the future when

Father is away and I shall not be obliged to return home so early.

Tuesday June 25ᵗʰ 1929

Another letter arrived from Torquay this morning. This time it was from Mother. She writes to say she is feeling a little better, largely due to a long spell of warm, dry weather. She says that she and Charlotte have enjoyed several walks through the Princess Gardens which are bounded on the sea front by exotic palm trees and, to the north, by a fine line of London planes. They are very taken by the splendid cast iron fountain surmounted by dolphins designed by Sir Reginald Blomfield, and by the impressive memorial to soldiers who lost their lives in the Great War. She concluded by saying how very much they are missing us and of their hope Father and I may be able to travel down to visit them before too many more days have passed. When I showed the letter to Father, his only comment was to say that he is far too busy at the office to contemplate a visit to Torquay at present. I reminded him that more than six weeks have passed since I first suggested we might drive down to see them, but he flew into a rage and said I had no idea how much he was required at the office, during these difficult economic times. I would gladly travel down to see them on my own but know he will never give his consent.

Sunday July 14ᵗʰ 1929

I was too tired to write in my diary when I arrived home yesterday evening for it was the day of our summer concert, and we did not return home until late. It was a most wonderful occasion. The splendid abbey was decked in flowers and I experienced a tingle of pleasure and pride when I saw the large poster in the porch announcing that, 'On Sunday July 14ᵗʰ at 7pm, a concert is to be given by the newly established Golden Valley Chorale, conducted by Miss Amelia Standish FRSM.'

We arrived for our final rehearsal to find the abbey bathed in sunlight which shone through the clear glass windows of what had originally been the abbey's south transept. 'The Chorale' was positioned on a low stage, facing the south door, with the altar and magnificent medieval choir stalls to our left. The rehearsal did not go too well, but Miss Standish told us not to be too concerned as she had every confidence in us, and was sure we would perform far better when it came to the actual performance

In the event the concert was a great success. I can honestly say that we sang our hearts out. In addition to the Vaughan Williams and Gibbons we had added an intriguing song 'Beware' by the youthful composer Benjamin Britten, Delius' enchanting 'Midsummer Song' and Elgar's 'Weary Wind of the West'. It was a challenging programme to say the least. We knew we were taking a bit of a risk introducing our audience to so many new pieces. However, we need not have worried. The church was packed and the audience applauded everything with great enthusiasm. The vicar said he had never seen the abbey so full and was overjoyed as all the ticket income was to go towards essential church restoration. My only disappointment was that neither Mother nor Charlotte were there. Father, of course, had shown little interest in supporting me when I first mentioned the performance to him, so I never bothered to ask if he would like to attend.

On the way home, William drove down a tiny side lane and we kissed. We were so elated by the excitement and success of the concert it was as though we had never kissed before.

Father had retired to bed when I finally returned home. I do not suppose he will ask me how the concert went.

Wednesday July 17th 1929
I was helping Mary in the kitchen when Father returned from Hereford this evening. From the grim look on his face, I feared that something was up as soon as I went to greet him in the hallway. He summoned me into his study and glared at me with ice-cold eyes. 'What's this I hear about you being seen about with that Cuddington fellow?'

he snapped at me. He said he supposed I thought I could do what I liked when he was out of the house and Mother and my sister were away. I was so taken aback that I was speechless. I could not imagine how, or from whom, he had heard I had been with William. Mary is sworn to secrecy and she would not betray me anyway. My heart was racing. What could anyone have overseen that led them to believe it was their duty to tell Father? I did not have to wait long for an answer. It seems that someone has informed him that they saw me in the company of William and another young couple on the day of the picnic, up the Olchon Valley. At least I was relieved to know we had not been seen on one of those occasions when we had been more intimate and alone. What really angered Father was that I had not asked his permission. I mumbled some excuse about the outing having been arranged at the last minute, and I had been unable to seek his approval because he had been away in Hereford at the time, working on the election. When I asked from where he had acquired this information, he said it was none of my business, but that I should hardly be surprised to have been observed, sitting in the front of William's Austin 7, with the roof down and for all the world to see. He banged his fist on the desk and shouted at me that people have eyes, and that not everyone in the village shared William's low sense of propriety.

However vehemently I protested, whatever I tried to say to defend poor William, Father would have none of it. He was in full flow by now and raged on about how William had campaigned for that 'young whippersnapper Owen' and had been seen handing out Liberal leaflets in the surrounding villages. He said William had only recently arrived in the County and yet had the impertinence to go about telling everyone how they should vote. Turning his back on me, he went to stare out of the window. I sensed he was preparing for a final onslaught. I knew what was coming and I didn't have to wait long. In a deathly, cold voice, but without turning to look at me, he said 'I absolutely forbid you to engage further with that detestable young man.' I ran out of the study and upstairs to my bedroom where I wept and wept until there were no tears left to fall.

I am calmer now and can see that nothing has really changed. Father was never likely to approve of my relationship with William and, no doubt, in his usual overbearing manner, he would have insisted on Mother's support too, had she been there. But if Father thinks he has ended our relationship he is very much mistaken. We shall have to be even more discreet but, thank goodness, we have our secret meeting place in the wood and I can depend on Mary to run messages between us.

Friday July 26th 1929

My time of the month has passed for a second time and there are still no traces of blood. I am almost certain I must be with child. The thought that I may be carrying William's child makes me want to sing with joy. And yet it is so heartbreaking that I cannot share my joy with anyone. It must even remain a secret from Mary because if Father found out she knew, without telling him, it would surely put her position in jeopardy. It is a secret that must be kept until I can be absolutely certain and, of course, until I have told William. If only Charlotte was here, for she is the one person in whom I could confide. But for now I must deal with it on my own. I must be strong and resolute.

Tuesday August 6th 1929

I was out in the garden today, watering the vegetables, when Father called for me. There was such a sense of urgency in his summons that I feared for the worst. He had tears in his eyes when he told me that Charlotte had just telephoned with the dreadful news that Mother has suffered a minor heart attack, and has been conveyed from the hotel to a nearby hospital in Torquay. He said we should try not to worry as Mother is being well cared for. However, the resident cardiologist has told Charlotte that there is little more they can do for Mother, and that she is likely to fare better at home, with a loving family to care for her. He has advised her that she should be ready to be discharged from the hospital in a few days, after she has recovered some of her strength.

Father stood by his desk, nervously rubbing his fingers over the corner of his blotting pad. He was deep in thought and seemed to be struggling with the reality of the situation. After a while he looked up at me and said that, of course, Mother must be brought home as soon as she is well enough to travel. He said he would arrange for a driver to take him down to Torquay to bring Mother and Charlotte back home. I had hoped he would ask me to go with him, but he insisted I remain at home to prepare everything for Mother's return. Father is rarely given to allowing his emotions to surface, but his every gesture spoke of a man whose mind is in turmoil. I assured him that he could depend on Charlotte and me to do everything we could to help to speed Mother's recovery.

I feel quite numb. Life can be too cruel at times. It is difficult to find words to describe my deeper inner feelings. At least Charlotte will soon be home and I shall be able to confide in her.

Friday August 9th 1929

Charlotte telephoned again early this morning to say that Mother has now sufficiently recovered to be brought home. A driver from the factory has been on stand-by for the last few days, so Father was able to set off on the long drive to Devon just after ten o'clock this morning. I passed the rest of the day helping Mary in the kitchen, ironing bed linen and making Mother's bed. This afternoon I cut some of Mother's favourite white Margaret Merril roses for her bedroom. She loves their strong and distinctive fragrance.

It has been an exhausting day. Father will not return with Mother and Charlotte until tomorrow. I shall go to bed with a copy of Villette. I need something to distract me from.

Saturday August 10th 1929

Yesterday I managed to complete all the preparations for Mother's return, so I was free to spend the morning writing to William. I had to let him know that some local busybody had seen us together on the day of the picnic and has told Father. He will find it hard to believe I have been forbidden ever to be with him again. I told him that, as far as it is in my power, nothing will keep us apart, that my love for him is undiminished and that I intend that we shall be together one day. I also told him that Mother is returning home from Torquay today, after suffering a heart attack, and begged him to be patient as it will, doubtless, be even more difficult for us to meet for a while. I tore up the letter and rewrote it several times, knowing how easily words on the page can be misconstrued. When I was finally satisfied, I gave the letter to Mary who promised to deliver it before the end of the day.

Father arrived home with Mother and Charlotte in the late afternoon. As we helped her out of the car, I thought how frail Mother was looking. She was unable to make the short walk from the car into the house without our support. Before we helped her up to her bed, she insisted on sitting in the drawing room with us for a while where Mary had laid out a light supper. I noticed how very short of breath she was. She was only able to speak to us in short sentences. But she was still able to warm our hearts with her beautiful smile, that so well reflects the sweetness and generosity of her nature. I sat next to her on the sofa where she held onto my hand all the while she remained with us. She listened attentively to our conversation until we saw her eyes begin to close. Charlotte took charge and insisted that she and I should take her upstairs to her bedroom, where she would be able to sleep in much greater comfort.

When we came back down again, we rejoined Father in the drawing room where we shared Mary's light supper together. It was such a relief to have Mother safely back home again, but we could all see how very poorly she is. We have little choice but to accept there is little likelihood of her making much of a recovery. Father told us he had spoken to the cardiologist at the hospital who had warned him Mother may suffer a further heart attack at any time, and that we should be prepared for the worst. Father and Charlotte were exhausted after their long journey and, much though I was longing to talk to Charlotte, I encouraged them both to take an early night.

I am so worried about Mother and, dear William, shall I ever see you again?

Sunday August 11th 1929

Charlotte and I spent the morning caring for Mother. She was in a deep sleep when I first went in to see her, early this morning. She lay with her hands clasped over her breast looking so pale and fragile that, for one dreadful moment, I feared she had passed away during the night. But, to my intense relief, when I knelt by her bedside, I could just hear her shallow, irregular, breathing. There was nothing I could do for her while she still slept, so I went down to breakfast. Father was distracted and had little to say. Charlotte, too, was unusually subdued. We all know Mother's condition is critical and it is as if a heavy pall of death already hangs over the house. We had just begun to clear the table when Father asked us to return to our seats. He said he was reluctant to leave the house, but that it was imperative he call in at the office as there were a number of serious matters there requiring his attention. He asked us to take good care of Mother while he was out and said that he expected to return home by the early evening.

Throughout the morning, Charlotte and I took it in turns to sit with Mother. She slept for much of the time and it wasn't until approaching midday that I saw her struggling to sit up. I did what I could to make her comfortable and managed to persuade her to consume a few spoons of the chicken broth, which Mary had specially prepared for her. When she spoke, it was in little more than a whisper, but she was able to tell us how grateful she was for all for our love and support. She asked if I would read to her from her collection of the poems of John Clare which is always by her bedside. I began by reading two of her favourites, 'The Yellowhammer's Nest' and 'Little Trotty Wagtail' and had just begun to read her 'The Badger', when I saw she had fallen back to sleep. I pulled up her bedclothes to cover her frail body, kissed her and quietly made my way downstairs.

I found Charlotte in the kitchen talking to Mary and told them Mother was sleeping. Neither Charlotte nor I were particularly hungry, but Mary insisted we take a bowl of the chicken broth which we sat and ate in the kitchen. Mary suggested it would do Charlotte and I good to go outside to get some fresh air. She said she was sure we must have a great deal of catching up to do after being apart for so long. Of course, she knew I would want to talk to Charlotte about William. In the meantime, she promised to keep an eye on Mother.

My mind was in a spin as we set off down the path towards the wood. I was far from sure how much it was wise to tell Charlotte at this stage. She chatted away incessantly as we ambled along the woodland path, telling me of the odd people she and Mother had met while staying in the hotel, of her attraction for a handsome Italian waiter who had served them at table, and of the long, drawn-out evenings she had spent reading in the hotel lounge and wishing she were somewhere else.

We reached the clearing in the wood where William and I have met and made love and I sensed his presence and the overwhelming power of our love for each other. It was then I knew I must open my heart to my sister. We sat, side by side, on the fallen ash tree. When I told her I had something important to tell her she looked a little taken aback, but encouraged me to continue. And then, it all came pouring out. I told her everything, absolutely everything. I told her of my chance encounter with William on the way to collect eggs from the farm; of our picnic up the Olchon Valley; of the first time we had made love in his cottage; of our secret meetings and love making here in the wood, near where we now sat; and of the precious moments we had spent together on the way back from choir rehearsals. Charlotte listened attentively and appeared to be remarkably undisturbed by what I had to tell her. It was not until I spoke to her of Father's fury at discovering I had been seen with William on the day of the picnic; of his vitriolic opposition to William's radical political ideals; and of his insistence that I should have no further contact with him, that she threw her hands up in horror and expressed her heartfelt concern for my situation. She said Father could be 'such a beast' and is so out of touch with modern day thinking it is hardly possible to believe. She said it is my misfortune that Mother should be so ill for she would assuredly have stood up for me but, in any event, was it not possible Father might come to accept the situation in the fullness of time, however reluctantly.

It was then I knew I had no choice. I had to tell her I was carrying William's child. How else could she possibly fully understand the gravity of my situation. It was easier to tell her than I had imagined. Of course, she wanted to know if I was quite certain of my condition, to which I could only say I was as certain as I could be. It was such a relief to see that she was not in the least sickened by what I had told her. On the contrary, she appeared to be delighted for me and threw her arms around me in the warmest of embraces. Of course, she wanted to know if William knew I was expecting his child and I explained that I had not yet had an opportunity to speak to him as I have been confined to the house, and under Father's strict command never to see him again. 'Well,' she said, 'if you truly love him and want to be with him, you must tell him, and you must not waste any time over it.' I told her how Mary has been my true and loyal friend and go-between but that it would be unfair to compromise her position any further. She chuckled, said this was no job for a cook-cum-postwoman and that, from now on, she herself would be my mouthpiece. She insisted we find a way for me to speak to William, and the sooner the better.

The rest of the day was devoted to attending to Mother, although she is so often asleep that her needs are few. Dinner was a further gloomy occasion. Father has retreated even further into the dark space he occupies.

Dear William when you fall asleep tonight will you dream of me as I know I shall dream of you?

Monday August 12th 1929

Dr Hutton called round this morning to see Mother. Afterwards, in the drawing room, he told us his main concern was over her difficulty in breathing which is due to a general weakening of her system since the heart attack. He deeply regretted that he could only advise us to prepare for the worst, as he agreed with the Torquay cardiologist that it was probable a second heart attack may soon follow. If this happens, he fears she is unlikely to come through. However, he said one could never be sure of these things and it was possible that, with our loving care, she may live for some weeks yet, even months.

We had all accepted the seriousness of Mother's condition but it came as a terrible blow to hear it stated so emphatically. When Dr Hutton had left, Father retreated into his study. Charlotte and I sat together in the drawing room for a while, vowing to give Mother all the love and attention we can, for as long as it may be required. Afterwards I went upstairs to sit with Mother until lunchtime.

Later this afternoon I told Charlotte that, with Mother's condition being so serious, I felt we must abandon our plan to visit William, at least for a few days, and she agreed. During the afternoon and evening we took it in turns to sit with Mother. She makes so few demands but continues to enjoy our reading to her.

Friday August 16th 1929

Father only goes up to Hereford occasionally these days. He says he needs to be near Mother, although he rarely goes up to see her. I think the truth is that he cannot bear to see her looking so poorly. I am surprised at how quickly Charlotte and I have slipped into a regular routine. We have established a kind of shift system which helps to ease the burden of looking after Mother, not that she is any real trouble, bless her. Indeed. much of the time she is barely conscious. In her waking moments she lies back, propped up on her pillows, with a sweet smile of appreciation on her face. We both read to her although I suspect she is able to take little of it in. Charlotte chooses items from the newspaper and *The Ideal Home* magazine, while I continue to read her the poems I know she loves. Mary has become a dab hand at dreaming up new recipes for soups and easily digestible dishes with which she hopes we shall be able to tempt Mother. Alas, her appetite is so poor, and she has such difficulty in swallowing, that much of what we serve her is returned to the kitchen.

After lunch, Charlotte prevailed upon me to delay no further in breaking the news of my condition to William. She said he would most likely be back from school soon after three o'clock and that, as it was one of Father's days up in Hereford, it was an opportunity not to be missed. She had already had a word with Mary who had willingly agreed to look after Mother while we were out. All my anxieties returned, but I knew Charlotte was right and that we must do as she urged.

We arrived at the cottage just before four o'clock. The front door was open and we could hear the sound of hammering from within. He must have heard us approaching because the hammering ceased and he emerged with a picture frame in his hand. 'Well, what a lucky man am I,' he said. 'It is not every day one is visited by the two most enchanting ladies in the parish!' He stepped forward to embrace us and then told us how sorry he was to hear that Mother was so unwell. He said it must be a very difficult time for us all. He invited us inside as the kettle was on the hob and he was about to make tea. Charlotte thanked him but said she knew there were intimate matters that he and I needed to discuss and that, in the meantime, she would like to take a walk in his garden.

Once we were alone, William told me how dismayed he had been to hear of Father's anger at our having been seen together on the day of the picnic, the more so as, far from being alone, we had been with the Powells. He said he understood how difficult it is for us to meet while I have Mother to care for. However, our not having been able to see each other over the past two weeks had helped him to appreciate how much he loved me, more than I could ever imagine. I was so happy to hear this that I burst into tears and was soon lost in the fold of his arms. When we drew apart, I finally plucked up the courage to tell him of my condition.

'William, my dearest William,' I said 'I'm going to have your baby.' I cannot adequately describe how moved he was at hearing these words tumble from my lips. Nor shall I ever forget the tears that rolled down his cheeks as he held me in his arms. 'Then we must be married,' he said, without a moment's hesitation. 'I shall go to speak to your Father, surely he cannot now deny us the right to be together.' Of course, I was overjoyed at William's resolution, but only too aware of how much Father detested him, and of the certainty of his request to marry me being refused. I begged him not to be too hasty as it would hardly be appropriate for him to approach Father at this difficult time. I said that, although I must be nearly three months into my pregnancy, the baby hardly shows as yet, and I was confident that I would be able to keep my condition secret for some weeks. William immediately grasped the import of what I had said and reluctantly agreed not to approach Father for the time being. However, when the time is right, he would let nothing come between us. I think Charlotte must have been listening outside for she came in now with a cheery smile on her face. She said how happy she was for us and promised to help us in any way she could. She reminded me that Father would soon be returning home and that we must be on our way. I was so sad to have leave, especially as I did not know when I would see William again.

I am indebted to Charlotte for all her loving support. She is my rock in these stormy seas.

Wednesday August 21ˢᵗ 1929

I fear Mother is sinking fast. She sleeps nearly all day, rarely opens her eyes and, even then, seems unaware of our presence. She has neither eaten nor drunk anything for two days. All we can do now is to moisten her lips with a little water. It is a slow, lingering death, but at least it would seem to be without pain. Dr Hutton called again this morning and said he doubted she would last the night through. Father has stayed home from work all week but rarely comes up to see Mother. To see her in this sorry state seems to be all too much for him to bear.

Thursday August 22ⁿᵈ 1929

Mother passed away in the early hours of this morning. Charlotte and I sat by her bed all night waiting for the awful moment which we knew must come. Her last breath came with no final death rattle, no muffled cry or whimper, just a sudden silence. Charlotte went to wake Father. I could hear him sobbing as he came from his bedroom, on the opposite side of the landing. He kneeled beside the bed and, with tears pouring down his cheeks, kissed her on the forehead. Unable to cope with his emotions, he then hurriedly left us and went downstairs to his study to mourn his wife's death in solitude. I closed Mother's eyes and laid her hands across her breast. Charlotte and I then kneeled down together to pray. After that, there was nothing left for us to do but to return to our beds in the hope of catching a few hours sleep before dawn. As I made my way up to my room, I could hear Father was still sobbing down below. I could not help wondering whether he was weeping for Mother or for himself.

I never realised how many things there are to do when someone dies. But, somehow, we got through it together.

Dr Hutton called to sign the death certificate; Father contacted the vicar to make arrangements for the funeral, while Charlotte and I wrote letters to everyone to inform them of the sad news. This has never been a happy house at the best of times and now, with Mother gone, I feel a sense of impending doom. Thank goodness for Charlotte, my loving sister and dearest and most loyal friend.

Friday August 30th 1929

Thankfully, the day Mother was laid to rest was blessed with glorious sunshine. It seemed so fitting for someone who has brought so much light into our lives. The little Church of St Clydog was packed with those who had come to pay their last respects. Many came because they knew and loved Mother, others came out of respect for Father and his position in the community. There was but a thin scattering of distant relatives, for neither Mother nor Father had brothers or sisters. The church was decked with the most beautiful flowers, and the cheerful hymns we had chosen made it more of a celebration than a wake. Charlotte and I struggled to hold back our tears during the committal at the graveside. We were thankful when it was all over and we were able to mingle with our guests. I was surprised to spot William out of the corner of my eye. He was talking to the parish clerk at the time, but looked in my direction and smiled. When I was sure Father was out of sight, I was finally able to have a few words with him. I told him how surprised I was to see him. He said it was only fitting that he should attend the funeral of the wife of one of the school's esteemed governors, besides which he had hoped to be able to have a few words with us to say how sorry he was for our loss. There was so much I wanted to say to him but we could not take the risk. I promised I would write to him soon and pleaded with him to be patient.

After the funeral we retired to the Cornewall Arms where Father had arranged for a modest buffet lunch to share with our relatives and a few of our closer acquaintances.

It was a sombre gathering. Father could hardly manage a smile for anyone and our guests were mostly elderly and cheerless. We were glad to return home and put our feet up in front of the drawing room fire. Father joined us for afternoon tea but then disappeared into his study once more. Charlotte said she had seen me talking with William and I told her he sent his sincere condolences. Otherwise, I said it had all been an awkward and unsatisfactory conversation as there was so much we wanted to say, but had been unable to do so, under the circumstances. Charlotte suggested we might play canasta to take our minds off things but I said I wasn't in the mood and was too tired, and so I came up to my room.

And now I can only think of William and of the future we long to share together.

Sunday September 1st 1929

I am more aware of how my body is changing with the passing of each day. When I looked at myself in the mirror this morning there could be no doubt, our baby is beginning to show. Soon I shall no longer be able to keep it a secret. Afraid of how Father is likely to react, I felt compelled to talk to Charlotte. Although Father will be strongly opposed to my marrying William, she believes that his sense of propriety may just persuade him to give his consent. She pleaded with me to be patient for a while, as Father is still in deep mourning. Reluctantly I agreed. However, it is so long since I have spoken to William that I begged her to call on him as soon as possible to explain the difficulty of our situation, and to assure him of my continuing love for him. This she most willing agreed to do.

Monday September 2nd 1929

Charlotte called to see William this afternoon. Although he is finding the waiting unbearable, she says that he accepts the need to delay a few more weeks before approaching Father. He begged Charlotte to tell me that he is determined we shall be married whatever Father's response, even if it means our running away together. He sent me a most lovely, fragrant red rose, plucked fresh from his garden as a token of his undying love. Oh, how I miss you my dear, sweet darling!

Monday September 9th 1929

I cannot stand the atmosphere in this house for much longer. Even Charlotte is subdued by Father's melancholy.

I dream of being far away from here with William by my side and our little baby cradled in my arms.

Tuesday September 10th 1929

Father has not gone up to Hereford since Mother died. He says he cannot abide the thought of the sympathetic faces that will greet him in the office and that, in any case, the state of the economy being so dire, there is little business to which he needs to attend.

It was not a particularly pleasant afternoon but Charlotte insisted we went for a walk in the woods. She was in a very jolly mood and I set off with her, not for a moment suspecting the surprise that awaited me. We were in sight of the fallen ash tree when strong hands clasped me from behind. I felt his lips on my cheek and my heart raced with excitement. It was such a joy to see William again. He was all laughter and smiles at first, but soon, with a frown, he gestured for Charlotte and I to sit down. He remained standing, with his arms folded, staring fixedly at the ground in front of him. After a while he looked up and told us he had been giving careful consideration to our impossible situation. He fully accepted that it would have been inappropriate to speak to Father in the days immediately following Mother's death. However, time was slipping by and he so very much wanted us to begin to make our home together, while our baby grows inside me. He felt it was no longer reasonable for us to allow Father to be a barrier to our love and commitment to each other. Surely there must be a possibility that, once he knew I was with child, he would consent to our getting married, however unwillingly.

I looked at Charlotte but she turned away. Although she had suggested this herself, I knew she was thinking, as was I, of how unlikely it was that Father would ever agree. With tears in my eyes, I told him so and said I was in despair as to what we should do. Such is her love for me, dear Charlotte was crying too. Meanwhile, William was anxiously pacing up and down. Finally, he stopped to look down at us with a determined look on his face. He said that if Father is going to refuse to give his permission, this is no less likely to be so in six months time, as it is now. He said he could wait no longer and was of a mind to speak to Father this very evening. Charlotte and I both could both see the logic of his argument but remained deeply apprehensive as to the outcome. 'But what if he does say no, what then?' Charlotte declared. 'Then we shall run away together for there will be no other choice left to us,' William replied. Charlotte and I stood up and the three of us drew together in a tight embrace. We parted with William insisting he would call to see Father at six o'clock this evening.

It is now only an hour until William is due to arrive and my stomach is churning at the prospect of his meeting with Father. Charlotte sat with me in the drawing room all afternoon in a vain attempt to distract me. I can think of nothing other than what is to come and I have a heavy heart.

Wednesday September 11th 1929

If only I could forever dismiss from my mind what happened yesterday evening. I have never felt so down-hearted. Charlotte and I were in the drawing room when William rang the doorbell and Mary opened the front door to him. I wanted to rush out to greet him, but Charlotte insisted it would be for the best if I remained with her until he had spoken to Father. We listened to their footsteps as they crossed the hallway, and to the sound of Mary knocking on Father's study door to announce he had a visitor. Once William had been admitted to the study and had closed the door behind him, we strained our ears, but could hear nothing but the sound of their muffled voices and the ticking of the grandfather clock.

At least five minutes must have passed before the tone of their distant voices changed. I had even begun to hope that, once he was aware of William's good intentions, Father might yet give his consent. But how sadly mistaken I was. All of a sudden there were angry raised voices, the study door was thrown open and we could hear Father shouting at William, demanding he leave the house at once and never return. Charlotte tried to hold me back, but I tore myself free from her and rushed out into the hallway where I saw William retreating backwards towards the front door, while Father rained further abuse at him. I tried to run to William but Father lunged forward and grabbed me by the arm, continuing to shout obscenities at my loved one. Father was so beside himself with anger I feared he might lash out at William at any moment. I could see that all was lost and so I pleaded with William to leave before they came to blows. Reluctantly, he heeded my advice and hurriedly departed with Father shouting after him never to darken our doorstep again. Once William had left, Father turned his anger on me, calling me 'a worthless whore', telling me I had betrayed his trust and forbidding me ever to see William again. He then ordered me out of his sight as he could not bear to look at me.

As I ran upstairs to my room, I could hear Father shouting at Charlotte, accusing her of duplicity and forbidding her to go anywhere near me. I threw myself onto my bed and wept the whole night through. Sometime in the early hours Charlotte tapped on my door, but I begged her to leave me alone. She returned before breakfast, and again at lunchtime, to tell me that Father had gone up to Hereford. She begged me to come down to eat but I sent her away, saying I was not in the least bit hungry. I feel completely numb as though life has gone out of me. My only thoughts are of my hatred for Father and of how I may escape from this prison.

Friday September 13ᵗʰ 1929

I must have finally fallen asleep last night although it cannot have been until the small hours. Apart from the deeply disturbed thoughts spinning around in my head, I felt physically sick and had a severe pain in my stomach. I was a little calmer when I woke this morning and my stomach cramps had eased. I no longer doubted what I have to do. I could not bear the thought of a further confrontation with Father and would not have gone down to breakfast if I had not heard him starting up his car to head off to the office. Charlotte gave me a big hug and Mary must have known what has happened for she fussed over me like a mother hen.

I told Charlotte that my mind is quite made up and that nothing will stop me from marrying William. If Father will not agree to our marriage, I shall marry him without his consent, even if it means running away with William. Charlotte understands how I feel but begged me to think about the baby. She said there is no certainty that William will be able to find a teaching post elsewhere and, under such circumstances, how would he be able to support us. She pleaded with me to be patient and to stay at home where she and Mary can look after me, at least until the baby is born. I said I doubted Father would agree to such a thing, but Charlotte believes he is hardly likely to send me away somewhere to have the baby in secret. She feels sure he will come round to the idea, once he recognises there is no real alternative. She said she was willing to speak to him on my behalf for which I shall be eternally grateful. Once we know the outcome, she promised to find a way of contacting William to let him know how things stand.

Father returned home soon after lunch. As I was anxious to provide Charlotte with an opportunity to speak to him first, I spent the rest of the afternoon in the garden, deadheading the roses and cutting back the honeysuckle which has grown so rampant over the summer months. It was late in the afternoon when Charlotte called me in to tell me that Father wished to speak to me. She gave me a reassuring hug but I was sick with apprehension as I knocked on his study door. To my surprise and relief he managed a weak smile when I entered and there was no sign of the anger which I had anticipated. However, he made it abundantly clear that, while he agreed to my remaining at home to have the baby, it was conditional on my promising to have no further contact with William, nor was I to leave the house without his permission. I have little choice but to agree to his conditions, for the time being at least.

As always, I am so grateful to Charlotte. She has managed to bring peace to a troubled situation. I know now that I shall receive all the support I need if I have our baby here at home. But I shall only rest when I know that William is in agreement. I shall write a letter explaining everything to him. Charlotte has to go up to Longtown tomorrow and has promised she will drop it off for him at the school.

Monday September 16th 1929

I cannot contain my anger and despair. Charlotte called at the school this afternoon as she had promised. She arrived just as the children were leaving for home and waited outside, expecting William to emerge at any moment. Once nearly all the children had left, and there was still no sign of him, she decided to approach the headmaster who was standing by the school gate in conversation with one of the mothers. When she enquired after William, she was appalled to learn that, following an extraordinary meeting of the school governors, he had been dismissed. She tried to question Mr Broadbent further but all he would say was that he had not been invited to attend the meeting, but that the chairman of the governors had subsequently informed him that William had been dismissed for 'improper conduct.' He had suggested that if she wished to know more, she should speak to her Father. For his part, he considered William to be an outstanding teacher who had been an inspiration to the children and he was sorry to lose him.

Charlotte was so shocked to hear this news that she had called at William's cottage on the way home, hoping to discover more, However, he was not at home at the time so she had pushed my letter under the door, and left a note of her own to say she would call again as soon as she was able. Of course, it is obvious who is responsible for William's dismissal, and I was all for challenging Father on the matter as soon as he returned home. However, Charlotte pleaded with me not to do so as she was sure it would only make matters worse. And so, for now, I shall bide my time. But I am determined to have it out with Father one of these days.

Tuesday 17th September 1929

As if my life isn't already sufficiently unbearable, I am now suffering from a most unpleasant pain in my abdomen. I first became aware of it over the weekend, but it is now much more severe and accompanied by constant waves of nausea. Charlotte is very concerned about my condition and says she will suggest to Father that he sends for Dr Hudson. However, I persuaded her to wait for a day or two as my discomfort is probably quite normal during pregnancy, and will most likely pass.

Wednesday 25th September 1929

Father hardly speaks to me these days. Breakfast is the only meal he regularly shares with us as he now prefers to take lunch and supper in his study. I rather think he is trying to avoid me but Charlotte insists that something else must be troubling him. She thinks it may be related to his business interests and the poor state of the national economy. Although we see so little of him, his gloomy presence continues to pervade the whole house. At least it no longer matters that I am not permitted to leave the

house as I rarely feel well enough to do so anyway. Thank
God, my stomach pains are less troubling than they were.

I am so desperate to know what has happened to
William. He has so little in the way of money or personal
possessions. I fear for his survival.

Friday 27ᵗʰ September 1929

We have just heard that William has been evicted from his
cottage! I can hardly countenance it, but Mary learned this
from one of her friends in the village and brought us the
dreadful news this morning. She tells me he was given but a
week's notice. I cannot imagine what fabricated reason his
landlord may have given him. However there can be little
doubt that, once more, Father is behind this. He will not
rest until William has been drummed out of the County.

I must find out where he has gone. Charlotte has to go
up to Longtown this afternoon to collect a blouse from
Mrs Prendergast. She promises to see what she can find
out.

Saturday 28ᵗʰ September 1929

Yesterday evening Charlotte didn't return home until just
before dinner. She told me she had bumped into Elizabeth
Powell while up in Longtown. The wonderful news is that
she and John have taken William in for the time being.
However, this is unlikely to be for very long as, with two
young children, they have little room in their small cottage.
Charlotte would have called to see William there and then
but Elizabeth informed her he had gone up to Hereford,
in the hope of selling some of his paintings. William has
told the Powells everything and they have promised to do
whatever they can to help. He has shown them my letter
and they have urged him to bide his time until our baby
has been born.

Wednesday 16ᵗʰ October 1929

I was so unwell this morning I had to retire to bed. I am
feeling a little better now but my stomach pains have

returned. I can feel our baby moving within the growing curve of my stomach and my heart cries out for you William, my only love.

Thursday 17th October 1929

Dr Hutton called this afternoon. He did not seem unduly concerned about my condition but, as I am now well into my pregnancy, said he would arrange for Mrs Benjamin, the midwife, to pay me a visit. Although I continue to be in considerable discomfort, Dr Hutton's opinion is most reassuring

Monday 21st October 1929

I do not question Mrs Benjamin's professional skills but she is a cold fish, utterly lacking in any humanity. She is unbelievably strait-laced and, although she refrained from making any direct comment on the matter, she was unable to conceal her disapproval of my condition. I found her visit thoroughly dispiriting. However, I must thank her for carrying out such a thorough examination. At least she has put my mind at rest over the discomfort I have been experiencing, which she says is not at all unusual at this stage in pregnancy.

It is an unbearable thought that I shall not see William until after our child is born.

Thursday 31st October 1929

Charlotte has been taken on as a part-time receptionist at Dr Hutton's surgery. I think she would have preferred to go full-time were it not for the duties she now has to carry out around the house. Of course, I feel guilty but she is so forgiving, not a cross word has passed her lips.

Her responsibilities at the surgery require her to go up to Longtown on three mornings a week. She has promised to take advantage of this to keep in touch with William. She starts her new role on Monday, so I shall write him a long letter over the weekend for her to take with her.

Tuesday 5th November 1929

Charlotte called on the Powells again today to find William packing his few belongings into his car. He told her he is moving to Hereford where he has been offered free accommodation and a modest wage, in exchange for a few hours each day, helping out in a bookshop in Widemarsh Street. As he will also be permitted to put his paintings on display there, he sees it as an opportunity he could not refuse. The Powells have been wonderfully kind in providing him shelter, but he is concerned not to outstay his welcome. He gave Charlotte his new address in Hereford and told her that the Powells are more than happy for us to use their postal address whenever he wishes to write to me. He asked Charlotte to tell me that not an hour goes by without him thinking of me, and wanting to be with me, and promised he will write to me as soon as he has settled in.

However much I wish William was still close b, I must try not to be too upset by this news, as I am sure it is for the best.

Monday 11th November 1929

This morning brings the first real touch of winter. There has been a heavy frost and the trees are veiled in white shrouds.

Father no longer goes up to Hereford. He says business is exceedingly slack in the steel industry and he can do what little has to be done from home. Charlotte and I are increasingly concerned for him as we suspect the Hereford steel factory may be in difficulty. We are not over-anxious about his financial situation for we believe he has a substantial portfolio of stocks and shares. But he is such a proud man, he will be devastated if his business goes under. Sadly, I dare not attempt to discuss such matters with him as it takes him all his time to tolerate my presence. I know he will never forgive me for my transgression, or for the disgrace I have brought upon the family name. He continues to keep himself much to himself. The house is so quiet on the days when Charlotte is up at the surgery. More often than not I retire to my bedroom after lunch. Here I can dream of my future with William and of the little house we shall set up together. I imagine us sitting out in our pretty little cottage garden. I shall hold our baby in my arms and recite Wordsworth or Keates while William sits on a stool beside me working on his latest painting. How often I find myself singing that haunting song I first heard William sing at Miss Blake's recital. It brings him closer to me. I have yet to hear from him. I do hope he writes soon. I long to hear all his news.

Thursday 14th November 1929

At last, Charlotte has brought home a letter from William. He is well and happily settling into his new life in Hereford. I am so pleased he is enjoying working in the bookshop, where he tells me he spends much of the time catching up on some of the classics of English literature that have previously passed him by. He has taken a particular liking to Charlotte Bronte who he finds to be more passionate and endearing than Jane Austin. The wonderful news is that he has already sold four of his watercolours, and has been commissioned to paint a series of oil paintings based on the mythological beasts and grotesques he showed us in the cathedral choirstalls. He says that the passing of each day brings us closer to the birth of our child and to the joyful day when we shall be reunited.

I shall write back to him this evening. I too dream of our future together even although it will not be easy. I know now that I cannot remain in this house to have our baby and must tell William I am ready to run away with him. I have £1,000 in the bank which dear Mother left me. We shall have enough money to rent a small cottage somewhere, and to get by on until William takes up a new position. Charlotte says it would be sensible for us to wait a week or two to give William time to look for our new home, as his accommodation over the bookshop is far from suitable. I shall send him a cheque for £50 when I write so that he will be able to put down a deposit. There will be no turning back once we have run away because Father will never forgive me. But, when the time comes, I shall not hesitate for, if I cannot be with William, I would rather be dead!

Thursday 21st November 1929

Charlotte called at the Powells again today and brought home a most heart-warming letter from William. As soon as he had heard from me, he had spoken to the owner of the bookshop who knows of a small property just outside Ledbury, belonging to a good friend of his, who has agreed to let it to us for just ten shillings a week. William has already driven over there to inspect the property which, he says, offers everything we could require. Downstairs it has a sizeable living room, a kitchen and a newly fitted bathroom to the rear, while upstairs there are two good-sized bedrooms. It is a mile outside the town in a small village with a public house and village store. The cottage has a small garden with a stream running along the bottom. William says he knows I will fall in love with it and has already laid down a modest deposit. It is only partially furnished, and so he will spend the next week or two buying the items we shall need. He says he is overjoyed at knowing we shall be together once the baby has been born. I can hardly believe our good fortune, the cottage sounds idyllic. All that remains for us to do now is to plan my escape from this house. Charlotte has promised to help. She says we must wait for a time when we know Father will be out of the house. As his visits to the office are now so rare, it will have to be an evening when he is attending a meeting of the parish council or school governors.

Wednesday 11th December 1929

I think Father has grown to detest me. There is nothing I can say that pleases him. Now that I am so much bigger with child he says he can hardly bear to look at me. But I shall not have to put up with him for much longer for

Charlotte has come up with a plan. She suggests I make my escape on Tuesday evening this coming week as Father will be attending a meeting of the Parish Council. I have written a note for Charlotte to post to William asking him to come for me at 6 o'clock. Charlotte is very downhearted at the thought of my departure, but agrees it will be for the best

Monday 16ᵗʰ December 1929

When Charlotte returned from Longtown this evening, she brought with her the letter from William for which I have waited all weekend with such longing and impatience. He promises he will come for me at 6 o'clock tomorrow as suggested and asks that I should be sure to be ready for him. He tells me he is overjoyed at the thought that we shall soon be together and to try not to worry In the meantime, as he is certain everything will work out for the good. Charlotte burst into tears when I showed her William's letter, and there were tears too from Mary when I broke the news to her. I have already packed the few things I shall need to take with me. My head is in turmoil, I know I shall not sleep tonight.

Conclusion

Chapter 16

NICK IMPATIENTLY TAPPED out rhythms on the steering wheel of the van. In his other hand he held his mobile phone, waiting for his sister to pick up the call. He'd had to drive some way up the lane to find a decent signal and was bursting to tell Kate about the contents of the diary. When she finally answered, and breathlessly enquired who was calling, he sensed he had caught her at a difficult moment.

'It's me, Nick, you sound out of breath, is everything all right?'

'Not really. I'm afraid I've just had a blazing row with Bill. He promised to be home this evening, but he's just called to say he has to attend an emergency meeting of the Constituency Executive. Apparently, there's been a fall-out amongst the local councillors, and he's been called in to try to bring the warring parties together. I wouldn't mind, but it's all about some stupid disagreement over who's going to serve on which committee and, as usual, it's more about individual egos than anything that really matters. I know these things happen, but I've hardly seen him over recent weeks.'

'Oh, I'm so sorry Kate. Would you rather I called at another time?'

'Actually no. It'll do me good to talk of other things, I've got the whole evening on my own ahead of me now and, in any case, I'm dying to know what's in that diary.'

'I'm not sure I know where to begin. The diary only covers a year or so, but Frances Whitmore would seem to have been the victim of a most unfortunate set of circumstances. I don't want to spoil it for you. You need to read it for yourself. All I will say, at this stage, is that the poor girl would appear to have had a miserable home life, much of which is dominated by an over-bearing father. The only real friend in her life is her sister Charlotte, that is until she meets a certain John

Cuddington, a teacher at the local Primary School, with whom she falls desperately in love.'

'Forgive me for asking, but why are you using the present tense. This all happened ages ago? You make it sound like the promotional synopsis on the back of a paperback!'

'Sorry, I didn't realise I was doing that. The truth is everything is so vividly described it feels like it's actually happening now. But, as I said, I don't want to spoil it for you; you have to read it yourself. I can't wait to hear what you make of it all. By the way, I found a tiny sepia photograph of a very attractive young woman, tucked inside the diary's cover, I assume it's Frances. It makes everything feel so much more real, if you know what I mean. She has the most gorgeous eyes and . . .'

'Hey, hold on, if I didn't know better, I'd say you're falling in love with her!'

'What me, falling in love with a disembodied spirit! I don't think so. But I can see what the schoolteacher must have seen in her.'

'So, what happens to Frances and her paramour?' Kate asked, unable to resist probing further. 'I assume her father strongly disapproves of the relationship, or something like that.'

'You bet, and what he doesn't know is that she's got herself pregnant. She manages to conceal this for months, that is until she and the schoolteacher finally decide the only way out is for them to run away together.'

'Sounds like an all too familiar love story to me. So how does it all end? I sense a tragedy in the making.'

'Judging by what we heard up in the attic, not so well, and that was real enough, wasn't it Kate?'

'You're kidding, I've never been so terrified in my life!'

'However, if you're looking for an answer to how it all ended in the diary, you won't find it. Her last entry is on 16th December 1929. Let me see, I've got it here somewhere, ah yes, here it is. She writes *'I have already packed the few things I shall need to take with me. My head is in turmoil, I know I shall not sleep tonight.'*

'Now you've got me really intrigued. I see I shall have to pluck up courage to come down again at the weekend to read the diary for myself. Have there been any further strange happenings, by the way?'

'Thankfully not, although I'm steering well clear of the attic.'

'We can't let this go Nick. I really want to find out more about this young woman and her lover and what happened to them.'

'I agree. I'm so pleased you want to come down again. When do you think you'll ger here?

'I thought I'd set off around mid-day on Friday to avoid the traffic. So, with any luck, I should make it by late afternoon. It looks like Bill's going to be tied up again most of the weekend and, frankly, in my current mood, I don't care one way or the other. I need some time apart from him. Perhaps then he'll appreciate what he's missing. Bloody politicians, they expect everyone to make excuses for them.'

'You'll enjoy the diary then. There's a fair deal of politics going on in the background. Frances' father was a diehard Tory of the old school, and young Cuddington was a radical, an active supporter of the Liberals. Frances writes quite extensively about the 1929 General Election. It seems that a journalist called Frank Owen won an unexpected victory for the Liberals in Hereford that year. No doubt this contributed to Frances's father's intense antagonism towards her lover.'

'Wow, I bet it did.'

'Listen, I was planning to call on the Benjamins to find out if they can tell us anything more about the Whitmores, and the house. Sam was very charming and welcoming, and all that, when I met him the first time, but I have a suspicion there is something he isn't telling us. How about I wait until you come down? We can walk over to their cottage together on Saturday morning to see what we can prise out of him.'

'That sounds like a good plan. Even if they're unaware of any paranormal activity in the house, they must know something about what happened to the Whitmores. Who knows, one or more of their descendants may still live in the area.'

'From what I remember from our conversation with Mr Prendergast, grandfather bought Mr Whitmore's business after it had become insolvent, and the house came as part of the package. If Frances's father went bankrupt, he must have taken quite a social tumble, from influential local businessman and leading member of the County Conservatives to someone in serious financial straits. It would have been incredibly humiliating. I can't imagine he'd want to stay in the area after such a fall.'

'You're probably right, but I'm even more intrigued to find out what happened to Frances and her lover. If the weird happenings we've experienced are anything to go by, their planned elopement must have gone horribly wrong.'

'Yes, I've been thinking that too. Anyway Kate, my battery's running low so I'm afraid we shall have to call it a day. I'll expect you for supper on Friday. Until then, big hugs and tell that husband of yours it's time he stepped up to his matrimonial responsibilities and spent a bit more time with you!'

'That'll be the day! Goodbye Nick. I think you're awfully brave staying in the house on your own. Take care now, won't you?'

'You can be sure of that. Goodbye Kate, love you to bits.'

It was with a mixed feeling of apprehension and excitement that Nick drove back to the house. He was more certain than ever that some terrible tragedy had befallen the Whitmore family. He was desperate to find out what had actually happened. Only once the truth was out was there any possibility of putting the anguished soul of Frances Whitmore to rest.

Chapter 17

DUE TO HEAVY traffic on the M40, Kate arrived at High House a little later on Friday than she had planned, but not too late to share supper with her brother. To Nick's delight, she came laden with the fruits of an extensive shopping spree in Waitrose, and they ate well. After they had eaten, they went out into the garden with their mugs of coffee to enjoy the last of the sun before it sank down behind the Black Hill.

'So, here it is,' Nick said, handing the diary to his sister. 'And this is the photograph I was telling you about, here, inside the front cover.'

'Gosh, I see what you mean. She certainly is very beautiful. Those high buttoned blouses of the twenties and thirties are so attractive and I like her hair tied up like that. You can't actually tell from a black and white photo, but she looks to have been exceptionally fair.'

'Yes, her hair looks like pure gold with the light glinting on it like that. You see, I wasn't exaggerating. She really is very lovely. Anyway, I'm sure you're dying to start reading the diary. Why don't I leave you to it while I go to start the generator. I've got it set up so that we have lights in the kitchen and study and there's another cable up to your bedroom, if you're happy to sleep up there tonight, that is?'

'I'd be happier if you slept up there with me.'

'I thought you might say that. I picked up a blow-up mattress the other day so I'll take it upstairs with my sleeping bag.'

Kate was soon so engrossed with the diary that she couldn't put it down. When it was too dark to continue reading outside, she went in to the study where she settled down in an armchair to read by the light of a desk lamp Nick had brought in from the workroom. She lost all sense of time and it was approaching midnight before she finally put the diary down. Her brother had been watching her for some time, sitting cross-legged on the other armchair.

'Well,' he said, 'what do you make of it?'

'It's an extraordinary story except, of course, it isn't a story. Poor girl, can you imagine what it must have been like for her, living here, with that awful father and a mother too sick to stand up for her.'

'Yes, I doubt she could have endured it if it wasn't for her sister Charlotte and the housekeeper Mary. At least there was someone she could talk to. Don't you think it's rather odd to think this all took place towards the end of the 1920's? Somehow, it feels much more Victorian, don't you think? Even Frances's language has something of the nineteenth century about it.'

'I know exactly what you mean. It feels a bit like a family that's been dragged, screaming, into the twentieth century.'

'I particularly like her description of the recital in the church in Longtown. I bet the audience wallowed in those Beethoven variations on the National Anthem. Incidentally, there's something I want to ask you. That song set to the Rossetti poem, you know, the one Cuddington sings, do you think that may be the same song you heard out in the garden?'

'Well, I can't be sure but I've been wondering that myself. The melody was clear enough but, as I've told you, I could hardly make out any of the words. However, bearing in mind Frances's passion for young Cuddington, I think it's a fair bet. I wrote the melody down in my notebook. It's in the workshop, but I can remember it clearly enough anyway.'

'Can you sing it for me?'

'All right. There's a sort of main theme followed by a chorus. It goes something like this,' Nick closed his eyes to concentrate and, taking in a deep breath, la-la'd his way through the melody.

'That's lovely Nick. It's sounds a bit like some sort of folk ballad. What a pity we don't have the words. I'm afraid I'm not familiar enough with Rossetti's poems.'

'The thing is, Kate, I haven't been able to get the tune out of my head. It's kind of inspired me to do something with it. I've been meaning to try my hand at something orchestral for some time now and, if we can only identify the words, I might see if I can develop it into a symphonic poem or something like that. I've been focussing on small scale music for far too long. You never know, I might even be able to persuade someone to commission it. I haven't had a commission for a while now, and I need to step up if I'm not to drop off my perch to join that great band of neglected middle-aged composers.'

'Fighting talk Nick, but it sounds like a great idea to me.'

'If you'll forgive the pun, on that score I suggest it's time for bed. We've got that visit to the Benjamins tomorrow and I want to have my wits about me.'

'I'm easily persuaded. I'm whacked after driving down here and the excitement of reading the diary. By the way, talking of the Benjamins, I expect you picked up on the fact that the midwife who called on Frances was also a Benjamin.'

'I did indeed. I gather it's a not uncommon surname in these parts, but I wouldn't be at all surprised to discover that Sam's related to her in some way.'

'Well, perhaps we shall be able to find that out tomorrow.

'Yes, that would make things even more interesting.'

Chapter 18

THEY WERE WOKEN the next morning by a shaft of late summer sun blazing through the bedroom window. The tall ash tree, closest to the front of the house, was swaying in the light breeze, casting moving shadows on the bedroom walls. It was too fine a morning to linger in bed and Nick and Kate were soon up and about. Kate was keen to visit the Benjamins as soon as they had finished breakfast, but Nick suggested they wait until the afternoon. He was sure they would be invited in and that the questions they wanted to ask would be better received over a cup of afternoon tea. They spent the morning scraping off several decades of accumulated dirt from the kitchen pipes and skirting boards in preparation for the challenge of redecorating the kitchen. They shared a light lunch before setting off for the village.

They found the Benjamins working in their back garden. Sam was mowing the lawn while his wife pruned a large rose bush covered in pale pink blooms. Nick opened the small side gate and they stood inside the garden wicket fence, waiting to be noticed by the industrious couple. Sam looked up when he reached the end of a run and, spotting them, turned off the mower engine and walked over to greet them.

'How very nice to see you again Nick and, let me see, yes, this must be your sister Kate, I can see the likeness. To what do we owe the pleasure of this visit.'

'Well, we were very much hoping to have a word with you about one or two things, but I can see you're busy. Perhaps we can call another time?'

'Nonsense, young man. Mrs Benjamin and I have been slaving away out here for long enough. Molly, look who's here; it's the young couple from High House. You've met Nick before and this is his sister Kate. How about I put the kettle on and we sit down to a cup of tea.'

'It's very nice to meet you Kate and to see you again Nick. It's such a lovely afternoon, let's sit at the table under the old apple tree. I baked some scones this morning Sam, you'll find them in the tin next to the toaster and there's butter and homemade strawberry jam in the fridge. Would you be a dear and set up the tea tray while I wipe down the table and the garden seats? It's bird droppings you know, I wipe them every day, but before you know it, one of those big fat pigeons has been at it again! Please do take a wander round the garden while we get everything ready. As you can see, we're rather fond of roses and we have quite a number of different varieties.'

Although small, the Benjamin's garden was full of a brightly coloured flowers. A long bed, comprising traditional cottage plants, ran the length of one side of the lawn. There was a large rose bed in front of the front door, and a small herb garden. At the far end of the garden, a well-stocked vegetable plot was half-concealed behind a wicker fence.

'What a charming garden,' Kate said to Molly as they sat down under the apple tree.

'You're not seeing it at its best, I'm afraid,' Molly said, smiling. 'It's getting towards the end of the season now and the annuals are looking a little sorry for themselves. Thank goodness for the roses; they keep on flowering from late Spring through to early Autumn. This has been such a good year for them. Mind you, we have to feed them regularly as there's a good deal of sand here, mixed in with the soil. Fortunately, there's a heavy layer of clay underneath which helps to retain the water.'

'So, who does most of the gardening?' Nick asked

'Well, we both love the garden, so it's fair to say it's very much a shared delight. Sam does most of the heavy work, leaving the lighter touches to me.'

'I understand you're an artist, Molly. What do you enjoy painting?' Kate asked.

'I've tried my hand at most things over the years, but now I mainly draw from nature, plants, trees, birds, wild life generally. I prefer working with watercolours. The texture suits my subjects better than oils or acrylics.'

'Molly's very modest about her work,' Sam said, having returned from the kitchen with a heavily-laden tray which he set down on the table. 'She's had quite a few exhibitions around the county you know.'

'I'd love to see some of your work, Molly,' Kate said enthusiastically.

'As it happens, quite a few of her paintings will be on show at an exhibition at The Courtyard in Hereford next month, if you have time to call by. Several other local artists will be showing at the same time.'

'That's quite enough about me, Sam,' Molly said, clearly embarrassed by her husband's pride in her work. 'Nick, I hear you're a composer and Kate, you must tell me all about yourself. It's such a pleasure to have some new faces in the village.'

Sam and Molly listened attentively while Nick and Kate told them a little about themselves and their respective backgrounds. Molly wanted to know more about Nick's compositions and he was surprised to discover how much she knew about contemporary classical music.

'I don't say I like it all,' she said 'but we both enjoy the challenge of being exposed to new music. We're regulars at the Three Choirs Festival and go over to Symphony Hall in Birmingham, once in a while. We have a great-niece who's studying 'cello at the Birmingham Conservatoire, so we've been there quite a few times too. On our last visit we met that nice Julian Lloyd-Webber. He's one of her tutors you know.'

Sam's ears pricked up when he heard that Kate's husband was a Labour MP. 'Let me see now, Bill Willoughby, I know the name. Isn't he hot on foreign affairs? He's a good speaker too. I was very impressed last time I saw him on 'Question Time'. I gather he's tipped for high office if Labour ever get back into power that is. But you won't find much Labour support round here I'm afraid.'

'I gather not,' Kate said, 'although it's not always been Tory here has it?'

'No, you're quite right. There was Frank Owen in the late twenties and more recently the Liberals took the seat again when young Paul Keetch was elected. That was back in 1997, at the time of Tony Blair's Labour landslide. Paul Keetch was a good constituency MP and held the seat until he stood down in 2010. But things are back to normal again now with a Conservative member sitting at Westminster with a sizeable majority. Anyway, enough of politics. How are you settling in at High House?'

Nick looked at his sister, he didn't know quite where to begin. She gave him an enouraging smile, so he decided not to hold back.

'Most of the time I'm at the house on my own. Kate is up in London and is only able to come down for the occasional weekend. I love the house, rather more than she does, to be honest. It's just the sort of retreat I've been looking for to get my creative juices flowing. We agreed, from the start, we'd give it a few months before deciding whether to keep the house or put it on the market. So, I'm doing my best to get the place up and running again, you know, water, electricity, telephone and broadband, that kind of thing. We decided we'd concentrate on decorating and furnishing just three or four rooms to start with. In that way we can at least have a few home comforts.'

'That all sounds very sensible,' Sam said, nodding his head thoughtfully. 'I gather young Bob Jenkins has been giving you a bit of a hand.'

'Yes, thank you so much for recommending him. He's been a huge help and, to be honest, I don't know how we could have managed without him. He's even found us a small generator. But, to come to the point of our visit, he's also been helping us try to uncover something very odd which we want to talk to you about.' Nick paused for a moment. 'You see, a few nights ago, Kate and I had a very unpleasant experience. It sounded like someone was crying and it was coming from up in the attic. It was pretty scary, I can tell you. However, we plucked up courage and went upstairs to investigate. The sound was coming from behind a locked door in the attic. It's the only room in the house to which we didn't have a key. To be honest, until then, we'd assumed it was just another empty bedroom and hadn't been particularly bothered.'

'Hearing that awful crying sound was a horrible experience, I can tell you,' Kate interjected. 'It was relentless, the sound of someone in dire distress, but not altogether of this world.'

'Goodness me!' Molly gasped, raising a hand to her mouth. 'What on earth did you do?'

'Nick went on to tell them about the violent commotion they had heard from downstairs, the angry voices, the hammering on the front door and of how, while they were still standing on the attic landing, a rush of ice-cold air had passed over them followed by a terrifying scream and the sound of someone falling down the stairs.

'I have never been so frightened in my life!' Kate exclaimed.

'Yes, it was truly horrific,' Nick continued. 'As it happens, Bob called by the following morning and so we told him what had happened. He was quite shocked and, despite our misgivings, persuaded us we simply had to find out what was behind that locked door in the attic. To be honest, Kate and I were pretty apprehensive about going back up there, but Bob was adamant. He said we couldn't leave things as they were, there were too many unanswered questions. He said he'd gladly help us to force the door open. Well, we knew he was right of course, so we went back upstairs and Bob, being of a sturdier frame than me, put the full force of his shoulder to the door. It flew open more easily than we'd expected. But what a surprise we got when we peered inside. The last thing we'd imagined was that we'd find a fully furnished bedroom. The furniture's all good quality, there are framed prints on the walls and a small bureau with a green marble ink stand. It's all a bit creepy, like a shrine to someone who's died, or left unexpectedly.'

'And you'll never guess what Nick found in the bureau,' Kate added excitedly. 'Frances Whitmore's diary which I've brought with me to show you. Look, the inscription inside the cover here tells us it was a twenty-first birthday present and she confirms this in her first entry in the diary, dated the 16th March 1929. The diary is a detailed account of ten months in the life of a young woman. A young woman walking in fear of a domineering father, who, with her sister Charlotte, nurses a dying mother, falls in love with a local schoolteacher, falls pregnant and is finally forced to plan to elope with her lover because her father makes it impossible for him to stay in the village. The only support she receives is from her sister Charlotte and from Mary, the housekeeper. It's an extraordinary story; you couldn't make it up.' Kate flicked through the pages of the diary until reaching the final entry. 'As you can see, the diary comes to a rather abrupt end with a final entry on 16 December, the day, it seems, she intended to elope with the schoolteacher.'

'What's really frustrating is not knowing what happened,' Nick said. 'Did she go off with her lover and leave the diary behind? If so, what happened to them? where did they go? and why was her bedroom left as it was? I'm sure you'll understand how much we want to find answers to these questions. That's why we've called to see you. I've had a couple of other odd experiences too which we can come to later. It seems we've inherited a house occupied by dead spirits. We're hoping you may be able to throw some light on the situation or, at least, be able to tell us something about the Whitmores.'

'Oh dear!' Sam exclaimed, raising his hands in consternation. 'I'm not quite sure what to say. You see, and Molly will back me up on this, you see there have been occasional accounts of unexplained happenings at High House. But this is one of those remote corners of England where old traditions die hard. Some of our local countryfolk still believe in witches and fairies and that kind of thing, and tales of supernatural happenings are not that uncommon. I've kept an eye on High House for a number of years now. I've been inside the house on many, many occasions and can honestly say I've never personally witnessed anything out of the ordinary. Well, that's not quite true. There was one occasion when I thought I heard what sounded like someone singing as I was leaving the house, but I don't know where it was coming from and I didn't see anyone. It was such a brief occurrence, the trees were full of birds calling out, so I put it down to my imagination.'

'That's really interesting because I've heard that voice twice. The melody was so captivating I jotted it down in my notebook. The first time I heard it, I thought it was coming from the attic or somewhere high up. The second time it was definitely outside, coming from the back of the house, and on that occasion, I actually saw something, a kind of misty human shape that almost instantly evaporated into the air in front of where I was standing.

'How very odd,' Sam said.

'Don't you think you should tell them about the young couple, Sam?' Molly asked, leaning forward and gripping her husband's arm.'

'Well, yes, my dear, I suppose I should. I've not mentioned this before because I didn't take it very seriously at the time. I'm sure you'll understand, the last thing I have wanted to do is to cause you any undue alarm and, to be honest, if there are any . . . what shall we call them . . . any unusual or inexplicable occurrences at High House, I thought it best you should find it out for yourselves.'

'So, tell us about the young couple' Kate said.

'Ah yes, the young couple. Well, some years ago, I went over to High House to carry out one of my routine checks. I was a little alarmed to find the back door wide open, you know, the one into the kitchen. I always made sure that all the outside doors were kept securely locked, not that there was ever anything of much value in the house but, you know what people are like, and we certainly didn't want any prowlers nosing around. As it happens, the lock on the kitchen door wasn't broken and it didn't look as though the door had been forced. I could only assume that whoever had broken in must have been a dab hand at lock picking. Anyway, when I went inside, I discovered someone had been sleeping in the old dining room. Whoever it was had dragged a mattress down from upstairs, and their belongings, such as they were, were strewn about all over the floor. I searched the house from top to bottom, but there was no-one there. I got the impression that whoever had been squatting in the house had left in a bit of a hurry. I thought they must have heard me approaching and scarpered. As there was no obvious damage, I didn't worry too much about it at the time, although I kept a more watchful eye on the house over the following weeks. Well, I was down at the Cornewell Arms one evening chatting to one or two of the locals about the incident. That was when I found out what must have actually happened. They told me about a young man and woman who had recently sought refuge at Monks Farm, just up the lane from you. They said they'd been camping out in a nearby abandoned house when they'd been disturbed by angry shouting and a loud banging on the front door. They were so terrified they'd fled, leaving most of their belongings behind. Well, I soon put two and two together of course and deduced it must have been they who had been camping out at High House.'

'The loud banging and shouting, that's just what we heard. What's it all about, that's what I want to know?' Kate said.

'Well, strange as it may seem, it does resonate with a quite dreadful chain of events that occurred at High House many years ago, but I'll tell you about that in a moment. I must say I'm astonished to hear what you found upstairs in that attic bedroom, and the diary in particular, fancy that turning up after all these years. I've been right through the house on many occasions checking for roof leaks and the like and, of course, I knew one of the attic bedrooms was locked but didn't really think much about why or what might be in there.'

'Can you tell us anything about the Whitmores? I mean, do you know if Frances eloped with the schoolteacher? If so, what happened to them and were they ever reconciled to Frances's father? It's such a romantic story but I sense it may have ended in tragedy,' Kate said, leaning forward with her hands clasped tightly together.

'Well, the events you tell me Frances recorded in her diary all happened some years before I was born. Indeed, I was only a small child at the time Mr Whitmore's business failed and he was forced to sell up. That would have been somewhere in the mid 1940's, just after the war. However, my father was quite active with the local Conservatives and knew old Mr Whitmore quite well, although I don't think he had a very high opinion of him. The Whitmore family saga is not a happy one and, as you've guessed, did not end well. It left such a deep impression on the village that it took the community some time to recover from the shock. Even today, some of the older folk prefer not to talk about it. It seems that, on the evening they had planned to elope, young Cuddington arrived at High House with the intention of taking Frances away with him. But, to his surprise and dismay, it was not Frances, but her father who opened the front door to him.'

'I thought he was supposed to be out at the time. According to her diary, they had deliberately chosen to make their escape when he would be at a parish council meeting.' Nick said

'Ah yes but unfortunately for the young couple the meeting had been called off at the last minute and Frances didn't have time to send a warning to her lover. It is generally believed that, far from holding back, young Cuddington boldly declared his intentions, and there was an almighty confrontation on the doorstep. Angry words were exchanged and William had the front door slammed in his face. We know all this because it was overheard by the housekeeper, and, as you can imagine, the story of the incident soon made its way round the village. Apparently Cuddington continued hammering on the door, demanding to see Frances until, finally, her father threatened to call the police.'

'This is all beginning to make sense,' Kate said. It certainly explains what we heard the other night and what made those squatters flee for their lives.'

'I'm afraid it does, doesn't it. Anyway, to continue with the housekeeper's account of what happened, Frances was waiting upstairs in her bedroom when Cuddington arrived. She had her bags packed and was ready to leave. Of course, She knew her Father was downstairs and must have been terrified at the thought of what would happen when he came to take her away. When she heard the commotion going on down below it seems she must have rushed out of her bedroom and, in her desperation to find out what was happening, must have tripped and fallen down the attic stairs. When she heard her sister scream, Charlotte ran upstairs and found Frances lying unconscious on the first-floor landing. Meanwhile, once Mr Whitmore had threatened to call the police, Cuddington had no choice but to make a hasty retreat, unaware of the dreadful accident that had befallen Frances.'

'How awful,' Kate said. 'I hardly dare ask what happened next.'

'It is indeed a very sad story and, I'm afraid, it has an even more tragic ending. You see, once he had seen off Cuddington, Mr Whitmore went upstairs to find Charlotte on her knees beside her sister who lay motionless on the floor. They managed to carry her to her bed where she lay unconscious until the early hours of the morning. When she finally regained consciousness she was badly bruised from head to toe and complaining of severe stomach pains. Mr Whitmore had the good sense to telephone Dr Hutton who, being in little doubt that Frances' pregnancy was at risk, immediately sent for the midwife, who, incidentally, was a distant relative of mine, on my Father's side.'

'Ah, we wondered if the Mrs Benjamin mentioned in the diary was a relative of yours.' Kate said.

'She was indeed, but I never met her. Anyway, if I may continue, Frances herself was so severely injured from the fall they feared both for her life and that of her child. Soon after the midwife arrived Frances gave birth to a baby girl born two months before her time. Miraculously the child survived but, owing to the loss of blood and her injuries, poor Frances herself only lived for a few more hours.

'What a very sad ending to a not very happy life. Do you know what happened to the baby?' Kate asked, with tears in her eyes.

'The story goes that old Percival Whitmore was so determined Cuddington shouldn't have the child that he wrote him a letter to tell him that Frances had died in childbirth and that the baby had died with her. He told Cuddington that he held him to be entirely responsible and threatened to take out a criminal prosecution against him unless he left the county immediately. I have no idea what the legal charge might have been, but the letter had the desired effect and it was the last the county saw of the unfortunate William Cuddington.'

'What a mean thing to do!' Kate said, aghast.

'Yes, it reveals a great deal about the nature of the man. As for the child, well, that's a happier tale. Charlotte undertook to look after her and bring her up as her own daughter. She married a Hereford solicitor by whom she had three more children and they lived happily together in a large house on Aylestone Hill. Some years later, her husband took up a partnership with a law firm, somewhere down in the West Country, and they all moved south.'

'And what about Whitmore? We know his business went bust and he was forced to sell up. What happened to him?' Nick asked.

'I'm afraid one tragedy followed another. After Charlotte left to get married, he lived on at the house in the sole company of the housekeeper. However, as his business began to fall apart, he became increasingly morose and withdrawn, so much so that, eventually, Mary left him, unable to put up with the unbearable atmosphere that pervaded the house. It's said that he neglected his business, but this only partly accounts for its failure. You see, as an engineering company manufacturing steel, the business had prospered before and during the war years, making components for military equipment. Once the war came to an end, their products were no longer in demand and they found it difficult to adapt to new lines of production. In the end, it all became too much for Whitmore and he took his own life, the very night before his business and High House were due to be taken into receivership. I suspect that he finally recognised there was nobody to blame for his daughter's death other than himself.'

'Did he take his own life in the house?' Kate exclaimed.

'No, thankfully, not in the house. He went for a walk in the woods and shot himself. The irony is that he used a Second-World-War military revolver, many of the parts of which had most probably been manufactured in his own factory.'

'Gosh, so that's where it all ended. What a harrowing tale and most of these terrible events happened in our house. No wonder the place is haunted!' Nick said, leaning back in his chair with a deep sigh.

'But it's not really over, is it?' Kate said, staring at her brother. 'Surely, we can't go on living in a house where these ghastly events are constantly recurring. If ever there was a need for proof that some souls are unable to find rest, we've found it. None of these happenings can be explained away by a trick of the light or one's imagination. There can't be any doubt. We're dealing with things we can never fully understand.' Kate shivered. 'It's all so creepy!'

'You poor dears!' Molly said 'You can't have known what you were letting yourselves in for when you came into your inheritance. But you know, there is something that can be done to put those souls to rest.'

'What do you mean?' Kate asked. 'If you're talking about exorcism, I thought that was something you only come across in horror movies!'

'Oh no, you're quite wrong there. Although it is only considered appropriate on the rarest of occasions, exorcism remains a recognised practice in the Roman Catholic and Anglican Churches. Believe it or not, we even have an official exorcist here in the Hereford Diocese. I read about her in the Hereford Times a few weeks ago. She's a vicar somewhere in the north of the county, a quite recent appointment. According to the article in the newspaper she's had an experience or two of the paranormal herself.'

'I think Molly's right,' Sam said. 'It would seem to me to be a sensible path to take. Mind you, it may not be all that straightforward as I expect the church authorities will take some convincing. If you decide to look into the possibility, why not start off by having a word with one of our parish priests? They're part of a team within The Black Mountains group of parishes. You'll find them very approachable.'

'Well, Kate and I need to think about this, but it sounds like it might be worth a try.' Nick said.

'All this morbid talk about such distressing matters and you've let your tea go cold. As my mother used to say, nothing cheers you up like a good cup of tea. Pass your cups and I'll pour you a fresh ones and, please, do have another scone.'

Chapter 19

THAT SAME EVENING, Nick and Kate sat outside watching the sun slowly dip down behind the Black Hill.

'What do you think we should do?' Kate asked.

'I think we should go for it. I mean what other options do we have?' Nick said.

'Reluctantly, I agree. We have to do something or else we'll never be able to live in this house and we'd certainly have difficulty selling it, even if we wanted to. Let's face it, before long, everyone in the village will be talking about the phantoms of High House and then what chance would we have of finding a buyer.'

'I guess that's the top and bottom of it. You know me, I still have serious aspirations of making something of this place – free of unwelcome spirits that is.'

'So, what's next? I have to get back to London tomorrow evening. Do you think you could search out the vicar and tell him of our plight?'

'Better than that, I happened to look at the church noticeboard the evening I went up to the pub to meet Bob Jenkins. As Sam told us, Clodock is part of the Black Mountain group of parishes. They don't have services here every week but, as luck would have it, there's Holy Communion at St Clydog's tomorrow morning at 9.30. Why don't we go along and introduce ourselves to the vicar?'

'Nick, I've only got the clothes I came down in, I can hardly turn up to church in a pair of baggy old jeans and a home-knitted cardigan.'

'This isn't your fashionable West End, you know. I don't suppose everyone dresses up for church in these parts, except perhaps for Christmas and Easter. They're probably grateful that anyone shows up at all, whatever they're wearing.'

'All right, if you say so. I can see it's going to take a while for me to adjust to country living.'

Sunday morning saw a sharp change in the weather. Dark clouds were gathering ominously over the Black Hill. With the threat of rain showers throughout the morning, Nick and Kate decided to drive to church in Kate's car.

Quite a few of the pews were already occupied when they entered St Clydog's. They were welcomed by a burly farmer wearing a brown tweed suit that had seen better days. He handed them copies of the Order of Service before showing them to a pew, half way down the aisle. They were fascinated to see the pew bore a number of carved symbols and initials. They assumed these must have belonged to the families that used to occupy them or 'probably still did', Nick observed.

'Just look at that magnificent pulpit,' Kate whispered, pointing to an impressive, triple-tier wooden structure, complete with sounding board. 'It must be eighteenth century, if not earlier, don't you think? I've never seen another one like it.'

'Designed for the days of the hour-long sermon no doubt. I hope they had cushions in these pews in those days.'

'They probably brought their own. It's a lovely little church isn't it. You know I'm not very good at these things, what is it, fourteenth century?'

'No, a little earlier I'd say, more like twelfth century.'

'To think that practically every village has a church, not all quite as special as this one of course, but, nevertheless, good business over the years for architects and builders, wouldn't you say.'

'And a mighty big drain on parish resources these days.' Nick replied, with a grin.

There was a sudden hush as the vicar entered and made his way to the altar. The service was unaccompanied by hymns or music, although they learned later that this was not usually the case. As Nick and Kate had been brought up within the more Catholic traditions of the Anglican Church, they were not familiar with the new Anglican Order of Service. However, they found something reassuring about the enthusiasm with which the parishioners participated. They took an immediate liking to the middle-aged cleric who conducted the service with warmth and sincerity, and who smiled benignly at his congregation, throughout his short address.

Once the service was over, they joined the queue of those waiting to shake hands with the vicar as they made their way out through the porch.

'Ah, new faces I see. Welcome to St Clydog's. I'm Tom Ellis, by the way, one of the team's parish priests. And what brings you to these parts?' he asked, noticing Kate's informal jeans and baggy jumper and assuming they were amongst the many holiday-makers who choose a walking holiday under the shadow of the Black Mountains.

'Well, actually, we've just moved into the village,' Nick said. 'Or, to be more precise, I have, for the time being at least. I'm Nick Mortimer and this is my sister Kate. She lives in London and is a more occasional visitor. We've recently inherited High House and are trying to make it habitable after years of it remaining empty.'

'I've driven past the place, although I've never been through the gates. Not much point as it's been empty for so long.'

'Look, we don't want to hold up the queue but we would very much like to have a word with you, when you've had a chance to speak to everyone else, that is. There's something rather important we'd like to discuss with you, if you have time, of course.'

'As it happens you're in luck. My wife's visiting her sister this morning and I'm at a bit of a loose end.'

'If you don't mind putting up with the somewhat primitive surroundings, we can offer you coffee and a piece of fruit cake back at High House,' Kate said.

'That sounds like an offer I can't refuse. I shall be interested to see the house. Just give me a few minutes to have a word with these good folk and I'll be right with you.'

'Actually, while we're waiting, there's a grave I'd like to show my sister,' Nick said, taking Kate's arm.

'By all means. Let's meet by the lychgate in fifteen minutes or so. Once I've had a word with everyone I need to pop back into the vestry to change out of my clerical garb.'

They made their way round the side of the church to the place where Nick had come across the young woman laying flowers by the graveside. It was exactly as Nick remembered it. The small glass jar containing the little bunch of wild flowers was still there, although the flowers themselves had long since faded and withered into little more than dry stalks.

Nick stood staring at the engraving on the headstone. 'Oh my Lord, just as I thought!' he exclaimed, 'Look, this is Frances's grave. This is where they buried the poor girl. I felt there was something special about the grave at the time and now it's all beginning to make sense.'

'Yes, but who was the young woman you saw. If you're an earthbound spirit I don't imagine you'd put flowers on your own grave. And, however dead those flowers may be, they and the glass jar are tangible enough.'

'Yes, I agree; this is altogether very confusing. Whoever she is or was, she bore a remarkable resemblance to the young woman I saw in the wood and, more to the point, to that photograph of Frances in the diary. It makes you question what's of this life and what's of the next.'

'Well, the singing voice, the weeping and sobbing and that dreadful hammering on the front door, they were definitely not of this world. As for the everything else, there has to be some kind of explanation, even if we can't fathom it.'

'It's all so strange, especially what I saw here by this graveside. You don't think I'm going potty do you?'

'Hardly, or at least, no more than usual.'

'Thank you, Sis, I love you too.'

'Come on, it's time to go and have a word with our friendly cleric.'

Chapter 20

'WELCOME TO OUR once grand but now humble abode,' Nick said, unlocking the back door. 'Do take a seat, I'll put the kettle on. I'm afraid it's mugs and plastic plates, not quite what you're used to on your parish rounds, I imagine.'

'There isn't so much of that sort of thing these days I'm afraid, not with several parishes to look after.'

'Yes, we gather you cover a large area. It must be something of a challenge ministering to some many different communities,' Kate said.

'Yes, we do cover quite a large area. There are seven churches in the group and they all present the usual problems of upkeep. Frankly, I have to spend far too much of my time worrying about such things, especially as the group includes several listed historic churches like St Clydog's and, of course, we're suffering from dwindling congregations. However, that being said, I love it out here and I wouldn't swap my living for anything. But tell me, there was a matter you wished to discuss with me?'

'It's probably not something that comes your way very often. You see we have good reason to believe this house is haunted. We've had a number of exceptionally odd and, in one case, really frightening experiences.' Kate said, studying the vicar's face and wondering how he would react.

'Haunted you say, my goodness! Now tell me, precisely what form do these hauntings take.'

'Well, it's quite a long story. You see we've had a number of weird and inexplicable experiences since we came down here in the early Summer.' With occasional promptings from Kate, Nick laid bare everything that had occurred since they had first moved into High House. He also spoke of what they had learned from their conversation with the Benjamins. 'Although what happened that night up in the attic was unbelievably frightening at the time, I don't actually believe we have much to fear from Frances, assuming it is her spirit that's somehow wandering about up there. It was much more frightening when we didn't know who or what it might be,' Nick concluded.

'My goodness, what a tale you have to tell, I've never heard anything quite like it. I believe what you've told me, of course, but it's rather outside my comfort zone. And what about the father? He was clearly an unhappy and deeply disturbed soul. Do you feel that his spirit lingers here too?'

'That, I can't say,' Nick said, 'although we did hear male voices shouting down in the hallway that time we were up in the attic. And Sam Benjamin has told us about a couple of young squatters who fled from the house to seek refuge at a neighbouring farm. Apparently, they too heard raised voices and a violent hammering on the front door. This seems to fit in with Mr Benjamin's description of what appears to have happened the night William came to the house with the intention of running away with Frances.'

The vicar closed his eyes and bowed his head, as if in prayer. When he looked up again he said 'So, the question is, what shall we do? I'm not equipped to deal with a situation like this but clearly something has to be done. These troubled souls need to find their rest. I can pray with you and I can pray for you, but I have neither the ability nor the authority to do more than that. The situation calls for the attention of someone with that authority.'

'Molly Benjamin tells us that the bishop has recently appointed a Diocesan exorcist. Do you think she may be able to help?'

'You're referring to the Reverend Lucy Edwards. Yes, I do believe she may be the right person to address this situation. But, the Ministry of Deliverance requires the formal approval of the bishop. You will appreciate these matters have to be handled with the utmost care.'

'So where do we go from here?' Nick asked. 'Should we contact the bishop?'

'I think it might be better coming from me. As it happens, I'll be seeing him next week, at a meeting of the rural deanery. Do you think you could provide me with a written account of your experiences, just as you've shared them with me?'

'Well, as the TV chefs say, 'here's one I prepared earlier,' Nick said with a grin. 'I wrote it all down yesterday evening. We thought it would be needed at some point.'

'That's all very clearly explained,' Tom said, after reading Nick's detailed account.

'I can't say how very grateful we are,' Kate said, looking relieved. 'This whole business has been unbelievably disturbing and we can't let things rest as they are.'

'Well, I can hardly say "it's all in a day's work". It is a very rare and unusual situation. Now, shall we say a little prayer together?'

Chapter 21

THE BISHOP'S APPROVAL was readily granted and the 'deliverance' of the souls of Frances Whitmore and her father Percival took place in mid-September. It was conducted by the Reverend Lucy Edwards with the assistance of the Reverend Tom Ellis. Nick was present at the time, but was advised not to attend the actual ritual. He had little idea what to expect but it soon became evident that he could put aside the classic image of 'bell, book and candle'. Lucy Edwards, a plump, middle-aged cleric, with a reassuring smile, explained that there was no set ritual for deliverance but that through prayer and divine intervention she trusted the troubled souls would be released from their earth-bound state.

Leaving the two clerics to perform their duties, Nick sat out in the garden, in the very spot where he had first heard the voice singing from above. Later that day, when it was all over, he called his sister to tell her of one last occurrence which he was sure would remain with him for ever.

'It was the strangest thing, Kate. I could hear the two clerics in the distance reciting that Compline prayer, you know the one, *'Visit, we beseech Thee, O Lord, this place, and drive from it all the snares of the enemy; let Thy holy angels dwell herein to preserve us in peace.'* Well, just as they were reaching the end of the prayer, I'm sure I heard Frances' voice again. It was magical. It was as if she was singing the song for me, one last time. But this time, she sounded happy, joyful even. It was so moving. I've still got a lump in my throat just telling you about it. But you probably think I'm going nuts!'

'What do you mean "going"; you've always been nuts. But, to be serious, I think that's really beautiful. You know what, Nick, you've rather fallen in love with Frances, haven't you? But I'm afraid she isn't available, not now anyway. Oh, I do hope it's worked. I'm so sorry to have chickened out of being there with you, but I didn't feel I could deal with a real live exorcism.'

'Actually, it was nothing like I'd expected. Tom was Wonderful. He's such a nice man, and Lucy Edwards – well, she's something else, so understanding, reassuring, confident and remarkably practical. I didn't attend the actual service, or whatever you call it, but it was all over surprisingly quickly, and we ended up having a jolly conversation over a cup of tea.'

'Is that it then? Is it all over do you think?'

'I guess only time will tell, but they seemed pretty confident. Lucy's dealt with several other cases before and certainly seemed to know what she was doing.'

'What a strange job, being a professional exorcist.'

'Well, it's hardly a full-time occupation. It must be a wonderful feeling to be able to liberate souls and to bring peace to troubled households. From what she told me afterwards, I gather most of the cases the church deals with are with the living and not the dead. You know, mental illness and that sort of thing.'

'I'm afraid I can't come down for a week or two, Nick. Bill's actually going to be around and he's filled my diary with theatre outings and dinners at our favourite restaurants. He says he wants to make up to me for having been away so much.'

'About time too! The good news is that we should have mains electricity in the house when you next come down. Western Power are planning to carry out the necessary work the week after next. Oh and, by the way, I'm actually calling you from the house. BT installed our new line this morning.'

'That's fantastic news. What about your music? I hope you're setting aside some time for that.'

'Not this week, but I am beginning to develop that idea I was telling you about for an orchestral work. But I don't really want to talk about it until it's a little clearer in my mind.'

'I understand. Anyway, thanks for the call and everything you've done and here's hoping there are no more ghostly appearances!'

'Here's hoping indeed!' Nick said, switching off his mobile 'phone and heading for the Cornewall Arms.

Chapter 22

AS SUMMER PASSED into autumn, the trees shed their leaves and the sun rose ever lower in the sky, Nick worked hard to ready the house for winter. Western Power had provided the house with an electricity supply and Bob was able to start work on rewiring the ground floor. By mid-October the study, the kitchen and the two remaining first floor bedrooms had all been redecorated and Kate had measured up for curtains. 'At last,' Nick said to Bob, 'the house is beginning to feel like a home again.'

'Well, you've certainly cracked the worst of it, but I can't help thinking you're going to be darned cold in the winter. It can blow pretty rough up hear you know and we nearly always get a good fall of snow, once the year's turned. You shouldn't really be lighting fires until you've had the chimneys swept. I know a guy who'll do that for you, if you like.'

'Good old Bob, you always know someone,' Nick said chuckling. 'But thanks, please let me have your contact and I'll get in touch. I've bought a couple of calor-gas heaters for the bedrooms.'

'I've been meaning to ask, how're you getting on with the boiler?'

'It's still working fine thanks. I only light it when I have to. Other than that, I make do with the kettle.'

'What this place really needs is a proper central heating system, but that'll cost you in a place this size.'

'I'm afraid that'll have to wait until we decide what we're going to do. It dawned on me the other day that it would make a perfect retreat for other artists to come and work. I still haven't quite convinced Kate that we should keep it, but she's beginning to soften. She's been so much happier since we had the place exorcised.'

'So it worked then. I've been meaning to ask.'

'Yes, I believe it has. There's a completely different atmosphere in the house now.'

'Funny you should say that. I can feel it too. There's something different about the place, like it wants to be lived in again.'

'Yes, that's exactly it.'

'Look, I've been thinking. I'm ready to start the rewiring next week. I don't want you to think I'm touting for work. Frankly, it doesn't make much difference to me either way, but I could rewire the whole house if you want me to. It's a pretty messy job as the plaster will have to be dug out to get at the old wiring and replace it with the new. But once it's done, it's done and I reckon it'll cost you less in the long run.'

'I can see that makes sense, but what are we talking about cost-wise?'

'Well, I need to go through the house with you, room by room, so we can agree on what you want in the way of power points and feeds for any lighting, but I reckon on somewhere in the region of £8,000.'

'Blimey, that's less than we'd expected. Look, I'll have to discuss this with Kate and get back to you, but thanks for the suggestion; it makes sense.'

'I suppose the point is that whether you choose to keep the house or sell up, it will have to be done anyway.'

'OK, leave it with me. I'll call Kate this evening and let you know. Perhaps we can meet up at the pub again? How are you fixed for tomorrow evening? I was thinking of going up there after supper, say about 8.30?'

'That's fine by me. See you tomorrow evening then.'

Nick dedicated the rest of the morning to chain-sawing fallen branches from the wood and stacking the logs at the end of the barn where the roof hadn't fallen in. It would take a year or two for most of it to season, but there was long-dead timber amongst it, enough to provide them with an ample supply for the boiler and study fireplace to take them through the winter. He spent the afternoon in the old store room which he had now successfully converted into his studio and which now housed the retuned baby grand piano. The melody of William Cuddington's song had been running through his head all morning. Everything they had uncovered about the tragic tale of Frances Whitmore and her lover added a remarkable poignancy to it. He felt compelled to really make something of the melody, to build it into a substantial composition. If only he had been able to hear enough of the words to identify the Rossetti poem. All he could clearly remember overhearing was that single phrase 'do not grieve', but what use was that?

And then he remembered the bookcase in Frances's bedroom and the many volumes of poetry that it contained. Surely, he would find a copy of Rossetti's poems amongst them. He hurried into the house and up to the attic, hardly able to contain his excitement. It was the first time he had been up there since the day of the exorcism and he couldn't avoid feeling a little apprehensive as he tentatively opened the door. But there was nothing to fear in there anymore. The late September sun filled the room with a lambent light and any shadows that had lurked in his mind were soon cast away. He knelt down in front of the bookcase and searched the titles, Milton, Spencer, Wordsworth, Byron, Keates, Tennyson, the works of an impressive range of Renaissance and Victorian poets lay, side by side, on the top shelf. The shelf below contained late nineteenth- and early twentieth-century collections, and it was amongst these that he found what he was looking for. It was tucked in between slim volumes of Elliott and Yeats, a fine leather-bound edition of Christina Rossetti's *Goblin Market and other Poems*.

Nick removed the volume from the shelf and blew off the many years of accumulated dust before carefully opening it. It was a second edition, published in 1865 by Macmillan & Co. On the bottom of the frontispiece there was a neat, hand-written inscription that read 'To my darling sister Frances in memory of a very special occasion, with fondest love, Charlotte.' Nick took in a deep breath. The last person to have touched this handsome little volume would have been Frances herself. It was difficult to control his excitement. He slowly turned the pages and scanned the text, certain that somewhere he would find the words he was looking for. At last, he came to a page where, written in a different hand to that which had inscribed the dedication on the frontispiece, was written 'I shall always hear your voice when I read this poem, my darling, my one true love'. The poem below was entitled 'Remember' and there, in the final verse, were the words he was looking for: He read the poem again. It was so poignant, given everything that had subsequently befallen Frances and her lover. Nor could he think of more appropriate words by which to remember Frances herself:

Remember me when I am gone away,
    Gone far away into the silent land;
When you can no more hold me by the hand,
    Nor I half turn to go yet turning stay.

Remember me when no more day by day
    You tell me of our future that you plann'd:
Only remember me; you understand
    It will be late to counsel then or pray.

Yet if you should forget me for a while
    And afterwards remember, do not grieve:
    For if the darkness and corruption leave
A vestige of the thoughts that once I had,
Better by far you should forget and smile
Than that you should remember and be sad.

Overjoyed at his good fortune in so easily finding the poem he had been looking for, Nick hurried back to the storeroom to put pen to paper, and began to sketch out some early ideas for his new composition. It was too early to know exactly what form it might take. From experience, he knew this was likely to change several times before he was finally satisfied. Of one thing he was certain: his muse, the true source of his inspiration, was Frances Whitmore of High House and she would guide him through the many weeks of laborious work that lay ahead.

EPILOGUE

WHEN THE FINAL notes have faded away, the Cathedral falls silent, there is not a sound or a movement. And then, all around them, members of the audience are standing up and applauding. There are shouts and screams of delight and people are hammering with their feet on the stone floor. Kate turns to look behind them and sees that the whole audience is on its feet. The conductor steps down from the rostrum and takes the hand of the soprano soloist. They stand there, side by side, acknowledging the enthusiastic applause. And then something happens that Kate has rarely seen before. Members of the orchestra have laid down their instruments and they too are standing and clapping enthusiastically to acknowledge their appreciation of her brother's new work. Soon Kate too is on her feet, clapping wildly with the others, overjoyed at her brother's success. She looks down at him. He is still sitting with his eyes closed and his hands clenched tightly together. Tears are trickling down his cheeks.

She bends down to whisper urgently in his ear. 'Look Nick, can't you see, he's calling for you, he wants you up on the stage. You must go now, they're all waiting for you.' Nick opens his eyes and looks up at his sister who is smiling down at him. When he stands up his legs are shaking. He is overcome by the warmth and generosity of the audience's response. With head bowed, he makes his way up onto the stage to further rapturous applause. He is warmly embraced by the conductor and soloist and shakes hands with the first violin and other orchestral principals, while the audience continues to clap, shout, cheer and whistle. Three times they exit from the stage and three times they are called back, the audience simply won't let them go.

Finally, it's all over and Kate makes her way to the hospitality marquee to re-join Nick for the post-concert reception. She finds him surrounded by his fellow composers who are enthusiastically congratulating him on his new composition. Kate can see this means more to him than any standing ovation. The head of BBC Radio 3 is there too, heaping praise on him, delighted with the success of their latest commission.

After a while, Nick turns to Kate and says 'do you think we can leave now? I don't think I can take much more of this, I'm not used to such adulation! It's all gone so well, it's an evening I'll never forget, but all I want to do now is to go somewhere quiet to find something to eat, I'm absolutely starving.'

They thank everyone profusely and, say their farewells. They are half way across the Cathedral Close, approaching Broad Street, when someone grasps Nick's arm from behind. He turns to face a young woman. She is smiling up at him. His hand goes to his mouth, he is so astonished he can hardly breathe. The girl bears such a remarkable resemblance to the young woman in the photograph.

'I'm so sorry. I didn't mean to startle you. I just wanted to have a word. There was an article in *The Times* last week all about your new composition and how you came to write it. I've travelled all the way up from Devon in the hope of meeting you. You see I'm Fran Cunningham and Frances Whitmore was my great-grandmother.'

Speechless, Nick stares down at the young woman, his mouth wide open in disbelief.

'You must forgive my brother,' Kate says. 'The thing is you look so very like your great-grandmother.'

'I know, everyone says so. We have a miniature portrait of her at home and when I look at it, it's rather like looking into a mirror,' she says, laughing. 'I absolutely loved the symphonic poem, by the way. It's so full of passion. It feels like you had a great deal of affection for Frances when you wrote it, if you don't mind my saying so.'

'I suppose, in a way, I did, still do indeed. It's the diary that brings her to life. A tale of such love and despair is bound to soften any man's heart.'

'I don't know all that much about my great-grandmother. I think the family must have been ashamed about what happened to her, and to her father of course. I'm so grateful to you for giving her back to us and for . . . for seeing she was finally laid to rest. And there's just one more thing. Do you think I might come to visit you while I'm up here? I'd so like to see the house where it all happened. I've been to the village. I drove up there earlier in the year to see if I could find where Frances was buried.'

'So it was you I saw putting those wild flowers by her graveside. That explains everything. What a strange coincidence that I should have been there at the time. Oh, yes, and of course you must come to High House, I would like that very much.'

Kate gives Nick a knowing smile. 'Look Fran, Nick and I are about to look for a nice quiet place where we can have something to eat. Why don't you join us, we have so much more to talk about.'

'Yes, I'd like that.' Fran said, 'I'd like that very much.'

BV - #0215 - 240223 - C0 - 229/152/13 - PB - 9781914424984 - Gloss Lamination